"Trust me

"I want to…" Dulcie began. It was time to admit the truth.

He rested his hand gently along the side of her face, loving the softness of her skin beneath his fingertips. He felt a flicker of hope. He would move slowly, patiently, so as not to frighten her again. "I can help you, Dulcie. Just tell me everything."

Her body strained toward his, and without realizing it, she lifted her face to him, hungry for the taste of his lips.

He stood very still, staring down into her eyes. But he made no move to kiss her.

She felt a wave of bitter disappointment. She had hoped to be able to lose herself in the mindless pleasure of passion. But he was not offering her passion.

What he was offering was trust.

And she knew with certainty that once he learned the truth he would turn away from her forever.…

Bride's Bay Resort

Dear Reader,

In this, the last in the Bride's Bay series for Harlequin, I take you back to the beginning. A country torn apart by bitter civil war. A South caught in the grip of death and destruction. And people, all hiding secrets, desperate to escape the insanity, who find not only purpose in their lives but also a measure of peace, joy and, most of all, love.

RUTH LANGAN

DULCIE'S GIFT

Harlequin Books

TORONTO • NEW YORK • LONDON
AMSTERDAM • PARIS • SYDNEY • HAMBURG
STOCKHOLM • ATHENS • TOKYO • MILAN
MADRID • WARSAW • BUDAPEST • AUCKLAND

ISBN 0-373-28924-3

DULCIE'S GIFT

Books by Ruth Langan

Harlequin Historicals

Mistress of the Seas #10
†*Texas Heart* #31
**Highland Barbarian* #41
*Highland Heather #65
*Highland Fire #91
*Highland Heart #111
†*Texas Healer* #131
Christmas Miracle #147
†*Texas Hero* #180
Deception #196
*The Highlander #228
Angel #245
*Highland Heaven #269
†† *Diamond* #305
Dulcie's Gift #324

†Texas Series
*The Highland Series
†† The Jewels of Texas

Harlequin Books

*Harlequin Historicals
Christmas Stories* 1990
  "Christmas at Bitter Creek"

Outlaw Brides
"Maverick Hearts"

RUTH LANGAN

traces her ancestry to Scotland and Ireland. It is no surprise, then, that she feels a kinship with the characters in her historical novels.

Married to her childhood sweetheart, she has raised five children and lives in Michigan, the state where she was born and raised.

To Anne Catherine Langan
Our newest blessing.
And her big brother, Tommy.
And her proud parents, Tom and Maureen.

And, of course, to Tom
Always to Tom.

Prologue

South Carolina
Spring, 1865

The ragged band of women and children broke free of the underbrush and stumbled toward the shore.

Dulcie, the group's acknowledged leader, spotted a boat and urged the others to climb aboard.

"But it isn't ours. We can't steal it," a solemn, dark-haired little girl challenged.

"We have no choice, Clara. Would you rather go back there?" Dulcie demanded, gathering her close.

"Look, Dulcie. Do you not see the storm?" The speaker was a young woman with hair the color of autumn leaves and a voice tinged with the lilt of Ireland.

"It can't be helped," Dulcie replied. Lifting one child on her back and another in her arms, she clambered over the edge and gratefully deposited her burdens on the rough wooden bottom of the boat. "There is nowhere else to go but out to sea. We dare not turn back now."

One of the older girls clutched the hand of a small boy and tried to back away, terrified by the heavy winds that caused the little craft to rock violently. "I can't, Dulcie. I'm ... so afraid."

Dulcie's voice took on a note of command. "Fiona, Nathaniel, help Starlight aboard. There is no time to waste." Her voice rose above the howling wind. "Remember what awaits us if we should tarry."

"Aye. Come on, lass." The Irish woman, bearing the weight of a six-year-old girl on her back, draped an arm around the pitifully frail shoulders of the younger woman and forced her to step into the angry, swirling surf. The little boy clung tightly to Starlight's other hand.

As soon as all of them had been helped aboard, Dulcie hauled anchor and pressed an oar into the sand. Setting the small craft afloat, she began to row.

"Now that we have escaped, we must make a pact." To convey the importance of her words, Dulcie deliberately met the wide, frightened stares of each member of the group. "No matter what happens, we must vow never to speak about what transpired back there."

"Isn't that the same as lying?" Once again, it was the earnest Clara who questioned their every move.

"That's just like a girl ..." Nathaniel began, but Dulcie shot him a look that silenced him.

"Listen to me, Clara," Dulcie continued. "Our very lives depend upon secrecy." At once the children began whimpering, and tears sprang to the eyes of the women. Dulcie's own lips trembled, but she forced herself to go on. "The danger is not past. Perhaps it never will be. But this much I know. We must never entrust our story to others. Do you understand? Now swear."

"I swear," Nathaniel said when Dulcie turned to him.

"And you, Belle?"

The auburn-haired six-year-old nodded.

"Emily?"

Frizzy blond curls bobbed up and down.

"Clara?"

The others held their breath until the somber little girl, who had become the voice of everyone's conscience, finally nodded in reluctant agreement. "I swear."

"I swear, as well," Fiona said.

"And I," said fifteen-year-old Starlight in hushed tones beside her.

"Good." Dulcie uncurled her fingers, which had been squeezed into such tight fists the nails had dug into her palms, drawing blood. She glanced around and realized that the shore was no longer visible. The wind and waves had dragged their little craft far out to sea. They were at the mercy of the storm.

"Now," she went on breathlessly, "we must pray for deliverance, for I fear we have exchanged one danger for another."

As they began the words of a familiar Bible verse, the storm broke directly overhead with such fury one oar was ripped from her grasp.

Fiona gathered the frightened children close, but as the small boat was tossed about like a piece of driftwood, she was flung backward, dragging Clara with her. Even the rumble of thunder couldn't drown out the terrible sound of their heads hitting the wood. As the next flash of lightning tore through the darkened sky, a thin line of blood could be seen trickling down Fiona's cheek. Beside her, Clara lay motionless in the bottom of the boat.

Dulcie wrapped them with her cape and petticoats to shield them from the full force of the storm. Then she took Fiona's place, draping her arms around the weeping chil-

dren. And though she was too frightened to speak, the
words of the psalm continued playing through her mind.

"Yea, though I walk through the shadow of the valley of
death, I will fear no evil . . ."

Chapter One

Jermain Island, South Carolina

The storm had lasted less than an hour, but its tremendous winds had uprooted trees and knocked down a storage shed, which had collapsed like a house of cards. Though rain still fell from a darkened sky, the worst of the downpour had blown out to sea.

Cal Jermain slogged his way through the flattened rows of tender seedlings to survey the damage. Frowning, he discovered evidence that confirmed his worst suspicions. The storm had completely wiped out days of backbreaking labor. The entire crop would have to be replanted if they were to have anything to harvest by late summer.

With a muttered oath he turned away and began to walk the shoreline, littered with debris. It was then that he spotted the flat-bottomed wooden boat bobbing in the surf.

"Any fool who can't take the time to tie up his craft deserves to lose it," he grumbled as he waded through the shallows to retrieve it.

He caught hold of the bow, then sucked in a quick breath.

Bodies were sprawled across the bottom of the craft. Three, six, seven of them in all. Women. Children. Bloodied. Battered. Sloshing in several inches of water that ran red with their blood.

He swore, loudly, savagely.

As he hauled the boat closer to the rough shore, he heard a low moan. Instantly he climbed over the edge of the craft to locate the survivor.

A young woman in a torn, sodden gown lifted her head. Hair as black as midnight hung in wet tendrils around a face devoid of color, except for two bright spots on her cheeks.

"Sarah!" The name was torn from Cal's lips in a breathless cry. "God in heaven. You've come..."

He scrambled to her side and dropped to his knees. In that instant he realized his mistake. Not Sarah. Up close, this stranger bore no resemblance. But his voice still trembled. "You're alive, then. Can you sit up?" He placed one arm carefully around the young woman's shoulders.

"I...Yes..." Dulcie's words trailed off as everything went black for a moment. Then a man's face came into focus. She had a quick impression of dark hair. Dark eyes. A tight angry mouth. A big man. Scowling. Threatening. Even kneeling, he filled her line of vision. She shrank from his touch, shivering violently.

The movement wasn't lost on Cal. There was a look of fear in her green eyes. A most unusual shade of green, which seemed to glow with some inner fire. Most probably fever. Or shock.

Very deliberately he lowered his hand to his side and backed away.

She relaxed her guard. "Where are we?"

The breathy voice was cultured, distinctly Southern. It whispered over his senses, touching a chord deep inside him. For as far back as he could remember, the women in his family had spoken in just such a soft, genteel manner.

"This bay is known as the Bay of Storms, and it's on Jermain Island. Off the coast of Charleston."

"How far from Charleston?" she asked a little too quickly.

At once he was alert to the terror that rippled through her. "An hour or more." He saw her fear slowly turn to relief. "But I would recommend a sturdier craft than this if you venture out to sea again. I don't know how you survived this wicked storm. You were indeed fortunate."

He glanced around as several of the others began to move or make little sounds of distress. Relief flooded through him. His first impression had been wrong. They were not dead. But barely alive, from the looks of them.

"I'll help you to shore."

As he reached for her, Dulcie realized with a shock that his left hand was missing. Instinctively she recoiled from his touch.

At her reaction, Cal went still.

It was an awkward, shattering moment. One that set both their faces to flame, hers in embarrassment, his in anger. Then, moving quickly to cover her feelings, Dulcie swept past him.

"I can manage, thank you." She was mortified by her reaction. Though it had been purely reflexive, it jarred her sense of fairness. After all, this stranger had already lost his hand. He should not have to suffer a loss of others' civility, as well. Nevertheless, she couldn't think of any way to make amends. "But if you would help the others..."

She scrambled over the edge of the boat and was nearly swamped by waves. Cal watched, making no effort to assist her, as the current tugged at her already soaked gown, dragging her to her knees before she managed to find her footing.

His eyes narrowed. He'd be damned if he'd offer his help a second time. Still, he kept careful watch to see that she made it to shore.

As soon as she dropped safely into the grass, he turned away and lifted out a small child who had begun to cry. When he'd carried the child to the grass, he returned to the boat again and again until all had been deposited on land. Assured now that everyone was alive, he called to Dulcie, who lay, breathing heavily, "I'll go now."

"Go?" She lifted her head in alarm, a challenge in her eyes.

As patiently as if he were addressing a child he said, "I have to go back to the barn and hitch the team if I'm to take all of you to safety."

"Oh." She turned her head, but not before he recognized the look of relief.

So, he thought as he trudged away, she'd expected to be abandoned. It was a typical reaction in the aftermath of the chaos that had swept the land. But it was not his problem, he reminded himself. There wasn't a soul left in these parts who hadn't been affected by the damnable war. And he certainly couldn't heal all the wounds. Hell, he couldn't even heal himself.

Leaning a shoulder into the heavy door, he entered the barn and breathed in the scents of warm dry hay, moist earth and dung. Scents that had been with him since his childhood on this island. Even now, all these years later, they soothed his troubled spirit.

Speaking softly to the horses, he hitched the team to the wagon, then hurried to the house for needed supplies.

When he returned a short time later, he found Dulcie kneeling in the midst of the others, soothing tears, calming fears. Most of them had managed to sit up. But two figures had not moved—the injured young woman and child.

"Which is the most seriously wounded?" Cal asked.

"Fiona." Dulcie knelt beside the slender figure and pressed her hand to Fiona's forehead. A low moan issued, but the woman's eyes remained closed.

Cal dropped to his knees beside her.

"A wave nearly swamped our boat. My friend was tossed about and hit her head as she fell. It was the last time she moved."

Cal lifted the young woman and placed her gently in the back of the wagon, which was strewn with an assortment of quilts and feather pillows.

"Clara was also thrown backward, and she's lost quite a bit of blood," Dulcie said, indicating the child lying in the grass.

Cal wrapped the child's arm in clean linen, then placed her beside Fiona. When he turned, Dulcie was urging the other children to their feet.

"Climb into the wagon," she called, and the little ones did as she bade, moving slowly, as though in a daze.

As Cal attempted to help Dulcie into the back of the wagon, she nearly slipped in the mud. At once he brought his other arm up to steady her.

The contact jolted them both.

Dulcie froze, unable to move, unable even to breathe, as his arm encircled her waist. Shock sliced through her, leaving her dazed. For a moment his face lowered to her, and she felt the warmth of his breath across her temple. Tiny sensations skittered along her spine.

Cal, too, seemed mesmerized by the touch of her. His hand lingered at her waist. Feelings long buried seemed to push their way to the surface of his mind, triggering half-remembered pleasures. He'd forgotten how soft a woman was. How warm her breath, how sweet her scent.

From behind came a little boy's innocent remark. "Sir, did you lose your hand in the war?"

At once the mood was shattered. Cal's mouth pressed into a grim, tight line.

"Hush, Nathaniel," Dulcie admonished.

But the damage had been done. Without a word Cal lifted Dulcie into the back of the wagon, then bent to the boy. When all were settled, he circled around and climbed into the driver's seat. With a crack of the whip, the team leaned into the harness and the wagon rolled through the mud with slow, lurching movements.

The little girls were weeping, and Dulcie drew them into her embrace, murmuring words of comfort.

"Look there. See?" She pointed to the darkened outline of the barn looming out of the curtain of rain. "Soon you'll be snug and dry and warm."

The horses continued past the barn toward another, larger structure. As they rolled closer, Dulcie made out a graceful old two-story house, with wooden shutters drawn over the windows against the storm. A veranda encircled both stories, the upper one supported by stately columns of pillars.

Though one wing of the house was gutted and appeared to have been burned, the main body of the building was intact.

This was even better than Dulcie had hoped for. It would have been enough to seek shelter in the barn. But a house! She gave a sigh of relief.

When the wagon jolted to a halt, the back door was opened wide. Light from a fireplace spilled into the growing darkness, illuminating several tall figures that stepped through the doorway onto the veranda. As the figures came down the steps to lend a hand, Dulcie realized they were young men no older than the driver. And like the driver, tight-lipped and unsmiling.

The women and children were helped from the wagon and led or carried inside to a room with wooden pegs along the wall that held an assortment of woolen cloaks. Along one wall stood a row of mud-spattered work boots of various sizes. Down the hall could be glimpsed a cozy parlor, where candles flickered in sconces along the wall, adding their warmth and light to the blaze in the fireplace.

"We must get these wet things off." A tall, sturdy woman strode into the room with an armload of blankets. Dark hair, shot with silver, framed a handsome face set in stern lines.

"Are you strong enough to assist me with these children?" she called to Dulcie.

"Of course."

Though Dulcie's head was spinning from all that had happened, she bent to her task with cool determination. After she stripped off the children's wet clothes, the woman wrapped them in warm, soft blankets. Each child was then handed off to one of the men and carried to the parlor. There the little ones curled up in front of the fire, and the youngest promptly fell asleep.

"This one is badly injured," Dulcie whispered. She and the woman worked together, gently removing the torn clothing from Clara and wrapping her tiny figure in a blanket.

The child was handed to Cal, who disappeared through a doorway.

When the children had been taken care of, Dulcie and the woman moved to either side of fifteen-year-old Starlight. At Dulcie's urging, the girl shed her soaked garments and gratefully accepted the blanket from her hostess. Then she was sent to join the children by the fire.

Finally they moved to the still form of Fiona. When her wet and bloodied clothing had been removed, the woman's

movements stilled as she studied the darkened bruises about
Fiona's back and shoulders, as well as a series of raised,
puckered scars. Without a word she gently wrapped Fiona
in a clean linen sheet, then covered her with a warm blanket, which quickly became stained with her blood. Again
Cal was called upon to carry her away.

"That's the lot of you?" the woman asked with a sigh.

"Yes. Thank you."

"Quickly now," the woman commanded. "Off with
those wet clothes."

Dulcie shed her soaked clothing and gratefully accepted
a blanket. The woman led the way to the parlor. Inside, two
men turned from inspecting the children to study Dulcie,
who was shivering violently.

"We are the Jermains," the woman said in her brisk tone.
"It would seem that nature has given you an inhospitable
time to visit. My name is Elizabeth Jermain, but everyone
calls me Aunt Bessie."

"I'm Dulcie Trenton. The injured woman is Fiona
O'Neil. And this," Dulcie said, touching a hand to the
younger woman's shoulder as she lay on a sofa by the fireplace, "is Starlight."

"What sort of name is that?" Aunt Bessie snapped.

At her harsh tone, Starlight's eyes seemed to glaze over,
and she focused her gaze on a single candle set in a sconce
on the wall. It was as though she'd gone off to another place
in her mind.

"It is the name she chose." Though Dulcie spoke softly,
there was a thread of steel in her voice, as though she dared
anyone to challenge her.

Starlight rewarded her a look of adoration before giving
in to the need to close her eyes.

"The boy?" Aunt Bessie demanded.

"The boy is Nathaniel."

"I'm eight and a half," he said proudly.

Dulcie tousled his hair and said, "The girls are Belle, who's six, and Emily, who's five." As their names were spoken, the children's gazes fastened adoringly on Dulcie.

"And the injured child," Dulcie continued, "is seven-year-old Clara. Where have you taken her?"

"To a bed." Aunt Bessie turned to indicate the two men. "These are my nephews, Barclay and Darwin."

"Everyone calls me Barc," said the shorter of the two.

Dulcie's hand was engulfed in a firm handshake, and she looked up into blue eyes set in a handsome, boyish face. Thick, brown hair curled wildly over the collar of his shirt. Despite his stern demeanor, there was a glint of wicked humor in his eyes. Was he amused by her appearance, she wondered, or by their unorthodox arrival? It didn't matter. She was too weary to care how she looked or what her rescuers thought.

"Darwin," Dulcie repeated as she accepted the handshake of the taller man, who appeared somewhat younger than Barclay.

"Dar, if you please," he muttered. His hair was jet black, his eyes as dark as a raven's. He had the rich, resonant voice of a preacher, and his bearing was rigid.

"We are most grateful for your hospitality." Dulcie glanced around. "I would like to thank the one who rescued us."

"Cal?" Barc gave a snort of laughter. "He would be offended by any display of gratitude, Miss Trenton. My older brother was merely doing his duty."

Brother. Though she was caught unawares, she could see the resemblance in the stern set of the jaw, the thick, unruly hair and the rough timbre of their voices. But where these two men were at least attempting to be cordial, their older brother had seemed angry, even hostile. And he had left without a word. He had not even had the good manners to linger long enough to be introduced.

She determined to put him out of her mind. "I would like to check on Fiona and Clara now."

"There is no need. They are in capable hands." Aunt Bessie turned to the dignified-looking black man who stood, ramrod straight, in the doorway.

"Robert, bring warm milk for the children and something stronger for the women. Wine perhaps, since they have need of a fire in their blood. And I would like a sip of spirits, as well."

"Yes, Miss Bessie." With a deferential nod, the man turned away.

"You'd best warm yourself," Aunt Bessie commanded imperiously.

"In a moment." With soft words and tender touches, Dulcie moved among the children, touching a hand to a forehead to check for fever, tucking a blanket more firmly around a small body, assuring herself that all was well.

Out of the corner of her eye she saw a figure in the doorway.

Before she could turn, she heard Cal's voice, tense, challenging. "How did you come to be out in that storm?"

At once the children looked nervously from one to the other and then to Dulcie. Their sudden mood switch was not lost on the Jermains, who were clearly puzzled. Just moments earlier these same children had been on the verge of sleep.

"We didn't do anything wrong," Nathaniel protested.

The two little girls began to cry.

"Hush now." Dulcie pressed a hand to Nathaniel's shoulder reassuringly, then knelt to soothe the weeping girls. "No one has accused us of any wrongdoing—" she lifted her head and met Cal's piercing stare "—have they?"

"I merely wondered why in hell anyone would be out in a small boat during such a storm."

"I—did not know the storm was coming," she said evasively.

"Even a fool could see—"

"The hour is late, Calhoun," Aunt Bessie chided gently. She had been watching and listening with great interest. "We will speak of this tomorrow. Right now what they need is rest." She turned to the young woman who was obviously the leader of this ragged band. "Miss Dulcie Trenton, may I present my oldest nephew, Calhoun Jermain."

Each regarded the other with wariness before giving a slight nod of acknowledgment.

"Thank you, Mr. Jermain, for rescuing us." Dulcie's words were stiff, formal. "I thank God that our boat drifted to your shore."

"You'd best thank Him for blowing the storm out to sea. I don't think that old battered craft would have stayed afloat much longer," Cal muttered. "And while you have His ear, you'd better ask for some common sense in the future or—"

"Sit, Miss Trenton." Aunt Bessie indicated a chair in front of the fireplace. Robert had just reentered, and taking a glass of ruby liquid from his tray, she handed it to the young woman with a terse "Drink."

Dulcie sank into the deep cushions and sipped, feeling the warmth of the wine trickle through her veins. She tried to hold on to her anger, but the warmth and the wine conspired against her. Heaven. She had just died and gone to heaven.

She heard the rumble of deep, masculine voices, as questions were asked. And the higher-pitched sounds of the children, as they answered.

"When did you last eat?" This from Aunt Bessie.

Nathaniel answered. "I don't remember."

"How long ago since you slept?" It was Barc's voice, low, almost conversational.

"Many hours, I think." Belle's voice trembled slightly.

"Where is your home?" Aunt Bessie challenged.

"We have no home," was Emily's response.

There was an awkward silence.

"And none of you saw the storm coming?"

Another silence.

"Do you all belong to Miss Trenton?" A man's voice, strong, demanding.

"Yes." This emphatic response from Nathaniel. It caused Dulcie's lips to curl in a dreamy smile. "Dulcie takes care of us."

She could hardly keep up with the words, but it didn't matter. For now, they were warm and dry and safe. That was all that mattered. And for one brief moment, she could relinquish her role as caretaker and relax her guard.

She glanced at the graceful curve of staircase that led to the second story. Perhaps they would be allowed to sleep here, curled up on the floor in front of the fireplace. If their hosts insisted upon seeing them to beds, she hoped she could just drift up, rather than climb, those stairs.

The voices seemed to fade. The half-empty glass was eased from her grip.

She must have slept, for when she opened her eyes, the fire had faded to embers and the candles had been snuffed. Against her will her lids flickered, then closed.

In the silence that followed, Dulcie felt herself being lifted in strong arms and cradled against a wall of chest. She smiled, remembering the way it had felt when Papa would carry her to her bed.

"Oh, Papa. You're home at last." With a sigh that arose from deep within her, she wrapped her arms around his neck and buried her lips against his throat, breathing deeply. The male, musky scent of him filled her heart and soul and brought her the first real peace she'd known in so many years. Years filled with uncertainty and hunger and fear. But now, all that was behind her. Papa was home.

She felt herself being lowered to her bed. The edge of the soft feather mattress shifted as he sat beside her and tucked the covers around her shoulders.

As he started to move away, she caught his hand and brought it to her lips. At once she heard the quick intake of breath and the muttered oath. Her lids fluttered open.

The figure was as tall as her father and as broad of shoulder. But where Papa's hair had been streaked with gray, this hair was as black as coal. The face unlined with age. The eyes hard, unblinking.

"You!" As before, she recoiled and felt her cheeks flame when the realization dawned. Sweet heaven. She had just made a fool of herself in front of a scowling, furious Cal Jermain.

Without a word he turned and stalked from the room, closing the door firmly behind him. Leaving her alone with her burning shame.

Cal shed his wet clothing and picked up a towel. As he dried himself, he moved to the window and watched the play of lights far out to sea. A torch flickered then died.

Only a fool or a villain would be out on such a night, he thought. So what did that make the women and children he'd rescued? Fools or...?

He leaned a hip against the sill. It was obvious they were frightened. He'd seen the same dazed looks in the eyes of hundreds of survivors across the South. Still, these seven seemed especially secretive. And what of Dulcie Trenton?

There was a toughness to her. As though she was ready to challenge anyone who threatened those in her care.

The war had done that to a lot of people, he thought with a growing sense of rage. It had torn this great nation apart, destroying entire families, turning them into something less than human.

He tried, without success, to put the dark-haired woman out of his mind. In that first instant when he'd seen her, he'd thought...God in heaven, what a fool he was. There was no place in his life now for a woman. Any woman. But especially one who reminded him of the past.

Still...

She'd called him Papa. And in her sleep she'd kissed him. A natural enough mistake. But his reaction to that kiss had been totally unexpected, and not at all paternal. Fool. With a hiss of anger he tossed the towel aside and strode naked to his bed. But sleep was a long time coming. As he tossed and turned, he could feel the press of her lips against his throat. And was forced to admit to himself the humiliation of his sudden, shocking arousal.

Chapter Two

Dulcie slipped from bed and crossed to the window. A spectacular sunrise was just visible on the horizon, and the land spread out below was still gilded with dew. She caught her breath at the sight of a herd of deer on a distant hillside. A cow was lowing nearby, and the birds had begun their morning symphony.

The newly plowed fields, a deep rich black, were divided by rows of gangling palmetto trees. Their fronds waved in the gentle breeze. An occasional live oak, dripping with Spanish moss, spread its branches in a graceful arc.

She had just discovered heaven. After the battle-scarred countryside she had left behind, this peaceful pastoral setting brought tears to her eyes.

Her prayers had been answered a hundredfold. And now she must find a way to remain in this Eden. Hadn't Papa always said that any fool could seize opportunity, but it took a wise man to create opportunity where none existed? She would have to get busy creating.

Dulcie turned away from the window, and for the first time noticed that her clothes were now washed and draped over a chair. Her chemise and petticoats were as clean as the day they'd been made. Her gown, though shabby, had been carefully pressed. Beside it were her old scuffed kid slippers, polished to a high shine.

She made her way to a basin of water that stood atop a low chest of drawers. Beside it was a cake of lavender soap and a soft linen towel. With a little smile of delight she set about washing herself.

Bless the Jermains, she thought. For all their stern posturing, they were being most kind. Now if only she could persuade them to be charitable, as well.

"She's lying." Cal's voice was rough with anger. In the thin light of morning he joined his aunt and brothers around the elegant dining-room table and filled his plate with corn bread, eggs and slabs of roasted pork.

"And the children?" Aunt Bessie whispered. "How do you explain their answers?"

"They're all lying."

"People have been caught unawares by storms before," Barc said logically.

"True—if the storm comes up unexpectedly. But this one gave plenty of warning. The skies over Charleston were black for days."

"So why do you think they took to the boat?"

"They're on the run. They refuse to talk about Charleston. Or the war. Most refugees are eager to talk about the people they lost, the homes, the belongings. I suspect something . . ."

"Something illegal perhaps?" Barc asked.

"Miss Trenton seems like a fine Southern lady," Aunt Bessie protested.

"And a fine Southern lady can do no wrong?" Cal gave a hollow laugh. "Look around you, Aunt Bessie. The war has made something less of all of us."

"Speak for yourself," Barc said with a sneer. "I rather like what I've become."

"You would. How much did you lose on your last trip to Charleston?" his older brother snapped.

"Enough to assure me an invitation to their next round of poker."

"I'm sure Nellie Simpson is thrilled at your patronage of her sporting house." Cal's features tightened.

"I only go for the games of chance," Barc insisted.

"I've heard a man gambles every time he samples Nellie's women," Dar put in.

At the young man's remark, Aunt Bessie's eyes flashed fire. "I'll not have such talk in my home, Darwin."

"Yes, ma'am. Sorry." Chastised, he lifted his cup to his lips and fixed his gaze on the spotless lace tablecloth.

"As for you, Barclay." The older woman turned her full wrath on the smiling charmer who was her middle nephew. "How can you stand to visit Charleston and see what General Sherman has done to that lovely city? It's—"

"We were talking about the women and children." Cal refused to allow her to dwell on her favorite source of irritation.

"Yes. Of course. Now, Calhoun," Aunt Bessie continued as though she'd never been sidetracked, "I don't see how we can turn them away."

"I'm not suggesting we turn them out in the cold." Cal sampled the corn bread and thought again how he'd missed such simple pleasures when he'd been away at war. So many things had been taken for granted until they were gone. A bed. Dry clothes. Corn bread warm from the oven. "At least not now," he added. "But as soon as the injured are well enough to travel, I want them returned to Charleston." The sooner the better, he thought, and felt a little flush of displeasure at the image that had come, unbidden, to mind. The image of a body pressed to his, lips buried against his throat, lashes whispering across his heated skin. Abruptly he lost his appetite and shoved aside his plate.

"You will see to them, won't you, Calhoun?" His aunt placed a hand over his.

At once she felt him pull back.

He had been this way since his return from the battle-field. Cold. Withdrawn. As though he could prove that he needed no sympathy for his loss. No comfort for his pain.

"I'll do what I can," he said, at the pleading look in her eyes.

"I'll be happy to take them back to Charleston when they're ready," Barc said with a smile.

"It will give you an excuse to try your hand at the cards again," Dar muttered.

"How soon do you think they can travel?" Aunt Bessie asked.

Cal shrugged. "A week or so, I should think. The child doesn't seem as badly hurt as the woman."

He stood, eager to keep his promise to his aunt so he could escape to the fields. His impatience wasn't lost on the others. Ever since their return from the war, each brother had taken refuge in his own way. The reclusive Dar had his precious books. Outgoing Barc had his whiskey and gambling. And Cal, angry and embittered, lost himself in the mind-numbing, physical demands of farming.

"Is there some potion or poultice Robert could prepare?" Aunt Bessie asked.

Cal shook his head. "There isn't any medicine that will erase a blow to the head."

"Well, I know you'll do the best you can," his aunt said solemnly.

Cal was already striding from the room and up the stairs.

As he entered the Irishwoman's room, he nearly collided with Dulcie. Instinctively his hand shot out to steady her.

The rush of feelings was the same. He felt the heat first and then the tiny current that seemed to pass from her to him and back again. He released her at once and took a step back.

It was obvious that her crimson satin gown had once been considered the height of fashion. Now one sleeve was torn, and the cuffs were frayed beyond repair.

Over her gown she had tied a simple white apron, which only served to emphasize her tiny waist.

But it was her face that held his gaze. Scrubbed clean of mud, her skin was flawless and as pale as alabaster. Burnished dark hair, brushed until it gleamed, fell in silky waves to below her waist. The striking green eyes were wide with surprise.

"What are you doing here?" she demanded.

"I promised my aunt I would look to our injured guests." He emphasized the word "guests" as he moved past Dulcie.

She stood with hands on hips, looking as if she would block his entrance. "Why?"

"I know a little about healing." He sat on the edge of the bed and touched a hand to Fiona's head, then gently lifted each eyelid, frowning as he studied her pupils.

Dulcie watched him, feeling a growing sense of panic. Of all the people in this house, why did it have to be this gruff, angry man who'd been sent to look after Fiona?

Well, this was his house. He had permitted them refuge from the storm. She had no right to interfere.

Nevertheless, she persisted. "Are you a doctor, Mr. Jermain?"

He shot her a quelling look. "I am a farmer, Miss Trenton. A simple farmer."

When he returned his attentions to Fiona, Dulcie clenched her hands at her sides. A farmer maybe. But simple? Never. There was so much anger in this complex man, so much hostility, it fairly burned to burst free.

"Miss O'Neil." Cal spoke sharply to the still figure in the bed. "Can you hear me, Miss O'Neil?"

Acting as a buffer between her friend and this stern stranger, Dulcie moved to the other side of the bed and reached out to clasp Fiona's hand. "Oh, Fiona," she whispered, "please, please hear me."

"You must speak in a normal tone, Miss Trenton."

Dulcie eyed him suspiciously. "Why?"

"Because your friend is in a deep sleep. You must find a way to penetrate the layers of pain. Each time you visit her bedside, you must attempt to engage her in conversation. Talk about things you both know. Things you've shared. Call to her. Invite her to reach out to you."

She stared down at her friend, as if willing the young woman her strength. "Yes. All right."

"Now, about those marks on her back..."

Dulcie's head came up sharply, and he could see her closing up before his eyes.

"It is obvious that not all of them were caused by the fall in the boat. How did she come by the others?"

"I have no right to violate her privacy. You will have to ask her when she awakes."

"I am asking you, Miss Trenton."

Dulcie gritted her teeth and held her silence.

"Very well." Cal stood and walked out of the room.

She released Fiona's hand and raced after him as he crossed the hallway to another bedroom. "Clara is sleeping. I would rather you not disturb..."

Ignoring her, he stepped into the room and approached the bedside where the little girl lay. From the doorway Dulcie watched as he lifted the child's hand and examined her injured arm. After applying a clean dressing, he felt her forehead, then gently rolled the sleeping child onto her stomach and ran his fingers along her spine. When at last he tucked the blankets around the little girl's shoulders and turned away, Dulcie confronted him.

"You call yourself a simple farmer, Mr. Jermain, yet your actions say otherwise. I do not believe you."

"Then we are even, Miss Trenton." He pinned her with his dark, penetrating look. "For when you say you did not see the storm approaching, I do not believe you."

Struck speechless, she could only stare after him as he moved around her and stalked away.

As Dulcie stepped into Starlight's room, where the others had gathered, she was pleasantly surprised. The young woman had supervised sponge baths for everyone, and all stood, neatly dressed, hair combed.

But despite their spotless appearance, they wore identical frowns of concern.

"You look splendid. But please, tell me what's wrong," Dulcie coaxed.

"We're afraid," Starlight explained. "The Jermains are such stern people. It's obvious they don't like having us here." She clutched Dulcie's arm. "Oh, Dulcie. What if they send us back today?"

Dulcie swallowed. She'd been asking herself the same question.

"I don't believe they will send us away until Fiona and Clara are capable of making the journey back to Charleston. So for a few days they will tolerate our presence on their island. And perhaps we can find a way to remain a little longer."

"But how?" Starlight asked.

Dulcie glanced around at her young charges. "God works in mysterious ways," she said as bravely as she could manage. Then, straightening her spine, she said, "Come along. It's time to greet our rescuers." And face their prying questions once more, she thought.

As she descended the stairs, her fears nagged at her. The Jermains would be eager to be done with the burden of so many extra mouths to feed. She had to think of a way to make the burden lighter. For she was determined to remain here as long as possible. No matter what price they were forced to pay, she and the others must not be returned to Charleston.

"Well." Aunt Bessie looked up from her mending. It was not one of her favorite tasks, but with all of the household work falling to Robert, she had no choice but to pitch in. "I see you are up and about at last."

"Yes. Thank you for your hospitality. For the beds we slept in. And for washing our clothes," Dulcie said as she shepherded the others into the room.

"For your clothes you can thank Robert. He was not happy with the muddy rags on his floor and thought it best to sacrifice a little sleep in order to achieve the cleanliness he desires."

Aunt Bessie set aside her basket of mending. Though the women and children wore clothes that were clean and pressed, they were indeed little more than rags. It offended her sense of dignity.

"There is hot food in the dining room. Come along."

All eyes widened when they entered the dining room and caught sight of the sideboard groaning under the weight of several silver trays.

"There is corn bread, roasted pork and coddled eggs," Aunt Bessie announced. "I sent Darwin to milk the cow. As I recall, children have need of such nourishment."

"That was kind of you." Dulcie handed each child a plate. But instead of filling them, the children began cramming the food into their mouths.

Aunt Bessie looked horrified. "I simply cannot abide such a lack of manners," she said with indignation. "Where were you children raised? In the streets?"

Dulcie bit back the words that sprang to her lips. Could the woman not see that the children were starving?

Taking charge, she admonished, "You will spoon the food onto your plates. Nathaniel, you may go back for seconds. But for now, take only what you can eat."

"Yes'm." He eyed the food with naked hunger.

"Emily and Belle, I think your eyes are bigger than your stomachs."

The two little girls reluctantly returned half their food to the silver trays, put the rest on their plates and made their way to the table.

Frail Starlight, on the other hand, spooned only a speck of food onto her plate. Dulcie took it from her hands and filled it, then returned it to the young woman. "See that you eat, Starlight. You need to regain your strength."

"I . . . I'll try."

When all were seated, Dulcie prepared a plate for herself and took a seat at the table. She bowed her head and the others did the same, clasping hands as Dulcie murmured, "We thank thee, Father, for this shelter from the storm and for this splendid food."

"Amen," the children intoned.

As the others began eating, Dulcie touched a hand almost lovingly to the lace tablecloth. "This is beautiful, Aunt Bessie."

It took the older woman a moment to gather her wits. She had been first moved to anger by the shocking lack of dining etiquette and was now moved by some other, deeper emotion at the touching scene of the women and children praying.

It had been a long time since she had heard such words in this house. She had never been one for outward signs of religious faith. Her nephews were especially resistant to any displays of religion since their return from the war.

"The lace was made in Belgium." As soon as she took her seat at the table, Robert appeared at her side with a steaming cup of tea. As always, his white shirt and dark pants were perfectly pressed, his shoes polished to a high shine.

A minute later Dar entered carrying a pitcher of milk. As he filled each child's glass, he kept his gaze averted, as though reluctant to look directly into their eyes. But he did glance at Starlight, who ate slowly, as though she'd had little experience at such a feat. Almost at once he looked away.

"Milk?" He paused beside her.

"Yes, please."

He filled her glass quickly, then moved on to Dulcie, who refused. She'd noted that Aunt Bessie had said cow. Singular. If, indeed, there was only one cow on the plantation, it would be important to save what little milk there was for the children who needed it.

His chore completed, Dar fled the room, obviously eager to get away from so many strangers. Perhaps, Dulcie thought, he did not like children. Nor, it seemed, did any of his family.

"Tea, missy?" Robert asked.

"Yes, thank you. And thank you for washing and pressing our clothes, Robert. That was very kind."

Except for a slight arching of his brow, Robert's handsome face remained expressionless.

As Dulcie bit into the coddled eggs, the first she'd actually tasted in months, and corn bread still warm from the oven, she couldn't help sighing. Leaning back, she sipped strong, hot tea. "This is wonderful, Aunt Bessie."

"Thanks to the Yankees who set fire to our home and helped themselves to most of our supplies, it's simple fare," the older woman snapped.

Out of the corner of her eye Dulcie saw the look that came over Starlight, and knew that Bessie's words had sent her retreating into a safe place in her mind. She knew she must deftly change the subject, or the young woman would retreat even farther.

"Simple to you, perhaps, but not to us. This food is heaven-sent." Dulcie glanced around the table, enjoying the way the children looked as they dug into their meal. It was the first time she'd seen them scrubbed clean, wearing crisply ironed clothes. They were, in Dulcie's eyes, a band of angels.

When she'd searched the upper rooms this morning, Dulcie discovered that she was not the only one with her own room, which opened onto a graceful balcony. Nathaniel and Starlight had been given rooms of their own. Emily and Belle had been given a room together. Though they had probably been placed in separate beds, Dulcie had found the two little girls lying together in one bed, their arms still wrapped around each other for comfort.

She could hardly blame them for being fearful. It had been a dangerous, exhausting journey, and she still found it hard to believe they had survived.

"I'm sure you are eager to return to Charleston," Aunt Bessie began. She caught the looks that passed between Dulcie and the others, and thought about what Cal had said over breakfast. She was not imagining the fear she saw in their faces. "But my nephew assures me that the woman and girl are not yet strong enough to make the trip. Therefore, it would appear that you will have to remain with us for a few days.''

Their relief was palpable.

For a moment no one spoke. Then Dulcie broke the silence. ''We wish to repay your kindness.''

''And you shall,'' Aunt Bessie said sternly. ''This is a large plantation. Since the war, we find ourselves without help. There are floors to scrub and rugs to beat. Dishes to wash and—''

''—clothes to mend,'' Dulcie put in, glancing down at her torn gown.

At the word ''mend,'' Aunt Bessie perked up. Perhaps she could be relieved of one of her dreaded chores. ''Can one of you actually sew?''

''I can,'' Starlight said softly as she finished her meal.

Aunt Bessie immediately warmed to the strange young woman. ''Fine, child. Come with me. The rest of you can offer your services to Robert. But beware,'' she cautioned, ''he is a harsh taskmaster. And I am even more so.''

''We are not afraid of hard work,'' Dulcie assured her.

As the children pushed away from the table, Dulcie called to them, ''Each of you will carry a tray laden with dishes to the kitchen. Papa always said, 'With many hands a burden is made light.' ''

In the kitchen, they found Robert busily wrapping food in a square of linen. He seemed genuinely surprised when Dulcie explained that she and the others intended to work in payment for their keep.

''Just tell us what to do and it will be done,'' she said simply.

He thought for several long moments, and it was plain to Dulcie that he was wondering whether he could entrust the care of this fine old house to such inexperienced hands. At length he nodded. "I will show the children what I want them to do. In the meantime, missy, this food must be taken to the men in the fields, along with a heavy jug of water. Can you manage?"

She nodded.

He glanced down at her kid slippers. "Then I would suggest you select a pair of boots from those in the cloakroom. After last night's rain, the fields will be muddy."

Dulcie made her way to the back hallway and pulled on a pair of oversize boots. Picking up the food and water, she stepped outside and began walking across the fields.

It was easy to see where the men were working. A horse plodded slowly across a distant field, with a man at the plow behind, churning up the rich black soil. In his wake walked two more men.

Despite the blazing sun overhead, the air was cooled by a fresh breeze off the water. Dulcie found herself savoring the chance to be alone with her thoughts while enjoying the beautiful day.

Oh, how Papa would have loved this! There was a time when the two of them could have stood here like this all day, enjoying the beauty of nature. Just thinking about those wonderful carefree days brought a smile to her lips. Then, remembering her duty, she walked on.

When she drew close to the two men, she saw they were Barc and Dar. They looked up in surprise.

"What are you doing here?" Barc called.

"I've brought you your midday meal."

"And none too soon." Barc crossed to sit in the shade of a live oak.

Dar dropped down beside him. Both men eagerly drank from the jug, then leaned back on their elbows to watch as Cal followed the horse toward them, etching a straight, perfect furrow as he did.

Dulcie stood there, grateful for the shade. As Cal came closer, she couldn't tear her gaze from him.

He was...magnificent. It was the first word that came to her mind. He had removed his shirt, and the muscles of his upper arms and shoulders bunched and tightened with every step. Sweat glistened in the dark hair that matted his chest. When he came abreast of them and reined in the horse, he lifted an arm to wipe the sweat from his brow.

"Robert has been replaced." Barc handed the water jug to his older brother. "And I, for one, am grateful. Miss Trenton is far easier to look upon."

At Barc's gentle teasing, Dulcie felt the heat rise to her cheeks.

"So I see." Cal balanced the heavy jug in one hand. Tilting back his head, he took a long, deep drink before returning the jug to Barc and wiping the back of his hand across his lips.

"Let's see what Robert sent us." Barc eagerly unwrapped the linen and helped himself to a chunk of corn bread and a slab of cold pork before passing it on to the others.

Cal sat down, leaning against the trunk of the tree. He stretched out his long legs and lazily crossed one foot over the other. "To what do we owe this pleasure, Miss Trenton?"

Dulcie's blush deepened. The sarcastic tone of his voice did not make it sound like a pleasure at all.

"Your aunt explained that if we were to remain here for several days, we might wish to earn our keep."

"And do you wish to earn your keep?" he asked, studying her until she was forced to look away in embarrassment.

"Of course," she said through gritted teeth. "It is not our intention to be a burden to anyone."

"If you were a burden, Miss Trenton," Barc said with a laugh, "you would at least be a most charming one."

Grateful for his glib tongue, she offered him a smile. "What are you planting, Barc?"

"At one time, all of these fields used to be filled with white gold—" Dulcie was familiar with this term for cotton "—but now, with no market for it, and no way to get foodstuffs from the North, we must grow everything we need. In this field we're planting sweet potatoes."

"What other crops do you plant?" Dulcie asked, eager to keep the conversation on less personal subjects.

"Okra, sorghum, corn, beans, grain." Barc pressed a hand to his back. "And anything else Cal can think of that'll keep us stooped over a furrow all day. Isn't that right, Dar?"

Dar only nodded and helped himself to more corn bread.

Cal finished his meal quickly and got to his feet. As he brushed past Dulcie, he muttered, "You may be able to earn your keep, Miss Trenton. But you'll never earn our trust."

He strode back to the waiting horse. Leaning into the harness, man and beast resumed the tedious, backbreaking job that seemed, given the vastness of the fields around them, never-ending.

Stung by Cal's abrupt dismissal, Dulcie gathered up the remains of their meal. Barc touched a hand to her arm. "Don't take offense, Miss Trenton. Cal...has not been himself since the war."

"The war affected all of us," she replied. As she turned to leave, she could feel Cal's dark, piercing stare burn into her, even from the distance that separated them. Lifting her chin, she returned his look before tossing her head and beginning the long walk back to the house.

It didn't matter, she told herself. She didn't care what Cal Jermain said to her or thought of her, just as long as she and the others were allowed to remain here.

She would work. She would endure. But she would never go back.

Chapter Three

"No, little missy, not like that." With a sigh of impatience, Robert took the feather duster from five-year-old Emily's hand and circled it lightly around the various objects that cluttered a tabletop in the formal parlor. "Like this."

The child watched for a moment, more interested in the array of glittering crystal animals than in his deft touch. "It's a bunny!" she cried in delight, lifting one of the pieces.

"You must not touch," Robert admonished sternly. He took the crystal rabbit from her and replaced it exactly as it had been. "Those things belong to Miss Bessie. They are not to be handled by anyone else."

She lowered her head. "Yes, sir."

"I am not a sir. I am just..." Frustrated, he searched for a word. "I am just Robert."

"Yes, sir."

With a shake of his head he handed her the duster and crossed the room to where Nathaniel knelt on the hearth scrubbing soot from the blackened fireplace. Though the fieldstone gleamed, the boy was black from head to foot. Even his blond hair was streaked with soot.

"How does it look?" Nathaniel asked with pride.

Robert took his time, examining the work carefully. The quality of the boy's work was a pleasant surprise.

He pointed to a far corner of the fireplace. "You forgot a spot."

For a moment Nathaniel seemed discouraged. Then he bent to his work once more, saying, "I'll get it so clean you'll be able to see your reflection."

"Eek!"

At Belle's cry of alarm from across the room, Robert raced to where the six-year-old was huddled, her eyes wide with terror. Her job had been a simple one: shake the dust and cobwebs from the heavy draperies and open all the windows to air out the parlor.

The servant drew aside the draperies to see what had caused such an uproar. "Why, it's just a dead mouse, little missy. He cannot hurt anyone."

His words, meant to reassure, only caused her to squeeze her eyes tightly shut and begin to weep and wail.

Nathaniel abandoned his post and hurried over. Seeing the mouse, he wrapped his soot-covered arms around the little girl, as he'd seen Dulcie do a hundred times, and pressed her face against his filthy shirt. Over her head he explained to a startled Robert, "When the soldiers came, Belle and her mother hid in their cellar for weeks. They had nothing to eat, so her mother was finally forced to cook whatever they could catch. Mice mostly. And then her mother died, and Belle was alone..." With all the wisdom of an eight-year-old, he patted Belle's head clumsily and whispered, "Don't cry, Belle. You're not alone now. Like Dulcie said, you'll always have us."

Watching the scene, Robert swallowed, then seemed to take an inordinately long time clearing his throat. At last he commanded imperiously, "You may go back to your chore, Nathaniel. Little missy, you come with me."

The little girl trailed behind his stiff figure, out of the parlor, along the hallway and into the kitchen, at the rear of the big house. While she stood trembling in the doorway, Robert crossed the room and lifted the heavy black kettle from the fireplace.

A wave of terror twisted Belle's dainty features. In her mind's eye she could already see this fearsome man cooking the dead mouse and forcing her to eat it as punishment for failing to complete her chores.

"Come here, little missy," he called sternly.

With slow, jerky movements she made her way to the table, where he stood waiting.

"Sit," he ordered.

Trembling violently, she did as she was told and watched as he placed a steaming cup in front of her.

She stared at him, uncomprehending.

"Tea," he said. "When Miss Bessie finds the day... upsetting, I always fix her tea."

The little girl stared at him, then at the cup. While she watched, he produced a plate on which rested two precious cookies still warm from the oven.

"When you finish your tea and cookies," he said, "you will find me in the parlor." And with that he strode from the room.

Throughout the long afternoon, Dulcie drove herself, beating rugs, scrubbing floors until they shone, rubbing Fiona's bloodied sheets on a scrubbing board until her knuckles were raw. And all the while she kept hearing Cal Jermain's taunting words. *You may earn your keep, Miss Trenton. But you will never earn our trust.*

What did it matter to her what that cruel, ignorant clod thought? As the sun made its arc across the sky, she snapped the sheets off the line and struggled to fold them in the stiff breeze. With each snap of the laundry she told herself that she cared not even that much about Cal Jermain's opinion.

When the last sheet was folded, she grabbed up the huge wicker basket and turned, only to find the object of her venom standing shirtless by the well, washing himself in a bucket of cold water.

For the space of a heartbeat she could do nothing more than stare at the ripple of muscles across his back as he plunged his arms deep into the water and splashed it over his face. Then, forcing herself to move, she started past him. At that moment he turned toward her.

"Miss Trenton. Earning your keep, I see."

She lifted her chin and held her silence. But as she took a step, his hand suddenly shot out, stopping her in midstride.

Shock waves vibrated through her at the strength of his touch. Perhaps it was the heat of the afternoon. Or exhaustion. But whatever, she lashed out at him in a tone usually reserved for Yankee soldiers and villains.

"Unhand me, Mr. Jermain."

Cal had intended to do just that. In fact, he had just broken his self-imposed rule against touching. But now that she was as mad as a spitting wildcat, he changed his mind. He enjoyed seeing her lose that infuriatingly cool composure. A hint of a smile curled his lips. "And if I don't?"

"How would you like to explain to your aunt how a basket of sheets happened to be dumped over you?"

Caught by surprise, he threw back his head and laughed. "Now how do I know you're serious?"

"You need only continue holding me, Mr. Jermain, and you will find out."

His laughter died, though his lips still curved invitingly. "By God, Miss Trenton, I think you'd do just that."

"Then you had best release me."

"I could." His voice lowered to a seductive purr. "Or I could call your bluff."

Using his good right hand, he hauled her roughly against him. She was so astonished by his actions, she dropped the basket, aware of nothing but a pair of dark eyes looking into hers. And lips, still carved in a dangerous smile.

And then his mouth was on hers and she forgot everything except the feel of his lips. Rough. Bruising. Hungry.

His hunger fueled her own. She knew that she should be offering resistance. Instead, her arms hung limply at her sides.

She heard a sound and realized it had come from deep inside her throat, like a growl of pain. Or pleasure. He answered with a moan of his own.

She was lost. Lost in the dark, mysterious taste of him. Lost in feelings unlike any she'd ever known before. Feelings that sent her pulse racing and her heart soaring. Feelings that whispered over her senses, seducing, arousing, making her forget everything except this man and his dangerous, intimate kiss.

Cal couldn't seem to find the will to stop. Holding her, kissing her, stirred up feelings he'd thought buried forever. He had the strangest urge to go on kissing her until night crept over the land and the two of them could get lost in the darkness.

The hunger gnawed at him, causing an ache in his chest. God in heaven, what was happening to him? Calling on all his willpower, he lifted his head, dropped his arms and took a step back.

Dulcie's eyes snapped open. In their depths he could read confusion—and something else. A slumbering sensuality. And then a sudden return of temper.

"I hope you'll forgive me, Miss Trenton." He was surprised at how difficult it was to speak.

"For which offense are you apologizing, Mr. Jermain?" Dulcie struggled to ignore the dryness in her throat. "The kiss? Or your cruel words?"

"I apologize for both, ma'am. I had no right."

Without taking time to think, she lifted the wicker basket and dumped the contents over his head.

"Apology accepted," she called over her shoulder as she turned and raced toward the house as quickly as her trembling legs would carry her.

"This is my favorite time of day." Aunt Bessie surveyed everyone seated around the table. "The day's chores are behind us, and the evening stretches before us like a gift to be savored."

A gift to be savored indeed, thought Dulcie. She'd been given to understand that she and the others were expected to make their appearance at supper and continue with their chores until bedtime.

What was even more difficult was having to face Cal Jermain. She would never be able to forget the scene at the well. Or the confusing feelings he'd stirred up in her.

She forced her attention away from him.

Aunt Bessie wore an elegant gown of black, watered silk with high, ruffled neckline and long, tapered sleeves. At her throat was a cameo broach, and at her earlobes, elegant pearl-and-jade earrings.

Her nephews had changed from their rough field garb to crisp white shirts and dark suits. Though Dulcie, Starlight and the children had no change of clothes, they, too, had taken great pains to wash and make themselves presentable.

Dulcie found herself seated on Cal's right, with Starlight and the girls alongside her. Nathaniel was seated on Cal's left, with Barclay and Darwin beside him. She noted that many of the china plates were cracked, and several of the crystal goblets were chipped. But the dozen candles in silver candelabra in the center of the table cast their golden glow over the lace tablecloth, making the setting appear truly festive.

Robert circled the table, pouring a small amount of wine into goblets. The children's glasses were filled with lemonade.

As Robert took his seat beside Starlight, Dulcie reached out her hands to those on either side of her as she always did. Starlight clasped her right hand, and the children followed suit. Dulcie said softly, "We would ask a blessing upon this food."

She could feel the astonished looks from the Jermain family at her boldness. She was, after all, not an honored guest at table. She was, in fact, an intruder.

Aunt Bessie, a stickler for propriety, said imperiously, "In this house we do our praying without such outward displays of artificial reverence."

"Artificial—!" Starlight began, but a look from Dulcie stopped her in midsentence.

Dulcie and the others lowered their hands to their laps. From his vantage point, however, Cal could plainly see that, under cover of the tablecloth, the young women and children reached out until their hands were once more clasped.

"Besides," Aunt Bessie said sternly, "I believe God has turned His back on us since this damnable war." She turned to her youngest nephew. "Darwin," she said dryly, "you will lead us in prayer."

"Bless this food," Dar intoned.

"Amen," his brothers said in unison, relieved that the prayer had been short and simple.

Aunt Bessie shot Dar a challenging look as she lifted her goblet of wine to her lips. "For a man trained to be elo-

quent, you were very brief. I suppose this is something you
learned while fighting Yankees."

Dar stared pointedly at the table, taking care not to look
at the others. Across from him, Starlight focused on the
candles blazing in their splendid silver holders, seemingly
oblivious to the words being spoken.

"We put in a hard day in the fields," Barc said in defense of his brother. He drained his goblet in one swallow.
"Besides, you know Dar isn't fond of public speaking."

"I notice you have no such problem," his aunt chided.

"None whatever." He turned his attention to Dulcie.
"How are the Irish girl, and the little one?"

"They're improving, thank you." Out of the corner of
her eye she saw Cal's head swivel toward her, but she deter-
minedly kept her gaze focused on his brother. She knew she
was blushing, and that only made the color deepen. "Fiona
isn't alert yet, but her eyes opened once and she managed a
few sounds. And Clara is awake, but she's too weak to eat
yet."

"That's good news—" Barc turned to his older brother
"—isn't it, Cal?"

"Mmm." His brother took a sip of wine before asking,
"What sort of sounds?"

"Moans, really." Dulcie swallowed, remembering the
look of pain that had crossed Fiona's face when she'd responded to Dulcie's voice. "And she squeezed my hand."

"Yes, that's a good sign."

"I hope Fiona wakes up soon," Emily chirped. "I miss
her songs. And the funny stories she tells."

"Do you remember the one—" Belle began, but Aunt
Bessie cut her off.

"I do believe that children should be seen and not heard.
Now sit up straight. And take your elbows off the table. As

long as you are under my roof, you will learn the proper way a young lady comports herself.''

The two little girls looked crestfallen as they struggled to obey. The older woman glanced at Robert. At once he hurried to the kitchen and returned with a tray of food, which he carried around so that the people at the table could serve themselves.

Dulcie glanced at the dour man beside her. As strange as it seemed, she drew comfort from Cal's simple words about Fiona's moans. Despite his lack of manners and his cool, angry demeanor, despite that kiss, which had shaken her to her very core, there was about him an aura of knowledge and solid dependability. Though she was loath to admit it, she trusted his opinion.

Forcing herself out of her musings, Dulcie smiled at the children as they feasted on thick slabs of roasted pork and corn bread smothered in hot gravy. She would take comfort in the fact that the food was good and plentiful. Given enough time here, they would all regain much-needed strength for the task ahead.

"This is truly a fine meal, Aunt Bessie. And a rare treat for all of us." Across the table she saw sunny little Emily cram an entire roll into her mouth and wash it down with lemonade. From the stern look on Aunt Bessie's face, she knew the older woman had seen it, too.

"I must apologize for the dullness of our meals," Aunt Bessie said. "There was a time when we would roast several geese, a wild deer and perhaps a whole pig for one evening's feast." She sighed, a deep sigh of remembrance or regret. "And we would drink champagne from France and wear gowns from Paris and London. Now, thanks to the war," she said wistfully, "it all seems like just a lovely dream. Who knows when we will be able to restore our poor little island to its former beauty." She fell silent for a long moment. "Once again it seems, I have forgotten my vow. I promised myself that if my beloved nephews were returned safely, I would never complain about another thing. And here we are, all together at last. For that I am most humbly grateful."

"You were all in the war?" Nathaniel asked. "Where?"

Cal swung his gaze to the boy. There was something in Nathaniel's tone. Something anguished, something... seeking.

For a moment no one responded to the question. At last Barc said, "I spent half the war in Richmond, then joined General Lee himself. Dar was with Pickett's forces at Gettysburg. Cal was with the Seventh under Stonewall Jackson until he...stayed a little too long at Chancellorsville."

Cal saw the boy lower his gaze to the table. Whatever he was seeking, he had not found it in Barc's words.

Although the children did not understand the importance of the places Barc had mentioned, the names were not lost on Dulcie. She felt saddened and shocked to think that all three brothers had faced such danger.

Aunt Bessie touched a napkin to her lips and spoke to Robert. "We will take our coffee and dessert in the main parlor, Robert."

"Yes, Miss Bessie."

She pushed away from the table and waited until Cal approached and offered his arm.

Dulcie had to rouse Starlight from the dark cloud that enveloped her, brought about by the talk of the war.

Her hand on Cal's sleeve, Aunt Bessie led the way along the hallway to a set of ornate double doors. Sliding the doors open, Cal stood aside and waited for the others to enter. Inside, candles had been lit in sconces along the walls and in an ornate candelabra atop a table. The floor and tabletops gleamed in the candle glow, and everything smelled of beeswax and lye soap.

"What happened to this room?" Barc lifted a brow in surprise.

"We cleaned it," Nathaniel said proudly. "I did the fireplace."

"I've never seen it so clean," Barc said.

"I did the tabletops and little glass animals," Emily said excitedly, her blond curls bobbing up and down.

"And a fine job you did," Barc assured her.

"I counted them," the little girl went on. "Starlight is teaching me to count. There were twenty-eleven of them," she declared.

Dar winced, but Barc smiled and prodded gently, "And can you name all of them?"

"There's a bunny and a turtle and a deer and..." Her voice faded for a moment, then she announced, "But the bunny is my favorite, even though I can't ever touch it."

"And why is that?" Barc asked.

"Mr. Robert said they belong to Aunt Bessie, and I must never, ever touch them."

"Quite right," Aunt Bessie said in her regal tones. She crossed the room and took a seat beside the table.

After everyone else was seated, Robert moved among them, offering coffee for the adults, glasses of milk for the children and cookies for everyone.

When Aunt Bessie saw Nathaniel reaching for a second cookie before he'd eaten his first, she admonished, "Nathaniel, it is polite to take only what you can eat."

"Yes'm. But I know I can eat two."

He glanced at Dulcie for permission. She gently shook her head. With reluctance he replaced the second cookie.

Beside him, Barc helped himself to two cookies and slipped one into the boy's hand. The look on Nathaniel's face spoke volumes.

Across the room, Cal stood alone, a cup in his hand, his left arm hanging stiffly at his side. When Dulcie glanced at him, she found him staring at her. A shiver passed through her and she looked away. But against her will she shot another glance in his direction. Cal bowed his head ever so slightly and lifted his cup in a salute. Her cheeks reddened, and she stiffened her back defiantly before turning away from him.

Across the room, Aunt Bessie watched, intrigued by what she saw. Her flinty nephew and that mysterious young woman struck sparks off each other every time they came close. They had best beware, she thought with a tightly clenched jaw. Sometimes, a single spark was all it took to ignite a forest fire.

Chapter Four

"I will say good-night now." Aunt Bessie handed her cup to Robert and made her way to the door. "Calhoun, will you see me to my room?"

"Of course." Her nephew put down his coffee and offered his arm.

As the two swept from the room and up the wide, curved staircase, Dulcie stifled a yawn. "Come, children," she said. "It's time for bed."

Lulled by the food, exhausted by their day's work, Starlight and the children offered no protest as they followed Dulcie out of the room and up the stairs. Dulcie tucked the two little girls in bed, kissed them, then proceeded to Nathaniel's room.

"Barc is nice, isn't he?" the child murmured as Dulcie smoothed the covers over him.

"Yes."

"He gave me one of his cookies."

"That was kind of him."

"You don't mind?"

Dulcie laughed. "No, Nathaniel, I don't mind. I just want you to remember your manners. These people are kind enough to offer us shelter, and in return we owe them some courtesy."

"I'll work hard, Dulcie."

She tousled his hair and leaned down to kiss his forehead. "I know you will. I'm very proud of you, Nathaniel. Good night."

"Good night, Dulcie."

She closed his door and made her way to the room where Clara lay sleeping. A touch to the child's forehead assured her that there was no fever. For long moments she stood beside the bed, listening to the slow, easy breathing, relieved that her young charge seemed to be mending.

Next she checked on Fiona. The room was in darkness except for a pale sliver of light, and she clasped her friend's hand as she stood by the bed. "Oh, Fiona, I'm frightened for you."

"Don't be." Cal's deep voice, directly behind her, made her gasp and spin around.

At her reaction he said, "Forgive me, Miss Trenton. I thought you'd seen me when you came in. I just thought I'd look in on your friend."

Cal studied Dulcie in the spill of moonlight. Though she resembled so many of the other refugees he'd seen clogging the roads in the South, there was a stubborn strength in her, a fierceness that said she would survive at any cost.

He had a wild impulse to plunge his hand into the silken waves of her dark hair, to feel its smooth texture against his skin. His gaze skimmed her mouth, and he felt his throat go dry at the thought of the kiss he had stolen earlier.

An awkward silence settled between them.

Dulcie studied the man who stood scant inches from her, half his face moonlit, half in shadow. That was how she saw him. A part of him solid and steady, another part dark and dangerous. What was most alarming was that she couldn't decide which side was most attractive to her.

"I'll say good-night now, Miss Trenton." He made no move to leave.

"Good night, Mr. Jermain." She stood very still, watching him.

The figure in the bed moaned, and they both turned, their shoulders brushing as they leaned close.

"Fiona," Dulcie whispered, "can you hear me?"

The young woman moaned again, then drifted back to sleep.

Dulcie gave a shaky sigh. "I suppose I must stop hoping for miracles."

Cal gave a harsh sound that might have been a laugh had it not been so filled with pain. "I gave up on miracles a long time ago."

Without thinking she glanced down at his sleeve. Seeing the direction of her gaze, he stiffened, then turned away.

She thought briefly about holding him back with a touch, a word. But what could she possibly do or say that would ease the awkwardness between them? She allowed the moment to pass.

Without a word he left.

For long minutes she remained, listening to her friend's breathing. The only other sound in the room was the pounding of her own heart.

Cal awoke from a deep sleep to the sound of feminine voices down the hall. Opening one eye, he peered through the gloom, then rolled over, determined to steal a little more rest.

There was a trill of laughter, then more talking.

So much for sleep, he thought as he crawled out of bed and snatched up a pair of trousers. He pulled on his boots, then made his way down the hall, pulling on a shirt as he did. Without bothering to button it, he paused outside a closed door, listening to the high-pitched voices. Though it was not yet dawn, they were chattering like magpies.

He twisted open the door and thundered, "Doesn't anyone care that there are people asleep in this house?"

The sight that greeted him was like a bucket of cold water to his heated temper. The young Irishwoman was propped up in her bed, with mounds of pillows supporting her. Beside her sat the little girl with the injured arm, Clara. Though both of them still looked pale, their eyes were crinkled with laughter. But it was the figure in the middle of the bed that caught and held his attention.

Dulcie sat, surrounded by all her charges, dressed in her chemise and petticoat and draped in a ragged shawl. Her waist-length hair spilled about her shoulders in a riot of curls.

They all looked up with alarm, their laughter quickly extinguished.

"Forgive me, Mr. Jermain," Dulcie said. "We were so happy to see Clara and Fiona recovered from their wounds that we forgot about you and your family."

"I see." He took a step closer to the bed and said to Fiona, "So, you are awake at last."

"Aye." Fiona studied him suspiciously. "And who might you be?"

"Fiona," Dulcie put in quickly, "this is Mr. Cal Jermain. He found our boat and brought us here to his plantation."

"Then I am in your debt, Mr. Jermain." Fiona extended her hand. She continued to watch him warily.

He accepted her handshake. But when he tried to touch a hand to Clara's forehead, the little girl shrank from him.

"It's all right," Dulcie said softly. "Mr. Jermain just wants to see if your fever has subsided."

Cal deliberately kept his touch gentle as he pressed his fingers to the young girl's skin. After the briefest of contacts, he lowered his hand. He saw her gaze follow his movement, then shift to his other arm, where the cuff of his shirt ended abruptly.

"You will require some nourishment," he said, turning away. "I'll wake Robert."

"No." Dulcie wriggled off the bed. "It's enough that we cost you your sleep. Please don't wake Robert. I can see to their needs."

He tried not to stare at the bare feet, the shapely ankles, peeking out from beneath her petticoat. "As you wish, Miss Trenton. Come along." He lifted a candle from the table beside Fiona's bed. "I'll give you some assistance."

Cal led the way to the kitchen and lit a lantern to dispel the gloom. Soon, with a fire on the hearth, the empty room took on a warm glow.

Without a word, Cal disappeared.

Dulcie filled a kettle from a bucket of water and placed it over the fire to boil. Then she split half a dozen biscuits and drizzled them with honey before placing them on a warming shelf above the fireplace.

When the water boiled, she wrapped a linen square around her hand and lifted the blackened kettle from the fire. Turning, she was surprised to see Cal standing at the table with a bucket of milk, which he poured into several glasses.

"I thought you'd gone to bed." She felt a flush creep into her cheeks.

"No point in trying to sleep now. Besides, the cow would need milking in a few hours. I thought I'd save Dar the trouble. And I figured the children might be feeling hungry."

He reached over her to a high shelf. As he did, his hand brushed the top of her head. The softness of her hair against his skin caused a pleasant sensation. Though he hadn't intended it, he slowed his movements in order to better enjoy the moment.

What was it about this woman that heightened all his senses? Standing here, barely touching, he became aware of the soft scent of her, like a meadow after a spring rain. Though the shawl preserved her modesty, he could tell that the body beneath the opaque chemise and petticoat was perfectly formed. Long legs. Rounded hips. A slender waist. A shadowy cleft between high, firm breasts. The pale column of throat. And a face so fair, so lovely, it made his heart skip a beat.

He removed a small pouch containing tea and spices. "Aunt Bessie swears by their healing properties," he said as he measured some into a cup.

Dulcie poured the water, inhaling their fragrance. "I don't know if this can truly heal, but it smells wonderful."

"Then fix yourself a cup. And one for me," he added impulsively, sprinkling the precious spiced tea into two more cups.

He couldn't imagine why he'd said that. It had been years since he'd tasted Aunt Bessie's tea. And even more years since he'd done something so spontaneous. But the tea and spices did smell wonderful. And it was a small compensation for having missed his sleep.

When everything was arranged on a heavy silver tray, Cal picked it up, deftly balancing one side on his maimed arm. He indicated the lantern. "Lead the way, Miss Trenton."

He followed her along the hallway and up the stairs, achingly aware of the sway of her hips beneath the petticoat. If the very proper Miss Dulcie Trenton knew what he was thinking, he would certainly taste her temper again. Only this time, instead of a basket of sheets, he might find himself wearing a tray of biscuits, milk and hot tea.

He could still taste that first shocking kiss. A second one would be worth whatever punishment she meted out. The thought brought a smile to his lips, which he quickly erased as she shoved open the door to Fiona's room.

At the sight of milk and biscuits, little Emily clapped her hands in delight. "Oh, Dulcie! Is this a party?"

"Indeed it is. We are celebrating Clara and Fiona's return to the land of the living." Dulcie made room on the nightstand, and Cal set down the tray.

"Aunt Bessie's spiced tea for you, Fiona," Dulcie announced as she handed her friend a cup.

"Aunt Bessie?"

"She is Mr. Jermain's aunt. She asked us to call her Aunt Bessie while we are here."

Clara accepted a glass of milk and asked solemnly, "How long will that be?"

Everyone glanced at Cal. Aware of the tense silence that had descended upon them, he weighed his words carefully. They were, after all, an inconvenience to him and his family. But it seemed unnecessary to spoil the moment.

"I'm sure you will be eager to leave as soon as both Fiona and Clara are strong enough to travel by boat to the mainland."

"Do you mean Charleston?" Clara asked.

"Yes. That would be the nearest town."

"But we can't—"

In a panic, Dulcie passed the plate under the child's nose and said firmly, "Have a biscuit, Clara."

Cal saw the worried glances the others exchanged.

The moment passed. Clara nibbled a biscuit and retreated into stony silence. The other children sat, heads bowed, avoiding his eyes. Even Starlight, nervously tracing a finger along the pattern on the quilt, refused to lift her head.

The little scene confirmed Cal's worst suspicions. This bunch was hiding something. Even innocent children had been coerced into keeping the secret.

He drained his cup without taking the time to taste the delicate spices. Then he placed it on the tray and said abruptly, "I'll bid you all good morning."

No one spoke as Cal's footsteps receded down the hallway.

Minutes later Dulcie gathered the empty glasses and cups and placed them on the silver tray. Turning, she kissed Clara and Fiona, then said to the others, "There's still time for an hour or more of sleep before the day begins. I suggest we put it to good use."

She lifted the candle and led her little party to their rooms. Then she headed downstairs with the tray. But as she stepped into the kitchen, she realized her mistake.

Cal had not gone back to bed. He was standing by the window, staring out over the moonlit fields. When he turned to her, there was an ominous look in his eyes.

"What is it you and the others are hiding, Miss Trenton?"

Dulcie's breath backed up in her throat. Setting down the tray, she turned away, intent on leaving without a response. But his hand on her sleeve stopped her.

"I demand an answer, Miss Trenton."

She lifted her chin in that infuriating way and turned to face him. "What you ask is none of your concern, Mr. Jermain."

"The fact that you have taken refuge in my home makes it my concern, Miss Trenton. I want no trouble brought to my doorstep. The war has left my family weary beyond belief."

Her own tone deepened with passion. "I will remind you that yours was not the only family touched by the war. We are all weary. But we must go on if we are to survive."

Anger made him careless. Without taking time to consider his actions, he dragged her close, until her face was mere inches from his. Hot breath fanned her cheek as he growled, "Woman, you try my patience to the limit. Now tell me what it is that sent you fleeing into the eye of a storm."

She tried to pull away, but his strength was too great. The fire in his eyes frightened her, but she would never let him know that. Instead, she fought back with haughty indignation. "You go too far, sir. Release me at once."

"Tell me why you are running."

Dulcie froze.

Seeing her reaction he said, "If it is in my power, I will help you. But you must be honest with me."

She struggled to push free of his arms, but he held her fast. "Damn you, woman. Trust me."

She gave a sound that might have been a harsh laugh. Her throat was so constricted she could barely get the words out. "If the war has taught me one thing, it is not to trust anyone." Anger darkened her eyes. "Certainly not a man who tries to force his will on me."

Cal's eyes narrowed as though he'd been struck. Without a word he turned away and strode from the kitchen, slamming the door behind him.

For long minutes Dulcie stood, listening to the sound of his footfall as he stalked to the barn. If only she was free to confide in him. But she dared not. She had sworn the others to secrecy. She would not be the one to break the vow.

For now, she must live in a prison of her own making. And there was no room in that prison for the embittered Cal Jermain.

Chapter Five

As Dulcie and Starlight entered the dining room for the morning meal, they were met by Aunt Bessie.

"Good morning." The older woman studied them both with a cool, calculating look that had Dulcie's cheeks blooming. "Are the children still abed?"

"Yes. I thought I would let them sleep awhile." Dulcie glanced around the table, noting with relief that Cal was missing. "I see they are not the only ones still sleeping."

Barc gave a short laugh. "If you mean my brother, Miss Trenton, you are mistaken. Cal has been out in the fields since sunup."

"Oh, dear. We disturbed his sleep, I fear," Starlight said in dismay.

"Cal?" Barclay shook his head. "I wouldn't worry about him. Since his return from the war, he rarely sleeps more than a few hours a night."

"Does his wound still pain him?" Starlight asked.

"To which wound do you refer?" Barc sipped hot, strong coffee and watched as the two young women helped themselves to food from the sideboard.

At Dulcie's urging, Starlight filled her plate. Satisfied that the girl was eating enough to regain her strength, Dulcie helped herself to eggs and a biscuit and took her seat at the table.

Starlight arched a brow. "I don't understand. How many wounds has your brother suffered?"

"There is the obvious one," Barc said, "and I suppose the loss of a hand would be enough to do in most men. But Cal carries other, hidden wounds, as well."

"Hidden?" Starlight said softly.

Beside her, Dulcie went very still.

Barc glanced at his aunt, who was frowning in disapproval.

"It is not proper to discuss such personal matters with strangers," she protested.

He shrugged. "Aunt Bessie, Cal is not the first man whose beloved refused to wait for him while he was off fighting the war."

His revelation had Dulcie reeling. She could imagine Cal's pain at returning, broken in body and spirit, only to find that the woman he loved had deserted him. That would explain at least some of his bitterness.

And then another thought intruded. *Sarah*. The woman's name was Sarah. That was what Cal had called her in the boat. She shivered, recalling dark, angry eyes, the threatening, ominous stance. Did she look like Sarah? she wondered. Was that why he was forever scowling at her?

"Fortunately," Barc added with a chuckle, "I do not share my brother's problems. In fact, quite the contrary. There were so many ladies waiting for my return I was forced to lavish attention on dozens of them. It's quite exhausting work, which continues to drain me more with each passing evening."

Dulcie managed to smile at his joke, grateful that he always seemed able to relieve the tension. But his aunt was still frowning.

When Robert appeared at Dulcie's side with a cup of tea, she accepted gratefully. "Thank you, Robert," she murmured. "Where would you like us to begin work today?"

He looked beyond her to Aunt Bessie, who said, "You can begin on the upper floor today. I would like the bedrooms thoroughly cleaned and aired." She wrinkled her nose and added, "Barclay's room positively reeks of cigar smoke whenever I pass by. And Darwin has accumulated so many books it's a wonder he is able to find his bed."

Across the table, Dar blushed clear to his toes, but as was his custom, he said nothing in his own defense.

Starlight's eyes danced with unconcealed joy. "You have books to read, Dar?"

When he merely nodded, Barc answered for him. "It's my younger brother's passion. I believe he would rather read than eat or sleep."

"I envy you," the young woman said shyly.

"Would . . . would you care to borrow one or two of my books?" Dar asked.

Starlight was suddenly as shy as he. "Oh, no. I couldn't possibly. But thank you."

Both of them seemed to become deeply engrossed in the food on their plates.

Barc pushed away from the table. "It's time we got to work. By now, Cal has probably plowed another acre. Or five. He seems in an especially dark mood today. That always means more work than usual."

Dar stood and followed him from the room without a word. For a moment Aunt Bessie watched them go with a look of sadness in her eyes. Then, as if pulling herself back from her thoughts, she faced the two young women.

"You may begin with Barclay's room. I'll send the children along to help after they've eaten their breakfast." As

Dulcie and Starlight got up from the table, she added, "But don't bother with Calhoun's room. He left word that he did not want anything disturbed."

Barc's room did indeed reek of cigar smoke. And whiskey. A crystal decanter of aged bourbon stood on the nightstand, along with an impressive array of legal tomes, which showed evidence of having been much read.

Dulcie and Starlight threw open the windows and stripped the bedding. At Dulcie's insistence, Starlight was allowed to help only with lighter tasks, which would not tax her fragile strength.

With Robert's help Dulcie hauled the feather mattress outside, where she beat it and left it in the sun to air. When the children had finished breakfast, they helped scrub the floors until they gleamed, under the stern, watchful eye of Aunt Bessie. Nathaniel again worked on the stones of the fireplace until all the soot had been removed.

In Dar's room Dulcie and Starlight found a lantern still burning beside a pile of books on his night table.

"Absentminded," Starlight muttered as she began to clean the blackened chimney of the lantern.

"Look at all the books!" Dulcie exclaimed.

There were history books stacked on the hearth. Books on astronomy, science, biology on a table near the window. Mathematics books, English textbooks, poetry peeking out from beneath his bed.

"Do you think anyone could read all these?" Starlight asked.

"Of course," Dulcie replied. "Why else would they be here?"

Starlight seemed awestruck as she flipped through the pages. "So many things to read. To understand. To know. He must be...brilliant."

Dulcie found herself agreeing, though she said nothing. The shy man who inhabited this room showed a curious, questing mind. It would seem, she thought as she and Starlight filled a pitcher with fresh water and returned clean rugs to the floor, that Dar Jermain was more complex than he appeared. Though the man said very little, he was obviously well versed on a variety of subjects.

Aunt Bessie's room was a curious mix of neatness and clutter. Her huge four-poster was mounded with pillows.

"Seven," Starlight exclaimed in surprise as she began removing them. "Imagine that. How can anyone use seven pillows?"

"Perhaps she's a restless sleeper," Dulcie said as she stripped the rest of the bedding.

Aunt Bessie's armoire was a model of efficiency, her gowns hung in orderly rows, shoes set in pairs beneath, hats and gloves laid out on a shelf above. Her jewelry, on the other hand, carelessly spilled from a satin case and covered almost every inch of her dressing table. The mantel above the fireplace was crammed with more crystal figurines, heavy silver candlesticks, various bric-a-brac and souvenirs from Bessie's world travels.

A chaise was pulled up in front of the fireplace. Tossed negligently over it was an ornate Oriental dressing gown.

"Dulcie," Starlight called, tracing a finger over the patterns on the silk, "whatever are these?"

"They would appear to be Chinese characters," Dulcie said.

"Do you think Aunt Bessie has been all the way to China?"

Dulcie smiled. "I wouldn't be at all surprised."

"Just think," Starlight said with a sigh. "She has led such an exciting life, and I've never been anywhere except Charleston. And, of course, this island."

Dulcie glanced out the window, her gaze drawn to the figures working in the distant field. "Papa used to say it doesn't matter where you live. It's how you live that counts."

It was dinnertime. Upstairs in the hallway Clara clutched Dulcie's hand so tightly her knuckles were white from the effort. She and Fiona were about to be presented to the household, and she was plainly nervous. Dulcie gave her a reassuring smile, and when Fiona and the others joined them, the group descended the stairs.

As they entered the dining room, Cal, Barc and Dar were standing to one side of the room talking among themselves. All three men had, as usual, changed from their work garb into white shirts and dark suits.

Aunt Bessie, already seated at the head of the table, wore a gown of black satin, with a rope of iridescent pearls that shimmered in the candlelight. Her hair had been swept up into an elegant knot secured with jeweled combs.

Dulcie led Fiona and Clara to her chair and said, "Aunt Bessie, this is my friend, Fiona O'Neil. And this," she said, keeping her hands on the little girl's shoulders to lend her courage, "is Clara."

"At last we can be formally introduced," Aunt Bessie said. "I am pleased you feel strong enough to join us." She made an elegant, sweeping gesture with her hand. "May I present my nephews, Calhoun, Barclay and Darwin."

The three men nodded stiffly.

"Come and sit," Aunt Bessie invited. "Miss O'Neil, take the seat beside me. I should like to hear more about the adventure that caused your injury."

Fiona shot a glance at Dulcie before taking the proffered chair. She was aware that the three men had suddenly taken a keen interest in her conversation as they seated themselves.

"Aye," Fiona said softly, "'Twas indeed an adventure. When the storm broke above us, I thought we'd breathed our last. Imagine my surprise at waking up in a fine bed surrounded by such luxury."

"Will your family not be worried?" Aunt Bessie asked sharply.

Fiona's brogue thickened. "I've no family here in America. And no one to worry over the likes of me. Only Dulcie and Starlight and the children. We look out for one another." Her loving gaze swept all of them.

The Jermain family saw that affection returned in the eyes of their guests.

Aunt Bessie summoned Robert, who entered carrying a silver tray. When he lifted the domed lid, the room was suddenly filled with the fragrance of roast turkey with sage dressing and wild rice.

"Robert can work wonders with wild game," Aunt Bessie boasted as he circled the table.

Dulcie was grateful for his presence. Though she had warned Fiona and Clara about Aunt Bessie's sharp tongue and keen powers of observation, she was not eager to see the little girl go through the same interrogation as Fiona. She was, in fact, determined to keep Clara as far away from Aunt Bessie as possible.

As if reading her mind, the older woman pinned Clara with a look and asked, "And how about you, child? Are you also without family?"

"This is my family," Clara said solemnly. "Dulcie and Fiona and Starlight, and Emily and Belle and...Nathaniel." The little boy's name was spoken reluctantly, as though she regretted having to consider him family.

"And no one searches for any of you?"

"Searches...?" Clara turned wide eyes on Dulcie before lowering her head to stare at a spot on the table.

Robert chose that moment to pause beside Clara's chair. "Help yourself, little missy."

When her hands began to tremble, Dulcie took the serving fork and filled Clara's plate and then her own.

"Thank you, Robert," she murmured. He would never know how grateful she was for that little interruption. Or had he done it deliberately?

As he took his seat at the table, Dulcie turned to Aunt Bessie. "I hope you don't mind if we ask a blessing upon our food?"

"Do you really believe He can keep track of so many of us, Miss Trenton?" Without waiting for a reply the older woman turned to her middle nephew. "Would you like to lead us in prayer, Barclay?"

"I'm out of practice," he said as Dulcie and the others clasped hands beneath the tablecloth, "but I'll do my best." He paused. "Heavenly Father, bless this charming company, especially the two who have been given the strength to finally join us, and bless this fine food, which You have so generously provided."

"Amen," chimed in the others.

"I see your oratorical skills did not fail you," Aunt Bessie said dryly. "Now if only you could pass them along to your brothers." She turned to Cal. "How is the planting coming?"

"Slow." He dragged his gaze from Dulcie, who had taken great pains to soothe the anxious little girl beside her. There was more going on here than met the eye. All of them were afraid of something or someone. He pulled his thoughts back to his aunt's question. "The storm ruined one field of seedlings. That set us back about a week or more. Looks like another storm is brewing. If it hits, we'll probably have another washout.''

"What we need are a dozen more field hands," Barc said wryly. "Dar and I can't keep up with Cal's plowing. He's like a man possessed, working from sunup to sundown. I believe he'd work through the night if he could."

Nathaniel's head came up. "I could help," he said around a mouthful of sweet potatoes.

Barc's eyes warmed with amusement. "You're not quite what I had in mind, lad."

"But I'm a good worker. Tell him, Dulcie," the boy pleaded. "Tell him I could help."

She studied his earnest expression a moment before saying softly, "Indeed you could, Nathaniel. In fact—" her voice rose with excitement "—we could all help with the planting."

"It isn't fit work for women and children," Cal said sternly.

"But—" Dulcie began.

"I quite agree," Aunt Bessie said emphatically.

From the tone of her voice, Dulcie knew the subject was closed.

"And furthermore," the older woman went on, "I have repeatedly instructed you children to speak only when spoken to. I hope I should not have to remind you again." She stared pointedly at Nathaniel. "Especially when your mouth is full."

"Yes'm," he said, ducking his head.

"Robert," Aunt Bessie said sharply, "we will take our coffee and dessert in the parlor."

With that command, she swooped from the room on Cal's arm, leaving the others to follow in her wake.

When they entered the parlor, Fiona decided to ask about the portrait above the fireplace. "Who are these handsome people?"

"Our parents." Barc's tone was warm with affection.

"Cal looks like his father," Starlight said.

"Indeed he does," Aunt Bessie agreed. "And he was named for him. My brother, Calhoun, was a well-respected judge here in the Carolinas. Barclay and Darwin more resemble their mother. Catherine was a true lady, educated in the finest schools and a much-loved teacher herself. From the day she married my brother, she became my best friend. I miss her every day."

"Have they been . . . gone long?" Starlight asked hesitantly.

"Three years now. Catherine followed Calhoun to the grave by less than a month. I will always believe she died of a broken heart." Aunt Bessie sighed. "Brought about, not only by the death of her dear husband, but by the fact that all three of her sons were off fighting, and not one of them could be here in her hour of need. That damnable war," she muttered as she sank into an overstuffed chair and was rewarded by a gasp from little Clara at her profanity. Her voice rose. "I shall never forgive those Yankees for what they did to my beloved South."

"Not all of the destruction was done by Yankees," Dulcie said sharply.

"What sort of traitorous talk is that, girl?" Aunt Bessie rounded on her. "Did you see what General Sherman did to our land? He ordered his soldiers to burn our crops, kill our flocks and level our buildings."

"I am aware of that," Dulcie said. "But I still say there were many who contributed to our downfall. And not all of them outsiders."

"You are quite right." Cal's words, spoken softly, had everyone turning to him. "There is no one alive in this country, North or South, who was untouched by the war."

"I suppose so." Aunt Bessie sighed, her sudden flare of anger deflected by her nephew's words. "And I have no right to complain, for our little family is intact."

Robert moved among them, dispensing coffee and milk and small plates on which rested thick slices of cake drizzled with raspberry preserves.

Clara, perched on a chaise between Fiona and Dulcie, stared long and hard at the precious cake on her plate, as if unable to believe her eyes.

"You mean I can eat all of it?" she whispered.

Cal, overhearing, watched as Dulcie assured the little girl that she could. When the child's cake had been devoured, Dulcie offered hers, as well, but Clara shook her head solemnly.

"It wouldn't be fair," she said.

Dulcie dared not argue with Clara's rigid sense of right and wrong. To appease her, she ate half her cake, then coaxed Clara to eat the other half by insisting that she was too full to eat another crumb. Soon the child's eyes fluttered closed, and she leaned her head on Dulcie's shoulder.

"Come, Clara," Dulcie whispered.

Before she could rouse the child, Cal scooped her into his arms. "If you'll lead the way, Miss Trenton, I'll carry her. I think she's had quite enough on her first day out of bed."

"Thank you." She lifted a candle from the table.

As she started toward the door, Fiona said, "There is no need to return for the other children, Dulcie. Starlight and I can see the children to their beds."

"I bid you all good-night then," Dulcie called from the doorway.

She led the way up the curving staircase, her heartbeat accelerating with every step. She pushed open the door to Clara's room, set the candle on the nightstand and drew back the covers, then stepped aside so that Cal could deposit the sleeping child in bed. Bending, she tucked the covers around Clara's shoulders and brushed a kiss over her forehead.

She straightened and turned. "Thank you," she whispered.

Cal didn't say a word. He merely stared at her in that deep, penetrating way that made her scalp prickle with discomfort.

Alarmed, she picked up the candle from the nightstand. "I will say good-night now, Mr. Jermain."

She was startled when, as she headed toward the door, he stopped her with a hand on her arm and blew out the candle, leaving them in only the faint light from the hallway. The candle slipped from her fingers and would have fallen to the floor had he not caught it and set it on the chest of drawers.

Then he lifted his hand to her cheek in an oddly tender gesture. She could not have been more thunderstruck if he had slapped her. The roughness of his palm against her smooth flesh caused a rush of feelings that left her shaken to her core.

Heat blazed through her veins, turning her blood to flame. Suddenly his touch was no longer gentle. His fingers cupped the back of her head and pulled her close.

"You must not—" she began, but the words died on her lips as his mouth covered hers.

There was no tenderness in the kiss, no gentleness. Only raw, hungry need. It flared between them like lightning on a sultry night, catching them both by surprise.

She thought about shoving him away, but as her hands came up to his chest, her fingers curled around the front of his shirt, clutching him like a lifeline.

The taste of him, dark, earthy, filled her, until she moaned softly.

That only served to inflame him further, and he savaged her mouth as, with teeth and tongue and lips, he took her on a wild, dizzying ride.

"Please," she whispered as she pushed ineffectively against him. "You must stop."

"Are you saying you don't like this?" His low tone was rough, challenging.

"No, but I can't think. I—" His mouth again moved over hers, swallowing her words, and she gave herself up once more to the pleasure of his kiss.

They clung together, their hearts beating wildly, their breathing ragged.

Then, as suddenly as the kiss had begun, it ended. Cal lifted his head and took a step back, as though afraid of being too close to the flame.

"Mr. Jermain, I—"

He placed a finger over her lips. "Hush, Miss Trenton."

Mesmerized, she stood very still as his hand lowered to her throat, where a little pulse jumped. There was no thought of running. She was unable to move, unable to speak. She could think of nothing except the touch of his fingertips as they moved over her.

"I don't know why you came here, Miss Trenton." His whispered words were fierce with meaning. He was surprised at how difficult it was to speak. "But I know that if you stay, we would ... we would both be lost. Do you understand?"

Dulcie shook her head, still unable to speak. She swallowed the knot of fear in her throat, struggling with feelings that were so new, so overpowering, she could not even give them a name. She was trembling on the brink of something so new, so momentous . . .

She knew she must break this spell. She stepped toward the door, eager to escape. Again his hand on her arm stopped her in midstride.

His voice was hushed, fierce. "Do you agree that Fiona and Clara are strong enough to make the journey by boat back to the mainland?"

His words caught her by surprise. He was speaking in riddles. If she stayed, they were lost. And so he was sending her away. But if she left here . . . Oh, sweet heaven. She would be lost either way.

She closed her eyes a moment against the pain and took a deep breath. "I . . ." She moistened her dry lips with her tongue and saw the way his gaze followed the movement. It only added to her nervousness. "I suppose they could endure the journey."

"Tomorrow, then." He nodded, having made up his mind. "I'll arrange for Barc to take you. He'll be only too happy to earn a reprieve from the farm chores."

His gaze swept over her, lingering on her mouth. She felt the heat as surely as if he was still kissing her.

She could see the longing in his eyes. A hungry, desperate look. She had an almost overpowering desire to reach out to him, to draw him close and offer comfort. But then he blinked and the look was gone.

Cal watched the play of emotions on her expressive features and knew the battle she was waging. There was fear there. But there was also slumbering passion. A passion that, once awakened, would be all a man could want.

"This is best." He seemed about to say something more. Then, thinking better of it, he clamped his mouth shut and turned away.

As his footsteps receded down the hall, Dulcie stood in the darkness of Clara's room for long, silent moments, willing her heart to return to a steady rhythm. She could feel the heat along her arm where he'd touched her. The taste of him still lingered on her lips.

In the space of just moments, the fate of all of them had been sealed. And it had something to do with her weakness. And his.

In the morning, they would return to hell.

Chapter Six

With a heavy heart Dulcie took a turn around the bedrooms, assuring herself that all the children were asleep. Once again, Belle had sought refuge in Emily's bed, and the two little girls slept locked in each other's arms. Sunny, sweet Emily was the perfect companion for the fearful Belle. Though both children had suffered greatly during the war, Belle now faced every day expecting the worst, terrified that the past would return to haunt her, while Emily sailed into each new morning, grateful that the past was behind her. Perhaps, in time, Dulcie thought, each would learn something of value from the other.

Nathaniel was sprawled lengthwise across his bed, one foot dangling over the edge. With a little effort Dulcie was able to nudge him into a more comfortable position and tuck the covers around him. She smoothed back a lock of hair and felt a rush of tenderness for the little boy so eager to become a man, even though he'd never had a chance at childhood.

Starlight's room was awash with moonlight. She had tied the heavy draperies back with cords and positioned her bed so that she could see out the window. Dulcie stood beside her bed and studied the sleeping figure. Starlight lay on her side, curled into a tight little ball. Both hands were knotted into fists. From one hand dangled a locket. From the other, a small, deadly knife.

Tears flooded Dulcie's eyes. Blinking them back, she turned away. How would Starlight take the news that they were leaving this safe haven? What would become of her? Of all of them?

With a prayer on her lips, Dulcie made her way to her own bed. But she knew that sleep would not visit her tonight.

The storm started sometime just before dawn.

Dulcie was startled by a sound unlike anything she'd ever heard before. A wind so terrible it bore down with the ferocity of a locomotive.

She leaped out of bed and ran to the window. Outside, giant trees bent low to the ground. While she watched, several snapped like twigs and were carried hundreds of yards before dropping, smashing everything that lay in their path.

Lightning danced across the sky and thunder shook the huge old house with such force it seemed to shudder. While she watched, a brilliant flash of lightning skittered along the lower veranda, followed by a puff of smoke.

"Oh, sweet heaven! Fire!" she screamed as she raced from her room and began pounding on closed doors. "Hurry. Hurry. The house is on fire!"

Soon doors opened. Everyone stumbled into the hallway, pulling on their clothes as they scrambled toward the stairs.

Robert emerged from his room off the kitchen and joined the others in gathering up as many buckets as they could find. A blur of figures hurried out to the well.

Outside the wind was so fierce they seemed to take two steps backward for every step forward. Bending almost double against the onslaught, Dulcie was tempted to order the children back inside. But it was too late. The little ones, holding hands with Starlight and Fiona, formed a human chain. While Robert filled their buckets, they passed them along from hand to hand.

With so many hands, the fire was quickly extinguished. But sparks borne on the wind were carried to the barn. Within minutes, they had ignited another full-blown blaze.

"The barn!" Dulcie shouted. "Quickly. There's another fire in the barn."

There was no time to catch their breaths. While Cal and Barc and Dar battled the flames with water, Dulcie and Aunt Bessie led the horses and cow to safety, sheltering them in a small shed. By the time they returned to the barn, it was engulfed in flames. But that didn't deter those who were doing battle.

The children continued passing buckets. Barc and Dar tossed a steady stream of water on the billowing flames. Cal had picked up a horse blanket and was beating it against the walls of the barn. Following suit, Dulcie grabbed up a blanket and joined him.

"Over there!" he shouted, and Dulcie saw a thin line of flame break out on a far wall. At once she raced to the spot and began to beat at it.

Soon Cal joined her and the two fought the blaze side by side until, whipped by the wind, it became a wall of flame.

"Get back!" Cal commanded. His voice roared above the sound of the storm.

Dulcie refused to give up. Instead, she renewed her efforts, beating back the fire until she thought her arms would surely fall off. But each time she managed to extinguish a flame in one place, the wind would rush and swirl, causing sparks to leap and dance, and fire would break out in another spot.

Fire raced through the wooden structure, igniting straw and stalls and snaking across the high wooden beams. Still,

Dulcie and Cal worked on relentlessly until, despite their efforts, the walls began to cave inward, and the roof began to collapse.

"It's no use. Run!" Amid a rain of fire, Cal caught Dulcie's arm and dragged her backward.

Running, stumbling, they retreated and joined the others who had gathered near the well to witness the fiery ending. Dulcie dropped into the grass beside Fiona and watched in horror as the last of the beams crashed into the inferno and flames leaped into the air. Fiery missiles streaked into the darkened sky and fell to earth in a shower of flaming embers.

At the same moment, the heavens opened up in a cloudburst. Though the rain was too late to save the barn, the exhausted little party let out a collective sigh of relief, for they knew that the fire would not spread to the other buildings.

"Come along." Aunt Bessie, buffeted by wind and rain, leaned heavily on Cal's arm as she led the bedraggled party toward the house.

Dulcie handed the children off to Starlight, then turned to Fiona, who continued to lie in the grass.

"What is it?" Dulcie cried as she knelt beside her friend.

"Now don't go fretting," Fiona whispered. "I'm just a little weak is all."

"Barc! Dar!" Dulcie shouted.

At once the two young men hurried to her side.

"Fiona needs help."

The two assisted Fiona to her feet. Barc, ignoring her protests, lifted her into his arms and carried her through the pouring rain to the house.

"I should have made you stay in bed," Dulcie muttered as she led the way to a chair.

"I'm fine now. Really I am," Fiona insisted.

"Barc, could you fetch a blanket please?" Dulcie said over her friend's objections.

"Of course." He returned within minutes and wrapped it around Fiona's trembling shoulders.

Dulcie appeared at her side with a steaming cup of tea, which Robert had prepared. "Drink this," she ordered.

Dulcie then turned her attention to the shivering children, who huddled around Starlight.

"Is everyone all right?" she asked.

"We're fine," Starlight assured her. "Just a little wet and cold."

The frail young woman actually seemed invigorated by the battle. It occurred to Dulcie that Starlight had been given the opportunity to fight back. And that act had given her a sense of power.

Dulcie hurried upstairs and returned carrying blankets. While Robert moved among them distributing tea laced with sugar and milk, she saw to it that they removed their wet clothes and were carefully wrapped in warmth.

The storm continued to rage, hurling wind and rain against the house with such force the windows rattled.

Belle and Clara began to whimper and snuggled closer to Starlight for comfort.

Aunt Bessie set down her cup of tea with a clatter. "I believe we will move to the parlor," she announced. "Robert, will you get a fire started in there, please?"

"Yes, ma'am."

"Darwin, fetch one of your books, if you please. Something appropriate for the little ones. Children, follow me," she commanded imperiously. "Calhoun, perhaps you and Barclay should help Fiona up to bed. Dulcie, you go along with them, in case your friend should have need of you."

"Yes, of course." Despite her weariness, Dulcie forced herself to move slowly behind the two men, who were assisting Fiona.

Upstairs, she turned down Fiona's bedding and helped her to settle into bed. Then she moved aside as Cal sat on the edge of the bed and touched a hand to her friend's forehead.

"You have a slight fever," he said. "But it could be due to all the excitement. I think the best remedy is sleep."

"I'll need no coaxing," Fiona said as her lids fluttered. But she opened her eyes long enough to whisper, "Thank you."

The two men nodded and started toward the door with Dulcie following. But as she stepped into the hallway, Cal caught her hand in his, turning it palm up.

Embarrassed, Dulcie tried to pull her hand away, but Cal held it firmly in his as he examined the raw, painful blisters.

"My God, woman, how can you ignore something like this?" Cal caught her roughly by the elbow and propelled her toward the stairs. "Barc, ask Robert to come to the kitchen. And tell him to fetch my ointments."

"It . . . doesn't matter," Dulcie said softly.

With a muttered oath Cal led her down to the kitchen and forced her into a chair. "Let me see those hands," he commanded.

Feeling her cheeks flame, she rested her soot-covered hands, palms up, on the table. Cal studied them for several minutes, then stalked away and returned with a basin of soapy water.

"This will sting," he cautioned as he plunged her hands into it one at a time.

Robert hurried into the room carrying a linen towel and several vials. Cal spread the towel alongside the basin, then opened the vials.

Despite her pain, Dulcie wrinkled her nose at the foul-smelling ointment. Cal's touch was tender as he began to spread the ointment over her palms. For a moment her flesh was on fire, and she let out a cry.

Aunt Bessie strode into the kitchen, then skidded to a halt at the sight that greeted her. "Barclay said Dulcie's hands were badly burned."

"I'll need clean dressings," he said to Robert.

Within minutes the older man returned with strips of white linen, which Cal used to cover the burns.

"I think Miss Trenton should go up to her bed now," Aunt Bessie said as he finished. "Perhaps you'd help her, Calhoun."

"But the children . . ." Dulcie began.

"The children are fine. Darwin is reading to them in the parlor. And from the looks of it, they are having a fine time, though my nephew seems quite ill at ease." Aunt Bessie's tone gentled, but only a fraction. "It's time you gave a thought to yourself instead."

Dulcie drifted in and out of sleep. Once, when she cried out in pain, she discovered Cal at her bedside, holding a glass of whiskey to her lips. By the time she drained the fiery liquid, the pain fled and she fell into a deep, dreamless sleep.

Another time she awoke to find Cal and Fiona standing over her. While Cal removed the soiled coverings on her hands, he instructed Fiona in the proper way to spread the ointment and apply fresh dressings. Dulcie thought to speak to them, but before she could form the words, her lids grew heavy and she gave up the effort.

When next she awoke, the sun was high in the sky. The house was strangely silent. She thought about getting out of bed to investigate, but was too weary. Instead, she lay, lulled by the singing of a bird outside her window.

The door to her room opened a crack, and Aunt Bessie peered in. Seeing Dulcie's eyes open, she threw the door wide and bustled inside.

"So. You have returned to us. Are you in any pain?"

"Some. But it's tolerable. Where are the children, Aunt Bessie?"

"They have gone with my nephews to the woods at the far side of the island, where they will begin to fell trees." The older woman took a seat beside Dulcie's bed. She appeared tired and a bit frazzled, but her morning dress of gray silk with gored skirt and fringed bodice was neatly pressed, and her hair was pulled into an impeccable coil at her nape. "Calhoun swears we will have a new barn before summer ends."

"That is good news. But why did he take the children?"

"He thought it would be an adventure for them. Besides," she said with a slight frown, "they were so concerned about you, we had a difficult time keeping them away from your room."

"What about Fiona and Starlight?"

"Starlight is doing some sewing for me." Aunt Bessie's tone revealed her pleasure. "I swear that young woman works magic with a needle and thread. As for Fiona, she insisted that she felt strong enough to help Robert with the kitchen chores."

"So the children are alone with your nephews." Dulcie felt a wave of alarm. It would have been better—safer—if Starlight or Fiona had gone with them, in case Cal decided to question them further about the storm and the stolen boat. "Do you think it's safe for little ones to be around falling trees?"

"As long as they are with Calhoun, you need not worry yourself. Now," Aunt Bessie said briskly, "here I am, forgetting my orders. Calhoun told me I must keep an eye on you. Do you feel up to some lunch?"

Dulcie shook her head, disturbed at the thoughts that tumbled about her mind. "Nothing yet, thank you."

"Then I'll leave you to your rest." Aunt Bessie heaved herself from the chair and made her way to the door. As soon as it closed, Dulcie's eyes fluttered closed. Despite her misgivings, within minutes she was fast asleep.

Chapter Seven

"Were you able to learn anything from the children?" Aunt Bessie asked Cal. She and her three nephews were gathered around the fireplace in the parlor. Fiona and Starlight had taken the children off to bed shortly after dinner, leaving the Jermain family alone for the first time since the fire. At Aunt Bessie's request, Robert had brought a decanter of bourbon and four tumblers, before retiring for the night.

"Not a word." Cal's glass sat untouched beside him. "They are as tight-lipped as Dulcie."

"You can tell they've been warned to say nothing," Barc put in. "Without the women to shield them, they are frightened of their own shadows. I found the girls looking to Nathaniel to speak for them whenever I asked them about their lives in Charleston."

"They revealed nothing?"

"Only what we already knew. That they have no families," Barc said. "That they look out for one another."

"Dulcie is the key," Cal added. "They are all adrift without her."

"Well, you may put your minds to rest about one thing," Aunt Bessie said in hushed tones. "I know for a fact they are not thieves. I gave them a test."

"A test?" For the first time, the reticent Dar joined in the conversation.

"I deliberately left my jewelry tumbled about my dressing table when I sent them to clean my room. And not a single piece was disturbed."

Dar seemed scandalized by his aunt's admission. "You tempted them?"

"I did. And they did not take even a nibble from the apple," she said proudly.

"So you have determined that they are not thieves." Cal picked up his glass. "That still doesn't answer what they are."

"No. But I cannot forget what they did last night." Aunt Bessie's voice softened to a fierce whisper. "This is not their home. And they know they have no future here. Yet they worked alongside us to quell the blaze. And lest we forget, one among them was badly injured."

Falling silent, Cal returned his glass to the table untouched. He stood. "I need to check on my patient."

When he left the room, his family glanced at each other in silence. It was Barc who finally spoke.

"Did I hear correctly? Did my big brother just say what I thought he said?"

Aunt Bessie was beaming. "I believe he called Miss Trenton his patient."

"This calls for another drink." Barc topped off his aunt's glass, then Dar's and his own. "Here's to Miss Trenton," he said. "Though Cal sees her as a tool of the devil, she may be heaven-sent."

Cal held the candle aloft as he crossed the room to the bed. He stared down at the sleeping figure.

Dulcie lay on her side facing him. Her dark hair spilled over one shoulder. She slept as peacefully as a baby.

He sat on the edge of the mattress. From his pocket he produced a pair of small, sharp scissors. Working quickly, he cut away the dressings that covered her hands. He set aside the scissors, then spread the contents of a vial over his fingers and rubbed the ointment into her palms. When he was done, he lifted one of her hands in his and turned it to the light. The raw, puckered skin had already turned from red to healthy pink.

Such a small hand, he thought as he continued to rest it on his. But it had taken on such enormous tasks. Not just the fire, though that in itself had been a courageous feat. But much more daunting was the care of four young children and two obviously fragile women.

How did they come to be in your care? he wondered. *And what did you do to earn such blind loyalty?*

As if his thoughts had been spoken aloud, Dulcie's eyes opened. For a moment she blinked against the candlelight. And then, suddenly aware of the hand holding hers, she snatched it away and shrank from him.

"What are you doing in my room?"

"I'm sorry I startled you." He remained seated on her bed. "I was checking your burns."

She glanced at the night table. The scissors, the vial, the small bundle of soiled dressings were proof of his claim. She swallowed back whatever protest she'd been about to make.

She sat up, shoving the hair from her eyes, unaware that her chemise offered little in the way of modest covering.

Flexing her fingers, she said, "Forgive me. The pain is almost gone. Once again, it seems, I am in your debt, Mr. Jermain."

She offered her hand, and Cal had no choice but to accept. Now, however, as her small palm rested in his, all he could think about was the sudden rush of heat that her

touch kindled. Against his will, his gaze was drawn to the
shadowed cleft between her breasts.

"I still think," she added, "that you made too much
fuss—"

Her words were stilled as his mouth covered hers. She
could make no sound of protest as his hand slid up her
throat to tangle in her hair. Once again she felt the threat
that she'd sensed the first time she'd seen him. There was
danger in this man. Darkness. Tightly coiled, carefully
controlled passion.

His lips were neither gentle nor persuasive, but rather,
they simply took possession. And though it was not her nature to be dominated, the pure, physical pleasure won out
over independence. With a sigh she gave herself up to his
kiss.

She tasted as she looked. As sweet, as innocent as a field
of wildflowers after a spring rain. But underneath the
sweetness was a wild sensuality and, beneath that, a layer of
mystery. She was a stubborn woman with a will of iron. She
would be a challenge to any man.

As the kiss deepened, he poured all his feelings into it.
Feelings he'd experienced in their first shocking kiss. Passion. Hunger. And a deep welling of desire.

When Cal ended the kiss as abruptly as he'd begun it,
Dulcie blinked and struggled to still her racing heart.

Very deliberately he got to his feet, towering over her. His
hand, he realized, was trembling. He closed it into a fist at
his side. "I don't want your thanks, Miss Trenton. Let's just
say that now we're even. For without your warning of the
fire, our home, and many lives, I fear, would have been lost.
I'll leave you to rest now." He spun on his heel and strode
to the door.

Dulcie remained very still, watching the play of light and shadow on her wall, caused by the moonlight streaming through the tree branches outside her window.

Had he been sitting on the side of her bed for a long time, gently holding her hand in his? Or had she only dreamed it? She shook her head to dispel such foolish thoughts. Before the fire, Cal Jermain had ordered her to return to the mainland. Despite their kiss, nothing had changed. Very soon now, she would be out of his life. And tossed back into the maelstrom from which she had escaped.

"Starlight, where is my gown?" Dulcie stood in the middle of the bedroom in her chemise and petticoat. She had been forced to remain in her room for several days, accepting a tray at mealtime and sleeping every afternoon like an infant. Today she had decided to rebel against her enforced idleness.

"It was badly damaged by the fire, I'm afraid. Aunt Bessie said it wasn't worth salvaging."

"She ordered my only gown destroyed?"

"Tossed it into the fireplace." The young woman held up a lovely rose-colored dress with matching fringed shawl. "But to replace it, she asked me to make this over to fit you."

"Oh—" Dulcie shook her head "—it's far too lovely to wear while I work."

"Aunt Bessie said you can't work until your hands are completely healed."

Dulcie held up her palms to show healthy pink flesh, crisscrossed with scars. "But they're nearly healed. If I can't work, what am I to do all day?"

Starlight laughed. "According to Aunt Bessie, you shall keep her company." Her voice lowered as she helped Dulcie into the gown. "If you ask me, she seemed to be secretly pleased with the prospect of having someone to talk to. She has even begun talking to the children, although she still insists that they speak only when spoken to."

While Starlight fastened the row of tiny buttons, Dulcie surveyed her reflection in the mirror. It was startling to see herself in such finery.

"Are the children dressed?" she asked.

"Fiona is helping them. They'll be along any minute now." Starlight lifted a brush to Dulcie's thick dark hair. "Sit and I'll have you finished in no time."

Dulcie fidgeted. "I'm not used to having anyone fuss over me."

"I can tell." Starlight swept the hair away from Dulcie's face with two mother-of-pearl combs, then stood back to survey her handiwork. "There now. Don't you look like a fine lady!"

Before Dulcie could make a reply, there was a knock on her door. Then it opened to Fiona and the children, who gave gasps of approval.

"My, don't you look splendid," Fiona said, hurrying over and hugging her friend.

The children's heads bobbed in agreement.

"It's far too fine for me," Dulcie declared, "but it seems I have no choice. My other gown was burned."

"And none too soon," Fiona said with a laugh.

As Dulcie followed everyone down the stairs, she dropped a hand onto Fiona's shoulder. "Have you grown stronger?"

"Aye. I feel I could scrub a hundred floors and milk a few dozen cows."

Dulcie laughed. "Be careful. The Jermains may have you chopping trees if they hear that."

"I'd even be willing to do that," Fiona returned. "I don't know if it's the fine food or the soft bed, but I haven't felt this strong in a very long time."

Dulcie could see the proof of her words. Fiona's cheeks bloomed with color, and her laughing blue eyes were no longer rimmed with dark circles.

"So," Aunt Bessie called as they entered the dining room, "you're finally ready to join us, Miss Trenton."

Her three nephews looked up.

"Yes. Thanks to all of you."

"I see Starlight was able to tailor that old dress to fit you." Aunt Bessie added with a huff, "It looks much better on you than it ever did on me."

"I wish you had something simpler to lend me, Aunt Bessie. This is far too lovely to wear." Dulcie felt Cal's gaze on her and cursed the betraying heat that rushed to her cheeks.

"Nonsense. That trunk filled with old gowns was just gathering dust in the attic until now. They may as well be put to good use. Now," Aunt Bessie said, patting the chair beside her, "come and eat, Miss Trenton. You've eaten practically nothing at all since the fire."

Dulcie supervised the children first before taking a small portion of eggs and corn bread for herself. When she was seated, she bowed her head and offered her hand to Nathaniel. Seeing Aunt Bessie's frown of disapproval, she lowered her other hand to her lap as she led them in prayer.

"We thank Thee, Father, for these good people who have given us shelter from the storm. And we thank Thee for this abundance of food."

Across the table, Cal and his brothers watched in silence.

Amid a chorus of amens, the children tucked into their breakfast.

"Are you planting today, Calhoun," his aunt asked, "or cutting timber?"

"We have no choice but to do both. We need to keep up the planting if we want to have anything to harvest. But we'll need to cut the timber soon if we hope to have a barn up before harvest time, or we'll have no place to store our crops." He shoved away from the table. "We'll plant this morning, then cut timber until dark."

"What you need is more hours in the day," his aunt commented dryly.

"And fewer storms. Come on," Cal said to his brothers. "We've wasted enough time."

Dulcie could hold her silence no longer. "If you'll recall, Mr. Jermain, Nathaniel offered you the perfect solution to your dilemma days ago. You and your brothers could be free to cut timber all day if you would allow us to plant the fields."

"As I said before—"

"That was before the fire," she interjected. "Then, the only thing that concerned you was planting your crops. But now you have the added burden of building a barn."

"And what do any of you know about planting?" he challenged.

"All children of Eire have ties to the soil," Fiona said grandly. "I could learn."

"My father... was a sharecropper," Starlight admitted haltingly. "I had no choice but to help."

"I've worked the fields," Nathaniel said proudly.

"As have I," Dulcie said softly.

She felt Cal's dark gaze boring into her. "When our men went off to fight, we took on their chores. Even those of us who lived on fine plantations." She lifted her chin defiantly. "Show us what you want planted, Mr. Jermain, and we will see to it."

Cal realized Dulcie had deliberately revealed a little of her past. It would seem that her father had been a man of some means. Yet, for all her privileged upbringing, she seemed exceptionally well adjusted to this new life of hardship.

Why did he always get the feeling that Miss Dulcie Trenton was an accomplished liar?

Cal glanced around the table and realized that everyone was awaiting his decision.

"Barc?" he challenged. "What do you think about this?"

His brother shrugged. "I don't see why they can't help if they are willing."

"Dar?"

The younger man fiddled with his spoon, refusing to look at anyone. In a choked voice he said, "Our grandmother used to boast that she could work the plow as well as any man."

"Better, if truth be told," Aunt Bessie put in sternly.

Cal pinned her with a look. "So Aunt Bessie, do you now think the women and children should be allowed to help in the fields?"

She met his look. "I had forgotten about your grandmother. I think we would be fools to refuse our...guests' generous offer."

The little group waited in silence.

"Very well, then." Cal avoided Dulcie's eyes. "All but Miss Trenton will follow me to the fields as soon as you've finished your morning meal."

"I am not ill, Mr. Jermain," Dulcie protested. "And it will not be harmful to my hands to accompany the others."

"I'll not have you rooting in the dirt with those wounds." His tone was brusque.

Hers was equally determined. "I will not be singled out for special treatment. My hands have healed nicely. And they're accustomed to hard work."

He gave a little sigh of disgust and clenched his fist at his side. Then in a flat tone he said, "I'll hitch the team. My

brothers and I will deposit you in the south field on our way
to cut timber."

"All of us?" Dulcie demanded.

"Yes, Miss Trenton." He said through gritted teeth, "all
of you."

While she finished her meal, Dulcie struggled not to appear too jubilant. As long as they were needed, they would
be staying. Papa used to say the best way to be a welcome
guest was to share the chores. Right now, she would do any
chore necessary to avoid returning to Charleston.

"You will each take a furrow," Cal said.

The women and children stood around him as he gave his
instructions. Robert had provided them with wide-brimmed
hats, which offered protection from the sun. And they had
all changed into the ragged clothes they'd been wearing
when they'd first arrived. All except Dulcie, who wore a
simple white blouse and dark, gored skirt that Aunt Bessie
had insisted she accept.

"It is better to take your time and sow the seeds carefully," Cal said, "than to race through the chore and find
that some of the seeds were not deep enough or covered by
only a thin layer of soil."

"Why must we cover them?" Belle asked.

Cal pointed. "Do you see those birds?"

The little girl shaded her eyes and peered skyward at the
flock circling overhead. "Yes."

"They are very clever," Cal said. "If you leave even one
seed uncovered, they will devour it. If the birds eat enough
seeds, there will be no crop to harvest."

The children seemed properly impressed.

"You have the sack of seed," Cal went on. "And the food
and water Robert provided. But if the sun should become
intolerable, I suggest you take a break and sit in the shade."

He climbed onto the wagon and picked up the reins. "One more thing," he said. "Keep an eye on the weather. At the first hint of a storm, return to the house." His gaze narrowed on Dulcie. "Is that clear?"

"Yes. Of course. I would never jeopardize the safety of the others."

As soon as the words were out of her mouth, she saw his eyes darken and knew he was thinking about their arrival—in a storm.

She draped an arm around Clara's shoulders. "Go along now, Mr. Jermain. We'll be just fine."

As the horses and wagon lurched ahead, Barc and Dar, seated in the back with axes and saws, lifted their hats and waved. The women and children waved back until they were out of sight.

Then they were alone. With the sun and the birds overhead, and acres of rich, black earth underfoot.

Chapter Eight

Dulcie inched along the furrow, bent nearly double as she deposited the seeds in neat, orderly lines. Despite the wide-brimmed hat, the sun seemed merciless.

Like the others, she had quickly removed her kid boots. At first the earth had felt refreshingly cool. Now, like everything else in the sun's path, the dirt was so hot it nearly burned her flesh with each step she took.

She straightened and pressed both hands to her aching back. Looking out across the field, she could see the others bent to their tasks. It had been at her insistence that they had been forced into menial labor. Still, if it had to be the price to remain in this Eden, she knew they were all willing to pay it.

At the far end of the field she spotted a line of trees, under which Cal had deposited their food and drinking water.

"Starlight," she called, "tell the children it is time to eat. We'll take shelter beneath those trees."

The younger woman nodded and started off across the field. By the time they all arrived, Dulcie had set out a meal of corn bread and thick slices of turkey, along with peach preserves and biscuits topped with sugar and cinnamon. Though the once cold well water had grown tepid, it was still a welcome relief, and they drank their fill.

"Ah." Fiona sighed as she lowered herself to the ground in the shade of a gnarled palmetto tree. "Now you know why so many were eager to leave my lovely green land. From morn till night, this was the sort of backbreaking labor required to keep it green."

Dulcie nodded. "And to think, we've only just begun."

Starlight groaned.

Dulcie glanced around at the children, sitting or lying in the shade, picking at their food. "After lunch, Starlight, I want you to remain here with the children while they rest."

"Naps are for babies and girls," Nathaniel protested. "I'm not staying with them. I want to plant."

"The sun is too hot at this time of the day," Dulcie explained patiently. "I want you to rest in the shade until the worst of the day's heat has passed."

"But—"

"I insist, Nathaniel," she said softly.

Starlight and the little girls offered no such protest. Even before they had finished their lunch, they were curled up, fast asleep. Dejected, Nathaniel squatted in the dirt and drew circles with a stick.

Dulcie knelt beside him and put an arm around his shoulder. "I'll feel better knowing you're here watching over Starlight and the girls while they sleep."

Immediately the little boy's attitude changed. Now that he knew how much Dulcie needed him here, he didn't mind staying behind.

Despite his objections, he had to admit that working in the sun had made him drowsy. Leaning his back against the trunk of a tree, he tipped his hat over his face. Within minutes he drifted off.

* * *

"That's it for today," Cal said, wiping sweat from his face with his sleeve. "By the time we load these, it'll be getting on to dusk."

The three brothers struggled under the weight of the fallen tree as they loaded it into the wagon alongside a half-dozen others.

Cal climbed into the driver's seat and picked up the reins. Barc and Dar straddled the logs, and the wagon rolled across the field.

"How do you think our new field hands survived?" Barc asked.

"We'll soon see." Far ahead, Cal could make out the little party of women and children, fanned out across the freshly turned furrows. His gaze fastened on one in particular, whose long dark hair swept forward each time she bent to her task.

When the wagon rolled up alongside the field where she worked, Dulcie straightened. She'd used her sash to hike up her skirt between her legs like wide-legged pantaloons. Her legs were bare from the knee down, a most enticing sight.

"Time to head home for supper," Cal called to her. His voice carried across the field, and soon the others were walking toward them.

While Cal remained in the wagon, Barc and Dar scrambled down and began helping the women and children into the back, where they made themselves comfortable on top of the logs.

Dulcie quickly untied her sash and lowered her skirts before scooping up her shoes.

"Up you go, Miss Trenton," Barc said as he assisted Dulcie to the seat alongside his older brother.

A moment later Nathaniel was lifted up beside her. She was wedged so close to Cal his thigh brushed hers.

Cal flicked the reins and the wagon moved along at a slow, lumbering pace.

"I'm surprised to see that you all can still stand." Barc's voice was warm with admiration. "My first day back in the fields, I thought I'd never be able to straighten up."

"Aye," Fiona said with a laugh. "I may yet fall over. But I think we managed to plant half a field. Is that a fair amount?"

"Better than fair," Barc assured her. "I'd say you've more than earned your keep."

Cal remained silent. But he was achingly aware of the woman beside him. Of the way her hair lifted on the breeze to whisper over his cheek. Of one small, dirt-stained hand resting in her lap. Of the grubby bare toes poking out from beneath the hem of her skirt.

"I can't wait to duck into a bucket of water," Barc said, wiping sweat from his forehead.

"I was thinking of a swim," Fiona put in with a laugh. "It's the only way I'll ever wash away all this rich black Carolina dirt."

"A swim?" Barc paused, considering. "Now that sounds even better. What do you say, Cal? Want to make a stop at the shore before we go up to the house?"

"We still have to unload this timber," Cal said. "But we could drop off the women and children near the shore."

"Not fair," Barc protested laughingly. "Why should they have all the fun? Come on, Cal," he urged. "We've earned a swim. Don't you agree, Dar?"

His younger brother only blushed.

"The thought of all that cool water is mighty tempting," Cal admitted.

"Let's do it, then!" Barc shouted, waving his hat in the air.

As he impulsively turned the team toward the shore, Cal knew he was behaving irrationally. But at this moment, he didn't care.

Fiona was the first to toss her shoes and bonnet aside and run headlong into the water. The waves rolled up to meet her, and she laughed delightedly as she plunged beneath the waves and came up sputtering, her long skirts nearly dragging her to her knees.

"Oh!" she cried. "It's heavenly!"

"Come, girls." Dulcie helped the three little ones out of their bulky gowns, and wished she, too, could have the freedom to swim in her chemise and petticoat. But modesty would not permit it. Tossing aside her boots and hat, she linked hands with Starlight, and the two led the timid little girls into the shallows. As the water lapped at their ankles, they squealed in delight.

Barclay and Darwin needed no coaxing to toss aside their shirts and shoes and dive in. They were soon out in the deep, frolicking like porpoises.

As Cal removed his shoes and shirt, he noticed Nathaniel sitting alone on shore.

"Aren't you coming in?" he asked.

The boy shook his head. "I . . . I'll just stay here."

"Can you swim?" Cal asked.

The boy shook his head.

"Have you ever tried?"

"Yes, sir." Nathaniel avoided his eyes. "But it was a long time ago."

"Then you'll remember. Want to try it again?"

Nathaniel gave a negligent shrug of his shoulders and grasped the hand that Cal offered.

They stepped into the shallows. "I'm not afraid," the boy said fiercely as a swell rolled toward them. Holding tightly to Cal's hand, he felt the water lift him and take him along, before dropping him back on solid ground.

When the wave had passed, Cal went to his knees beside the boy and turned him to face him. "Remember this, Nathaniel. There's nothing wrong with being afraid."

"You mean I'm not a coward if I'm afraid of the water?"

"Of course not." Cal got to his feet, still holding the boy's hand. "It's natural to be afraid of things we can't control."

"Like the ocean? Like the weather?"

Cal nodded. "But instead of fearing them, we can learn a healthy respect." While he spoke, he continued leading the boy deeper into the water.

"When I was about your age," Cal said softly, "my father brought me here to this very spot and told me that the water surrounding my island would be my friend or my enemy. The choice was mine."

"What did you do?" Nathaniel's eyes were round with interest.

"I decided to make it my friend. I decided, there and then, that my first step was to learn to swim. Would you like to try to swim?"

Nathaniel hesitated for only a moment before saying, "Yes, sir."

Cal tightened his grasp on the boy's hand. "Then let's begin your first lesson."

Chapter Nine

"What on earth...?"

Aunt Bessie stared in consternation as the young women made their way up the stairs, lifting their sodden skirts to keep them from dripping all over the floor. The children followed, carrying armloads of wet, sandy clothing.

"We took a swim to cool off," Starlight explained.

The older woman looked horrified. "Thank heaven no one was around to witness such a spectacle."

Dulcie's cheeks flooded with color, and she herded her young charges up the stairs quickly, before they could say something that would embarrass them all.

"Where are my nephews?" Aunt Bessie called after her.

"Unloading timber from the wagon," Dulcie replied over her shoulder. "They'll be along shortly."

When they were gone, Robert moved a mop across the kitchen floor, obliterating their wet footprints. Just as he finished, Cal, Barc and Dar entered, creating fresh tracks. The older man followed in their wake, slowly moving the mop back and forth across the offensive sight.

Aunt Bessie's eyes widened in disbelief. "Please do not tell me you were swimming."

"I cannot tell a lie," Barc said with a devilish grin. "Besides, our wet clothes give us away."

"While there were young ladies in the water? Oh, my word!" his aunt moaned. "What other terrible things did you learn in that wicked war?"

Barc's eyes danced with amusement as he brushed a kiss on her cheek. "Are you going to blame this on those damned Yankees, too, Aunt Bessie?"

"And why not? Now get away, you scoundrel." She gave him a playful shove and watched as he followed his brothers up the stairs.

When she was alone, she picked up a fan and made her way to the parlor. The evening was uncommonly hot, with not the slightest breeze stirring the curtains. She supposed, if she'd been forced to work outdoors in the hot sun, she would have craved a chance to cool off, too, no matter how awkward the circumstances.

Shirtless, Cal lathered his face and picked up his straight razor. When he'd first returned from the horrors of war, he found his aunt's insistence upon formality at dinner frivolous and foolish, and he had chafed at her demands. But slowly, he'd begun to see the wisdom of such a routine. The orderliness of their existence had become a soothing, healing balm.

But now, he thought as he moved the razor up his throat in smooth, easy strokes, with the introduction of Dulcie Trenton and her little band, order had disappeared. In its place was...

What? His hand paused in midair. What had she brought into their lives? Not chaos exactly, but a disruption of that order. And the realization that even here on their little island, there was no escaping the realities of the war.

He finished shaving and wiped the lather from his face, then crossed to the window. He had come home to heal. Not true, he corrected as he leaned a hip against the sill. He'd really come home to hide. This island had become his refuge from reality. And now, Dulcie and the others had brought it all back to him. And he resented it. He didn't want to care about a boy who was trying desperately to be a man. Didn't want to see fear and torment in the eyes of little girls. Didn't want to watch one persistent young woman sharing her strength, her determination, with others who seemed to have lost theirs.

Most of all, he didn't want to have his heart race every time she walked into the room. And he certainly didn't want to have to fight for his very sanity every time he got too close to her.

He had no right to such feelings. For nothing could ever come of them. What woman in her right mind would want him the way he was now?

The sound of the children's voices filtered across the veranda and he ducked back into the shadows just as they appeared outside his window. From the other direction came Dulcie. The children lined up for her inspection, and she paused to straighten a hair ribbon, tie a sash, hook the back of Nathaniel's suspenders.

When she was satisfied with their appearance, she caught their hands and led them toward her room. "Come along," she said. "Robert will be summoning us to dinner soon. And you don't want to keep Aunt Bessie waiting."

Cal buttoned his shirt and pulled on his jacket. He had to admit mealtime had become much more lively since the arrival of Miss Dulcie Trenton and her ragtag band.

Aunt Bessie surveyed the freshly scrubbed faces around the table. The women and children in their new clothes scavenged from the trunks upstairs, and the men in their starched white shirts and dark suits, added a festive note to an otherwise ordinary meal. "I'd say this is an improvement over what I glimpsed a short while ago." She wrinkled her nose at the memory.

"Cal taught me how to swim," Nathaniel said proudly.

"Did he now?" Aunt Bessie recognized the adoring look in the little boy's eyes and turned to study her nephew, who seemed more ill at ease than she could ever recall. Had he actually gone out of his way to help the boy? Could it be that Nathaniel had found an opening in that wall her nephew had built?

"You already knew how to swim," Cal said. "I just helped you remember."

Nathaniel grinned.

"I can't swim yet," Emily said. "But Dulcie said that when I'm bigger, she'll teach me."

"I don't ever want to swim." Belle's eyes were wide with fear. "Out in the deep, the water is dark. And you can't see the things that are there waiting for you."

"What things?" Emily asked.

"Big fish like sharks and whales and—" she struggled with the word "—octopussies."

Across the table, Dar winced.

"What are octopussies?" Little Emily's eyes widened.

"They're big and fuzzy and have whiskers and tents that grab you and choke you."

While the others merely smiled, Dar could contain himself no longer. "The correct term is octopus. They're harmless, and their eight arms are called tentacles, not tents, Belle."

"Are they big and fuzzy?" Emily asked.

"Actually they're smooth, like an eel. Would you like to see a picture of one?" Dar asked.

"Oh, yes!" the children cried, clapping their hands in delight.

"I'll fetch one of my books after supper, and we can look at it in the parlor."

Dulcie was surprised by this spirited exchange between the shy, quiet Dar and the children. And even more surprised that Aunt Bessie had not intervened, only stared at her youngest nephew in stunned amazement. And as Robert began to circle the table with his silver tray, the older woman lifted her napkin to dab at the corner of her eye.

"Here is an octopus. And this is a squid."

While Dulcie and Fiona helped Aunt Bessie with her knitting, the children clustered around the sofa where Dar held court, nodding and murmuring as he pointed to the various pictures in his book.

He had pulled from his pocket a pair of spectacles, which gave him an owlish, yet oddly appealing look.

Starlight, seated in their midst with her basket of sewing, let out an exclamation of surprise. "Oh, it looks mean!"

"It really isn't," Dar assured her. "If it crossed paths with you in the water, there's no telling who would be more afraid. You or the octopus."

"Me," Starlight said, to the amusement of the others. "I'd be paddling away as fast as my arms and legs could take me."

"So would the octopus," Dar said with a laugh. "And he'd be headed in the opposite direction."

"That's good to know." Starlight looked relieved as she threaded her needle and began to hem one of Aunt Bessie's cast-off gowns.

"Dar, how did you get to know so much about everything?" Nathaniel asked.

"I... had fine teachers." Suddenly the laughter died in Dar's eyes, and he closed the book with a snap. "I'll say my good-nights now."

As he launched himself from the sofa and crossed the room, Starlight and the children watched with matching frowns of concern.

After he left the room, Starlight asked shyly, "Was it something I said, Aunt Bessie?"

The older woman shook her head. "You need not blame yourself. It is just Darwin's way. He needs to be alone now."

"But it was so much fun seeing the pictures in his book," Emily said. "Why should that make him want to be alone?"

Solemn little Clara, who had been silent throughout the evening, said with all the wisdom of a child, "You wouldn't understand, Emily. You only remember the happy times. But some of us still carry the bad times inside our heads. And sometimes, even when everyone around us is laughing, we feel like crying."

Dulcie felt as though a knife had pierced her heart. Then, forcing herself into action, she crossed the room and drew the little girl close.

"We all have some unhappy memories, Clara. And it's all right to cry about them."

"Even grown-ups?" the little girl asked.

"Yes. Even grown-ups."

"Then why doesn't Dar just cry so he'll feel better?"

"Papa used to say that some pain is too deep for tears." Dulcie pressed her lips to Clara's temple. "Anyway, I think it's time for bed."

The little girl nodded and allowed herself to be led away. With quiet murmurs of good-night, the others followed.

When they had left, Aunt Bessie rang for Robert. When he entered, Cal and Barc accepted tumblers of whiskey from his tray and sipped in thoughtful silence.

"Out of the mouths of babes . . ." Aunt Bessie began before her voice trailed off.

Cal wandered to the window and peered out into the darkened sky. He idly rubbed his left arm, feeling the phantom pain where his hand used to be. Maybe they were all suffering phantom pains. The loss of home and family and everything familiar would cause untold pain for many years to come. A lifetime perhaps. For some, the pain would never end.

Behind him Barc drained his glass in one long swallow and set it down with a clatter. Then he turned on his heel and headed for the door.

"Where are you going?" Aunt Bessie demanded.

"To bed. I intend to get an early start in the morning." He paused at the doorway. Seeing her arched brow, he added, "I'm tired of playing the role of the lowly farmer. It's been too long since I visited Charleston and tried my luck at Nellie Simpson's. I need to be around people who know how to laugh and talk and drink. I want to hear music and smell perfume and feel a deck of cards in my hands. I intend to get roaring drunk. And maybe, if I'm lucky, I'll even win some money."

Before his aunt could utter a word of protest he had disappeared, leaving his family in shocked silence.

Dulcie touched a hand to the delicately embroidered nightgown, which she'd unearthed from Aunt Bessie's trunk. There had been a time, not so long ago, when she had taken such finery for granted.

She walked to the window, deep in thought. But that had been before. Before the world had gone mad. Before her father had donned his splendid Confederate uniform and ridden off to join the fighting, never to return.

Her gaze was drawn to the peaceful scene below. Moonlight gilded the fields and the waters that lapped the shore. The rows of palmetto trees stood like silent sentinels.

Sometimes, when the house was quiet and darkness covered the land, she could almost convince herself that none of it had happened and that they were truly safe.

Oh, to be safe. It was all she wanted for herself and the others.

She stepped out onto the balcony and watched an owl in silent flight.

"Wishing you could fly like that?"

At the sound of the deep voice, she whirled.

Directly behind her, Cal stood leaning against the railing, one foot crossed casually over the other. In his hand was a cigar. The smoke curled like a wreath over his head, before dissipating into the night air. He was naked to the waist, a fact that had Dulcie's heart working overtime.

"I've often wished I could fly," she admitted.

"If you could, where would you go?"

She shrugged, avoiding his eyes. "Somewhere safe. Untouched by the war. A place where parents never die. Where children could dream of a better future." Now she looked up at him. "What about you?"

"I guess I've seen enough of other places. I'm in no hurry to go anywhere again. I'll stay on my little island. As for the future..." He stared off into the distance. "Dreams are for children. For myself, I see only hard work and a constant battle against the forces of nature."

"There must have been things you wanted when you were young."

"Maybe." He studied the way the moonlight sparkled like diamonds in her hair, turning the ends to blue-black. "But the war changed all that."

She heard the pain he tried to hide. Without thinking she touched a hand to his arm. "It doesn't have to be. You still have your home, your family, your island."

He could feel the softness of her touch, and with it, the heat. He steeled himself to feel nothing. His tone was rougher than he intended. "Whatever dreams I had, Miss Trenton, they weren't about this island."

"Forgive me. I had no right..." She started to step back, but in the blink of an eye, he tossed aside his cigar. His hand snaked out. Strong fingers closed around her wrist, holding her.

"No right? That's never stopped the bold Miss Dulcie Trenton before, has it?" He drew her fractionally closer. "You had no right to take those innocents out in a storm. But you did. You had no right to intrude into our lives. But you did." His eyes were chips of steel as he dragged her even closer. "And you have no right to remind me of the futility of my dreams. But every time you look at me, you do."

"Please..."

He hauled her against him, his voice was a rasp of pain. "You asked me what I dreamed of. I'll tell you. A good woman, warm and soft and willing, who would choose to be my wife. Children. Lots of children, who would tumble around us like leaves from a tree. And the chance to work. Satisfying work. The work I was trained to do."

"Then why—"

His words, spoken in a fierce whisper, cut her off. "Instead, I find myself tormented by a temptress with the voice of an angel and the heart of the devil. A woman who lies, who plots and schemes."

She lifted her hand to slap him. "How dare—"

This time he cut her off with a hard, punishing kiss.

She balled her hands into fists, determined to fight him. But her hands betrayed her, splaying across his chest, tingling at the contact with the rough hair that curled there.

Cal had known passion before. And desire. But never this. Need, hard, driving need clawed at him, begging for release. And as his mouth moved over hers, as his body strained toward hers, he thought he must have her. Or go mad.

He felt the gradual change in her as her body melted into his. First there had been the fear. Always that fear he could taste and feel and sense. But now her fingers dug into his shoulders, clinging to him as though clinging to life itself. Her lips softened, parted, and her tongue met his.

Without realizing it, his touch gentled. His hand tangled in her hair, and he marveled at the softness of it. With a moan of pleasure he ran nibbling kisses down her throat and was rewarded by her soft sighs.

She felt the gradual change in him as his hand moved down her back, his fingertips tracing her spine with feathery touches. His lips, too, had softened.

This wasn't what he wanted, he reminded himself. But in the same instant his lips closed over hers again, he knew he was lying to himself. This was everything he wanted. *She* was everything he wanted.

He gathered her close, until he could feel her heartbeat. Or was that his own heart that was beating so wildly? It didn't matter. Nothing mattered except this. This heat. This desire building, building until it became a passion that bordered on desperation.

Dulcie knew she could handle his insults. She could deal with his anger, his bitterness. But she had no defense against this tenderness. She knew she could go on forever being held this way, as though she were one of Aunt Bessie's fragile glass figurines. He made her feel so alive. And safe. How strange that this darkly dangerous man should be the one to make her feel that way.

Pulling his mouth away and resting his forehead against hers, Cal took in several long, deep breaths, as though gathering his courage. Then he took a step back.

He could read the confusion in Dulcie's eyes and cursed himself for his clumsiness. He'd taken her too far too fast. With a tenderness he didn't even know he possessed, he brought a finger to her cheek.

"I'm right, you know, Miss Dulcie Trenton. You did plot and scheme. And from the moment you arrived here, you've been lying."

This time she offered not a word in her defense.

He touched a thumb to her lower lip, tracing its fullness. His eyes suddenly narrowed, and with a muttered oath, he dragged her close and kissed her one last time until they were both breathless.

Then, without another word, he turned her toward her bedroom and released her. When she paused and turned to him, he said gruffly, "Go now, Dulcie. Before I do something we'll both regret."

In the stunned silence that followed, she hesitated, then as if in a daze, walked into her bedroom, leaving him alone on the balcony.

He stared into the distance toward Charleston. God in heaven, what was happening to him? He had almost taken her here like some sort of madman. He was aware of her innocence. He had no right to take advantage of her like this. And there was something else. Her fear. Something had happened to her that left her afraid to trust.

It was best this way, he thought. It was imperative he find a way to resist temptation. For even though they could offer each other momentary pleasure, they could have no future. There had already been too much in their past.

Chapter Ten

Cal cracked the whip, and the horses leaned into the harness, hauling their precious cargo of logs.

All around them, little green seedlings poked their way through the ground. For as far as the eye could see, the rich black earth sprouted a blanket of green.

The heat had intensified over the past weeks, and even the nights were hot and steamy. The storms, which blew in from the ocean with more frequency, failed to cool the air. And though the heat and rain made for excellent growing conditions, they brought unwanted guests.

"Ach. Weeds," Fiona said with disgust.

Beside her, Dulcie wielded her hoe like the sword of righteousness. "If we don't get them now, they'll choke the life out of our precious plants."

From his position on the wagon, Cal overheard and felt a warm trickle of pleasure. *Our precious plants,* was it? When had these fields become Dulcie's personal domain?

She had a right, he supposed. She and the others had managed to plant every single plowed field. And now, with the planting completed, they had to nurture the seedlings and save them from weeds, rodents and the elements.

He glanced at the single wall of the barn in the distance. Though it was slow going with only three of them to cut timbers and tend to the building, the barn was gradually being rebuilt. If they kept to their schedule, it would be ready before harvest.

There had been no more talk of sending the women and children back to Charleston. Right now, every willing hand was needed to see them through the growing season. They knew that the departure was inevitable, but everyone seemed to have reached an unspoken agreement. The women and children would be allowed to remain until the crops were harvested.

"I'll help you aboard," Barc called as the wagon came to a halt.

Starlight and the children emerged from the shade of a live oak, where Dulcie had ordered them to rest. They moved slowly, their energy sapped by the heat and the labors of the day.

Dulcie swept off her wide-brimmed hat and ran her fingers through her damp, matted hair. When Barc lifted her to the wagon seat, she felt the jolt as her shoulder brushed Cal's.

It had been nearly two weeks now since their encounter on the balcony. Since then, they had carefully avoided all contact. But each time she was forced to be in his company, Dulcie thought about the kiss they had shared. And experienced again the thrill.

As for Cal, she had to concede that he seemed to feel nothing at all for her. He still frowned whenever he looked her way. And he rarely spoke directly to her, choosing to speak to the others, instead.

"I'm glad to see that you children are taking brief rests," Barc commented.

"Dulcie insisted," Starlight said softly. "But I've found a way to put our resting time to good use," she added with a trace of pride.

"Don't tell me you're doing Aunt Bessie's sewing?" Barc teased.

"Of course not," the frail young woman replied. "You know I do that every night after supper."

She spoke so sincerely Barc couldn't help grinning. He'd been doing a lot of that lately. Since his return from Charleston, he'd been in fine humor, teasing the women, playing games with the children in the evenings. He'd even taught them how to play poker, much to his aunt's dismay. He found the Irishwoman to be an especially apt pupil. If he wasn't careful, she'd soon be beating him at his own game.

"So what is it you're doing while you're supposed to be resting?" he asked.

"I'm teaching the children."

Beside him, Dar sat up a little straighter.

"Teaching them what?" Barc asked.

Starlight shrugged. "Whatever I can. Spelling and sums mostly."

"Well, now. Isn't that fine." Barc turned to Nathaniel. "What did you learn today?"

"Starlight taught me how to spell my name and write it in the sand."

"That's great. Let me hear you," Barc urged.

"N-a-t..." Nathaniel paused a moment, glancing toward Starlight for approval. She nodded her head encouragingly, and he finished in a rush, "...a-n-y-u-l."

Barc didn't know whether to laugh or be horrified. At eight years old, he and his brothers had already been introduced to mathematics and science, and had begun mastering the intricacies of Greek and Latin. And this boy couldn't even spell his own name. What was even worse, neither could his teacher.

"Calhoun, can you spare the women and children tomorrow?" Aunt Bessie asked as they gathered in the parlor after supper. "I need their help with some household chores."

"Can't the chores wait? The weeds have a way of getting ahead of us this time of year, and everyone's needed in the fields."

"I will remind you that I have an entire plantation to oversee, Calhoun," his aunt replied. "And I need the women and children to help me."

"Yes, ma'am."

"Then you will spare the women tomorrow?"

He winked at his brothers. "Yes, ma'am," he repeated.

"Thank you." She sat down stiffly in her favorite chair and glanced toward the corner, where Barc was teaching the children a game of cards. Fiona had joined them and seemed to be enjoying herself immensely. "What is that you're playing?" Aunt Bessie called.

"Cutthroat," Belle answered innocently.

"Deuces wild," little Emily added.

"Oh, my." Aunt Bessie fanned herself furiously and summoned Robert.

When he entered, she said, "I would have a sip of spirits, Robert. Quickly, quickly."

"Yes, Miss Bessie."

After pouring a tumbler of whiskey for Aunt Bessie and her nephews, he offered tea to Dulcie and Fiona. Everyone sipped in companionable silence for several minutes.

Dulcie glanced around at the peaceful scene and found herself once again marveling that they had managed to find such a haven. However difficult their labors, the reward was great. And she knew she would work twice as hard just to assure herself she could always hear the sound of the children's laughter and see the happiness in their eyes.

"I forgot to tell you, Calhoun," Aunt Bessie said, breaking into Dulcie's reverie. "There was a boat just offshore today. I saw several men aboard and thought at first they might drop anchor and pay us a visit."

Across the room, Cal saw the delicate cup Dulcie had been in the process of bringing to her lips give a sudden jerk. Scalding tea sloshed over the rim, though she seemed unaware. She was staring at his aunt as if at a ghost.

"Do you think they were peddlers?" he asked.

"It was hard to tell. But they were definitely Southerners. I could see that some of them still wore the remnants of Confederate uniforms."

Across the room Starlight had gone into a trance, fixing her gaze on the blaze of candles and rocking gently back and forth.

"One of them stood up and seemed to be searching for something," Aunt Bessie went on. "I saw him glance toward the fields. Then they turned the boat around and headed back toward Charleston."

Cal was still watching Dulcie. Her face had gone the color of chalk. The cup slipped from her nerveless fingers and fell to the floor, where it shattered.

"Oh!" she cried. "Forgive me. I...don't know what came over me."

She dropped to her knees, but Robert took the shards from her hands. Clara, meanwhile, had begun to cry. "You'd better see to the little missy," he said.

"Yes. Of course." She crossed the room and gathered the sobbing Clara into her arms.

"I believe we'll go up to bed now if you don't mind." With a terse, "Come, children," she hustled them out of the room and up the stairs.

Fiona wrapped her arms around Starlight and forced her to follow.

When they were alone, Aunt Bessie turned to her oldest nephew. "Now what in heaven's name brought that about?

The child was absolutely terrified," Aunt Bessie said with a sigh.

And so was Dulcie, Cal thought with a frown. But he doubted there was any point in asking her for an explanation. She had become very adept at lying or at least evading the truth.

Dulcie knelt by the window in her darkened room and watched the path of a shooting star. Then she squeezed her eyes tightly shut and made a wish. It gave her no comfort. It was, after all, just a silly superstition. Like this island. It gave the illusion of safety. But in truth, there was no safety to be found anywhere.

It had taken her almost two hours to get the children to settle down and fall asleep. Starlight, too terrified to be alone, had sought shelter in Fiona's room.

Dulcie found her own room hot and airless, but she was afraid to go out on the veranda. Cal might be there, waiting in the darkness to confront her. And so she remained huddled by the window, staring at the night sky, praying for wisdom, for courage. For safety.

Cal paced the upper veranda, alternately cursing the woman in the next room and worrying about her.

When she'd heard about the boatload of men, she'd been genuinely frightened. As had the others. So much for their lie that no one was following them.

But what was he going to do about it? He thought of the rifle he kept beside his bed. He'd seen enough dead and dying in the battlefield to last him a lifetime. And he'd vowed that once he returned to his island refuge, there would be no more violence. But sometimes life didn't offer a man much choice.

Damn these women! What plague had they brought to his doorstep?

He swore fiercely. He'd do his best to keep the women and children safe. But his first obligation was to his own family. How could he be certain that these men, whoever they were, wouldn't harm his brothers and Aunt Bessie and Robert in their quest for his uninvited guests?

He would let Dulcie Trenton know that he would tolerate no more lies. She would, by God, tell him the truth. And when he had the facts, he would decide if she and the children would be allowed to stay or if they would have to go, for the safety of his own loved ones.

The decision gave him no peace. In fact, he was more agitated than ever. He tossed his cigar aside and stalked into his room. He may as well dress and start the day's chores. There would be no sleep for him this night.

Chapter Eleven

"Did you manage to sleep a bit?" Fiona asked as Dulcie entered her room in the morning.

"Some." Dulcie felt weighted down by the cares of the world. Outside the window, the sun climbed steadily over the horizon, promising another hot, muggy day.

The others, freshly scrubbed and carefully dressed, had gathered around the Irishwoman's bed. Their faces revealed their concern. Aunt Bessie's revelation had once again cut them adrift from their safe harbor.

"Do you think those men will come back, Dulcie?" Clara twisted her hands together nervously.

"I think—" Dulcie licked her lips and repeated what her papa had always said "—that we must put yesterday's fears behind us and get on with today."

"But those men ..."

"They could be peddlers, bringing their wares to the island. Or fishermen. Or men searching for their families. Come," Dulcie said firmly. "It's time to begin a new day. Let's see what chores Aunt Bessie has in store for us."

They tramped down the stairs, then paused. Dulcie peered into the dining room. Aunt Bessie and her nephews were seated around the table. Dulcie knew, by the look on Cal's face, that he was in a fierce, black mood. A tiny shiver snaked along her spine.

She wanted to flee, but pride and common sense would not permit it. For the sake of the others, she would have to bluff her way through this first confrontation.

"Good morning," Aunt Bessie greeted them as they entered. She seemed determined to put on a cheerful face.

Dulcie followed suit. "Good morning."

As she took her seat she was grateful that she wouldn't have to accompany the men to the fields today.

"Tea, missy?"

At the sound of Robert's voice beside her, she dropped her fork with a clatter and looked up to find everyone staring at her. "Yes, please."

Embarrassed, she ducked her head, but not before she caught the look Cal shot her.

"I would have a word with you after breakfast, Miss Trenton." His tone left no doubt as to his intentions.

"Oh, dear," Aunt Bessie said. "I'm afraid whatever you have to say to Miss Trenton will have to wait until tonight, Calhoun." She was delighted to have the women at her disposal for the day and was not about to sacrifice a single minute. She knew exactly what was on her nephew's mind, and she intended to put off the inevitable until after the work was completed to her satisfaction. "Robert and I have so many chores we'll have to get started immediately if we're to see them all to their conclusion by bedtime."

Cal scraped back his chair and stood. With a slight nod of his head he said, "It seems you've won a reprieve, Miss Trenton."

Her lips curved in a half smile until he added, "But only until tonight. Then you and I will have our talk."

He stomped from the room and his brothers followed.

* * *

Dulcie and the others finished their meals and cleared the table. While Fiona and the little girls began making candles under Aunt Bessie's watchful eye, Dulcie and Nathaniel churned butter. Starlight settled herself near the window and picked up the basket of mending. Though it was a chore that seemed never-ending, the young woman found it soothing. When she glanced around at the others, she took great comfort in the familiar scene. For a moment it almost seemed like home, with Daddy and Mama and her sisters...

Aunt Bessie was the first to notice the change in Starlight. The hand holding the needle had stilled. She sat rigid, unmoving. Her eyes stared unblinking at the bright sunlight outside the window.

"What is it, child?" Aunt Bessie asked softly.

There was no response.

Dulcie, busy at the churn, paid scant attention as the older woman bent to Starlight and placed a hand on her shoulder. Abruptly Starlight jerked away from the touch and jumped to her feet, dropping the basket of mending and sending spools of thread, buttons and needles skittering across the floor.

Starlight's mouth opened, but the sound she made bore little resemblance to a human cry. It was more like that of a wild creature in the throes of agony. Aunt Bessie leaped back, her trembling hands clutched to her bosom.

Dulcie raced to the girl's side and gathered her close, murmuring words meant to soothe. Starlight's cries faded to a whimper, then to stillness.

Dulcie released her, and Starlight blinked and looked around at the items littering the floor. "What is this?" she asked in dismay. "Did I do this?"

"Hush," Dulcie whispered. "It's nothing. Just an accident."

"But I don't remember. I don't even remember getting out of my chair."

"It doesn't matter," Dulcie assured her. "You see? I'll have it all picked up in a moment." She bent to her task, and when Robert joined her, she said in an aside, "I think Starlight might like one of your special cups of tea."

"Yes, missy." He hurried from the room.

When he returned with a steaming cup, Starlight was calmly seated in her chair, the basket of mending in her lap.

And Aunt Bessie was left to ponder yet another piece of this strange puzzle.

Fiona and the girls cleaned the kitchen until it gleamed, freeing Robert to spend the morning fishing. Though the housework was difficult, the change of pace made everyone more relaxed. The house seemed cool after their weeks spent in the blazing sun.

When Robert returned, he taught the children how to scale the fish he'd caught and fillet them for frying. Then he set about baking biscuits, while Fiona lowered a crock of buttermilk into the well to chill.

On the surface, it was a scene of domestic tranquility. But beneath the surface, simmered a cauldron of mixed passions.

"Would you like these rooms cleaned, Aunt Bessie?"

Dulcie, who had been scrubbing the downstairs hallway on her hands and knees, paused outside a set of ornate double doors.

"Oh, no. It would be impossible, I fear." Aunt Bessie stood outside the door, wringing her hands.

"Isn't this where the fire did some damage?" Dulcie asked.

"Yes." The older woman took a deep breath, then twisted the knob and gave the door a shove. As it swung open, she peered inside almost hesitantly. "This...used to be our grand ballroom."

She paused in the doorway and lifted a hand to her throat, jolted by the sight. "I haven't come here since the fire. It is too disheartening."

She sighed as she stared around at the charred, blackened ruins. Though she was reluctant to enter, something drew her inside. "The marble floors are from Italy," she said as she lifted her skirts and stepped over a burned wooden beam.

Dulcie followed her, moving carefully through the debris and rubble. Despite the mess, it was easy to imagine how opulent the room must have been.

The outer walls, though blackened, remained intact. There were graceful curved arches over the doors and windows, enhanced by elegant scrollwork. All of them were charred and blackened. Part of the ceiling had collapsed, littering the floor with plaster and shards of crystal from a once splendid chandelier. In the center of the room, two fluted columns remained upright. The other two lay in pieces. A tall, floor-to-ceiling window had shattered. Part of the curtain still clung to a broken rod. The tattered lace edges fluttered in the breeze. In one corner a piano was nearly buried in plaster dust. Several sheets of music were scattered haphazardly on the music stand. The piano bench lay on its side, one leg missing.

"You cannot imagine the grand parties my parents hosted here."

Dulcie saw the way the older woman struggled with the memories as she stood in the middle of the room. "Father brought the piano from Paris for my mother, who was quite an accomplished musician. Every Christmas he threw a gala ball and hired half-a-dozen boats just to bring the guests over from Charleston. Oh, the times we had . . .'' Her voice trailed off and she bent to retrieve something from the floor.

''What is it, Aunt Bessie?''

''Just an old button,'' she said softly.

But from the way she said it, Dulcie knew it carried special meaning for the older woman.

''Is it from one of your gowns?'' she asked.

''No. From my . . . my brother's suit.'' Suddenly Aunt Bessie's shoulders sagged. In the blink of an eye she appeared stooped and weary. ''I believe I'll go up to my room and rest.''

''Yes, ma'am.''

Dulcie watched as she picked her way carefully through the clutter and made her way from the ballroom. For long minutes after Aunt Bessie left, Dulcie stared around, imagining the room as it had once been. Then, as an idea took shape, she hurried to find the others.

Aunt Bessie remained in her room and refused to come downstairs for lunch. The women and children took their meal with Robert at the big scarred table in the kitchen. Afterward, at Dulcie's invitation, everyone followed her to the ballroom.

When she suggested cleaning it as a surprise for Aunt Bessie, Robert shook his head. ''There is far too much work needed here, missy.''

''But there are many willing hands.''

He stared around, his eyes as sad and haunted as Aunt Bessie's had been. Perhaps, Dulcie thought, he, too, was seeing it in its former glory.

"We can't make it as elegant as it once was," she said softly, "but we can clean it enough so that Aunt Bessie won't feel so much pain when she comes in here."

He continued to resist. "We cannot shirk our other duties."

"I wouldn't suggest such a thing. But the candles are made, the butter is churned, the floors are scrubbed, and the food is ready for tonight's supper. Please, Robert, allow us to try."

He thought about it for several moments. At last he shrugged his shoulders in defeat. "If you wish. But I warn you, it will be next to impossible to make a difference in this room by the end of the day."

Dulcie could have hugged him. Instead, she said simply, "Thank you, Robert. We'll do our best."

She turned to the others. "What do you think?"

Nathaniel was the first to respond. "I think we should get started."

For the next few hours the women and children made endless trips outside, clearing the huge room of debris. When it was empty, they set about scrubbing the floor, the ceiling and walls of all traces of soot and grime.

Robert helped Nathaniel to nail boards over the broken window, and Fiona and the girls washed the torn curtains and hung them outside. When they were dry, Starlight sewed the ragged bits together until they looked almost as good as new. After Robert ironed them, they were hung in such a way that they hid the rough boards, making it appear that the window was intact.

Fiona and Starlight then set about mending and patching the charred upholstery on the chairs and sofas. Dulcie and the girls painstakingly gathered the broken crystal into several buckets, in the hopes that the once elegant chandelier could someday be restored.

By the time Robert left them to prepare for supper, their surroundings were much improved, and they gazed around with a feeling of satisfaction.

"I've never seen anything so lovely," Dulcie breathed as she stared around at the stately columns, the gleaming marble floor and the graceful curving arches, now free of dirt and soot.

"No wonder Aunt Bessie took to her bed," Fiona said. "'Twould break any heart to see such destruction."

"Come," Dulcie said, leading the way to the well. "It's time to wash and help Robert set the table."

And get ready to face Cal Jermain's questions, she thought. But this time, he would demand answers. Answers that, given truthfully, would surely send them packing for good.

"We will take our coffee in the parlor, Robert," Aunt Bessie announced at the end of supper.

"Yes, ma'am."

Not one word had been said about the restored ballroom. It had been decided that they would surprise Aunt Bessie with their secret.

Despite the fact that her labors should have stimulated her appetite, Dulcie hadn't been able to swallow more than a few bites. It seemed like only minutes ago that she had sat down, still undecided about what she would tell Cal. But now the moment she had dreaded was upon her, and she was still unprepared.

"Barc will escort you, Aunt Bessie," Cal said. "Miss Trenton and I will remain here for a few minutes while we have our little talk."

Dulcie didn't even look up when Cal spoke, but kept her gaze locked firmly on her plate.

Clinging to Barc's arm, Aunt Bessie swept from the room with the others following.

"Dulcie?" Clara turned back, but Fiona took the little girl firmly by the hand and hauled her away before she could say another word.

Robert picked up a silver tray laden with desserts and coffee and walked stiffly from the room.

And then they were alone.

Dulcie sat up straighter, squaring her shoulders, lifting her chin defiantly.

Across the table, Cal watched her in silence. He sat very still, his hand resting lightly on the lace cloth. Dulcie found herself studying the contrast between his work-roughened hand and the delicate lace.

"It is time for an explanation, Miss Trenton."

At his softly spoken words she looked up at him, then away. It was impossible to meet that dark, knowing gaze.

When she said nothing, he decided to prompt her. He stood and walked to the window, turning his back for a moment to give her time to compose herself. "Let us begin with one undeniable fact." He turned to face her. "From your reaction to my aunt's mention of the boat last night, it is obvious that you believe those men were looking for you."

She picked up an ornate silver spoon and studied it in silence.

"Why would they be looking for you?"

She switched the spoon to her other hand, running her thumb along the raised design.

He clenched his hand at his side and tried another tack. He would dare her to deny the truth. "I know you are being followed, Miss Trenton."

She nodded.

The first crack in her wall. He struggled to keep his tone even. "Why?"

She swallowed. "The . . . boat we came here in."

"What about it?"

"It was not mine to use. I . . . stole it."

He let out a breath. At last. An admission of sorts. "I see. You stole the boat. That would explain why you were out in the storm." He waited, studying her with that narrow, watchful gaze. "And you think one of those men could be the owner?"

Her head came up sharply, as though she hadn't thought of that. "Of course. I mean . . . yes. Don't you see? Aunt Bessie said they seemed to be searching for someone—something," she corrected. "They probably spotted the boat on shore and recognized it as theirs."

"Then why did they not simply come to shore and claim it?"

Her mind raced feverishly for a reasonable response. "Perhaps they thought they might have to fight for it and were unprepared. Or perhaps they thought to wait until dark."

He turned for a moment, glancing out the window, then swiveled back to her. His voice took on a challenging tone. "The boat is still there, Miss Trenton. If they intended to retrieve their stolen property under cover of darkness, they would have done so last night."

"Perhaps the tide was too high. Or the water too rough. Perhaps they were otherwise engaged last night."

"And perhaps they want more than the boat." His tone lowered with sudden frustration. "Why do you keep evading the truth, Miss Trenton?"

As he started toward her, she jumped up, knocking over the chair. Before she could escape, he reached out and caught her by the arm. "Our little discussion is not over yet."

"I've told you the truth." She tried to pull free, but his fingers tightened. "You're hurting me!" she cried.

Though he loosened his grip just a little, he refused to release her. Instead, he hauled her close until their faces were inches apart.

Her voice lowered to a whisper. "Isn't it enough to know that I stole the boat? Must you humiliate me further?"

"I am not interested in your humiliation, Miss Trenton. I care only for our safety here on the island. You have failed to explain one very important thing."

"And what is that?" She tossed her head, determined to face him down. Like any cornered creature, she was prepared to fight back any way she could, even using false bravado.

He gave her a dangerous smile, and she felt her heart stop. "You still haven't told me why you stole the boat."

Chapter Twelve

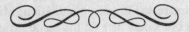

Dulcie's throat went dry. She could hear Papa's voice. "Oh, what a tangled web we weave when first we practice to deceive."

Forgive me, Papa.

"It . . . was necessary," Dulcie said softly. "We had to escape Charleston."

"Why?"

"Because I—" she swallowed "—stole." The words were spilling from her lips now, tumbling one over the other. "Yes. I stole. Food. For the children. They were hungry." She looked up in time to see him blanch.

He lowered his hand to his side and took a step back.

Like a carefully aimed dagger, her words had found their mark. Her heart began to race. She had uncovered his weakness. Even while she rejoiced at her good fortune, she felt a pang of remorse. She was now reduced to lying in order to keep her young charges safe. But it was nothing to what she had already done. Lying, cheating, stealing. Cal had been right when he'd accused her. She was absolutely shameless.

She took a deep breath and began rubbing her arm. "There. I've told you. And while I'm at it, I'll admit something else." Her voice grew stronger with every word. She could see the effect it had on him. He had already made up his mind to believe her. And why not? In her own mind, the lie grew until she could almost believe it herself. "I'm not sorry for what I did. If I had to, I'd do it again."

While her confidence grew, so did his remorse. "I'm sorry, Miss Trenton. I had no right to force such an embarrassing confession from you."

"Then you... don't think I'm a wicked person? For stealing, I mean?"

"You were only doing what was necessary to survive. I suppose, living here on our island, with more than enough to eat and a roof over our heads, we tend to forget how much this war has affected others. Of course you would steal in order to feed the children. I don't think less of you for it. I would have done the same."

She brightened. "You would?"

"Of course."

"Then we can stay? You won't send us away?"

For the first time he smiled. He found that her relief at having admitted her guilt was contagious. He felt equally relieved. He'd hoped all along that her crimes were minor. He wanted to believe, despite his misgivings, that she was an honest, God-fearing woman.

But, he told himself, his relief was not only for himself. Aunt Bessie was growing fond of these strangers, as were his brothers. "You have made yourselves indispensable for the moment. Until the barn is completed and my brothers and I can return to the fields, I suppose we must keep you on."

Having regained her confidence, Dulcie faced the last hurdle. "What of those men? Are you not concerned that they might return?"

"If they looked closely, they must have seen that their boat was badly damaged by the storm and almost completely submerged. It would do them no good now. They wouldn't get it halfway home before it would sink. I'm sure that's why they left without approaching shore. They were convinced of the futility of retrieving it." Cal crossed the room and held the door. "Let's join the others. I'm sure they're eager to hear the outcome of our little discussion."

Dulcie swept past him and started toward the parlor. And prayed that the trembling in her legs would go unnoticed by the man who followed closely behind.

The women and children clustered around her the moment she entered the parlor. Across the room, Cal's family gathered around him to hear the outcome of his confrontation. They were holding a lengthy whispered discussion.

"Was it terrible?" Starlight asked in a low voice. "Was he horrified when you told him?"

"Hush, now," Fiona admonished her. She had seen the flush on Dulcie's cheeks and knew her friend was in a highly emotional state. "We'll speak no more about it." To Dulcie she whispered, "I told the children to be prepared to leave in the morning. We'll find shelter—somewhere."

Emily and Belle began to weep. And though Nathaniel struggled to put on a brave face, his lower lip quivered.

"That won't be necessary," Dulcie murmured. "We're staying."

There was a moment of stunned silence.

It was Clara who finally spoke. "You didn't tell him the truth, did you, Dulcie?"

"Of course I . . ." She stared down into the child's trusting eyes and swallowed her protest. "No, Clara, I couldn't. I lied. I'm sorry."

Everyone gasped at her admission.

For a moment the little girl frowned. Then she caught Dulcie's hand and squeezed it, just the way Dulcie always did when she was trying to reassure one of them. "It's all right, Dulcie. I know God understands that it was the only way you could keep us all safe. I know He'll forgive you."

For a moment Dulcie couldn't find her voice. Blinking rapidly, she finally managed, "Thank you, Clara. That means more to me than you will ever know."

Robert approached Dulcie and leaned close. "All is in readiness, missy."

"Thank you, Robert." Dulcie drained her coffee, feeling all of her confidence returning. She turned to Aunt Bessie. "We've been saving a very special surprise for you." One that she had feared would be a farewell gift.

The older woman was feeling greatly relieved now that her nephew had assured her that the women and children would be staying. It was not the loss of their company, she told herself. It was the loss of good help. But for some unknown reason, she was feeling especially lighthearted.

"A surprise?" Aunt Bessie clapped her hands. "How delightful. What is it?"

"You'll have to come with us," Dulcie said. "Nathaniel, will you do the honors?"

The little boy gravely walked to Aunt Bessie's side and offered his arm as he'd seen Cal do. Mystified, the older woman tucked her hand into the crook of his arm and allowed him to lead her out of the parlor. The others followed. When they reached the closed door of the ballroom, they paused.

Robert opened the door, then stood aside as the others entered. For a moment Aunt Bessie held back, afraid to look. Then, urged on by the little boy, she stepped inside.

Lighted candles rested in sconces along the walls, casting a golden glow over the room. A silver candelabra, ablaze with light, stood atop the piano. Though the furniture had been hastily repaired and much of it was still shabby and damaged, the marble floors, as well as the walls and ceiling, gleamed in the glow of candlelight.

A round table, covered with crisp linens, held crystal tumblers of whiskey, and for the children, glasses of lemonade and cookies still warm from the oven.

"Oh, my! However did you manage this?" Aunt Bessie cried.

"We worked all afternoon while you were in your room," little Emily chirped.

Tears shimmered on Aunt Bessie's lashes, and she blinked them away.

"Don't cry, Aunt Bessie," Belle said. "We did this so you wouldn't have to feel sad anymore."

"Oh, you dear, dear children." With a cry, Aunt Bessie knelt and gathered them all close. The tears rolled unchecked down her cheeks as she murmured, "I'm not weeping because I'm sad. I'm weeping because you've made me so very happy."

As she hugged them, she looked over their heads to where the three young women stood together, smiling and clasping hands. What a strange band they were. Secretive, yet openly loving. Homeless, destitute, but generous to a fault.

"I will never forget this," she said as she got to her feet. "And now, I think we must celebrate."

"How?" Clara asked.

"How indeed?" Aunt Bessie smoothed the dark hair from the girl's forehead and gave a sudden bright smile. "I know. We shall dance. After all, this is a ballroom."

"Don't we need music to dance?" Emily asked.

"That we do." Aunt Bessie looked around. "What shall we do for music?"

"I can play the piano," Fiona admitted.

"Good girl." Barc caught her arm and led her across the room. The two of them began to sort through the sheet music.

Fiona looked slightly flustered as she settled herself at the piano and ran her fingers over the keys. Dulcie couldn't tell if her unease was due to the unfamiliar instrument or the attentions of the handsome, charming Barc. Whatever the reason, Fiona's cheeks were highly colored, her face radiant as she began to play. The strains of a waltz filled the air.

Aunt Bessie made her way to her oldest nephew and opened her arms. Cal bowed formally, then led her through the steps of the dance.

It was plain that they had danced often. In Cal's arms, the tall woman appeared as graceful as a fawn. And Cal, in black suit and crisp white shirt, looked every inch the lord of his manor.

As they whirled round and round, the children clapped in appreciation. Aunt Bessie, smiling and laughing, whispered something to Cal. Suddenly they separated, and Aunt Bessie turned to Nathaniel and offered her hand. Amid peals of laughter, they began the waltz.

Cal bowed stiffly in front of Clara and said, "May I have this dance, miss?"

The little girl giggled as she was swept away in his arms.

A few minutes later the partners separated again. Aunt Bessie danced with Darwin, while Nathaniel bowed in front of Starlight. Clara chose Emily, and Cal bowed in front of shy Belle. Barc, who had been turning pages for Fiona and whispering things that made her blush and laugh, spotted Dulcie standing alone. He hurried across the room and bowed grandly before sweeping her into his arms. Soon they were all flushed and laughing as they twirled and dipped their way around the elegant ballroom.

Fiona began a new piece, and Aunt Bessie announced that they must all change partners again. Dulcie danced with Nathaniel, who was having a grand time. His cheeks were pink, his eyes bright with excitement. But after a few turns around the room, it was time to change partners again. This time Dulcie found herself in Cal's arms.

"You are indeed a woman of many surprises," he murmured against her temple as they began to move to the music.

"I think Aunt Bessie is pleased."

"Pleased?" He lifted his head and gazed down into her eyes. "My aunt is delighted. This was an enormous undertaking. It was a very kind thing to do, Miss Trenton."

She felt a warm glow at his words of praise. "I had feared a scant hour ago that it would be my last chance to repay her kindness," she admitted softly, "before I was banished forever from your island."

"If this is a sample of the work you and the others are capable of, Miss Trenton, then I am doubly pleased that you are staying."

"Doubly pleased?"

He smiled. "Pleased for my aunt's sake and pleased for my own."

She thought nothing could make her happier than she was at this moment. But when he drew her close and began to move slowly through the dance, she thought her heart might explode from sheer happiness. With his hand holding hers, his cheek pressed to her temple, she felt more alive than she would have dreamed possible. She closed her eyes, loving the dizzying feelings that assaulted her as they twirled. She thought she could go on like this forever, as long as Cal Jermain held her in his arms.

"I'm sorry I misjudged you, Dulcie," he whispered against her temple.

She ignored the little twinge of conscience. "You had every right to wonder about us." She lifted her face to him and was rewarded by a sudden rush of heat as his lips whispered over her cheek.

"But I thought you might even be desperate women, the sort who would—"

She ignored the pain, sharp and stinging, and touched a finger to his lips to silence him. "Let's speak no more of such things."

He caught her hand and pressed a kiss to the palm. She felt the tremor all the way to her toes.

"You're right. Forgive me. Let's just enjoy the moment." He drew her close and she was achingly aware of the hard press of his thigh, the length of his leg against hers. His lips teased her ear as he turned her and led her through an intricate step. With a sigh she clung to him and moved with him and wished the music and the dance would go on forever.

When at last they were forced to change partners again, she smiled up at him and was rewarded by a parting smile. She floated into Barc's arms and was soon laughing delightedly as he lifted her off her feet and whirled her around the floor.

Across the room she watched as Aunt Bessie urged shy Starlight into Dar's arms. The two moved awkwardly, as though afraid to touch. And when the music ended, they stepped apart so quickly they nearly stumbled.

It was past midnight when Robert passed among them with a silver tray, offering a last chance at refreshments. Though the children were still delighted with their party, they were having a hard time hiding their yawns.

"Unfortunately all good things must come to an end," Aunt Bessie announced. She turned to Fiona. "I hope you will entertain us again soon."

"It would be my pleasure," the young woman said. "It's been a long time since I've had the opportunity to make music."

"You aren't one to boast, are you, Miss O'Neil?" Barc said as he caught both her hands in his and brought them to his lips. "You truly do have many talents."

The bloom on Fiona's cheeks matched the color of her hair.

"Was this a fine surprise, Aunt Bessie?" Nathaniel asked.

"Indeed it was. I thank all of you for this delightful evening. I shall not soon forget it." She turned to her nephew. "And now, Calhoun, if you will assist me, I will say goodnight."

She placed her hand on his sleeve and walked grandly from the ballroom, with the others not far behind. At the doorway she turned for a last glimpse. Her eyes sparkled with tears of joy. Without a word she departed and headed for her room.

Cal stood on the balcony listening to the whispered voices as the children were tucked into their beds. He could make out bits and pieces of prayers, followed by muffled goodnights. A trill of laughter drifted on the air, followed by a command to hush.

He exhaled a puff of rich cigar smoke and stared into the darkness. There was something satisfying about the presence of so many people in the house. Looking back, he realized that this old plantation had felt cold and lifeless ever since his return from the war. He'd blamed it on the fact that his parents were gone. But it was more than that. Much more. Since the arrival of Dulcie and the others, this house once again teemed with life, with love and laughter and tears. It had been reborn.

As had he.

That thought startled him. What nonsense. He was the same man he'd been yesterday. The same man who'd come home from the war maimed in body and spirit. And tomorrow, when he awoke, he would still be less than the man he'd been before the war.

He drew deeply on his cigar, wondering why such thoughts hadn't summoned the familiar bitterness. Could it be he was beginning to trust again? Could the reason for that trust be Miss Dulcie Trenton?

The flicker of candlelight drew his gaze to her window. He could see her, dressed in her nightgown, neatly folding back the bed covers. That done, she sat at her dressing table and ran a brush through her hair. With each stroke, he felt something tighten inside him.

While he watched, she crossed to her nightstand and blew out the candle. In the darkness he could hear the soft rustling as she settled herself into bed.

Tossing aside his cigar, he remained on the balcony a long time. While the darkness closed in around him, he struggled with demons he'd thought long buried.

Chapter Thirteen

"Nathaniel," Cal asked one morning as the wagon lumbered toward the fields, "how would you like to work with us today?"

"You mean it?" The little boy's eyes danced with unconcealed excitement.

"I do." Cal glanced toward Dulcie. "That is, if the women can spare you."

Dulcie was horrified. "You want Nathaniel to cut timber?"

"There's a lot more to what we do than just chopping down trees. There are roots to be dug, branches to be removed and seedlings to be planted. Quite a lot for three men."

"But he's just a little boy," she protested.

"Aw, Dulcie. You make me sound like a baby." Nathaniel's face fell.

At once she regretted her protest. He wanted so badly to be a man. And this would give him an opportunity to spend the entire day around the ones he most admired.

"Forgive me, Nathaniel." She dropped an arm around his shoulders. "I'm sure you could be a great help." She glanced over his head toward Cal, who was holding the reins and awaiting her reply. "Of course he can go with you."

"Thanks, Dulcie." The boy impulsively hugged her, and she prayed she'd made the right choice.

As Barc helped her and the others down from the wagon, she said, "You'll see that he rests during the hottest part of the day?"

"Aw, Dulcie," Nathaniel moaned. "There you go again, making me out to be a baby."

"I'll see to it," Cal said.

"Don't forget your lessons," Starlight put in.

"What lessons?" Barc asked good-naturedly as the wagon rumbled away.

"We're learning sums." Picking his way carefully, Nathaniel climbed over the wagon seat and settled himself in the back beside Barc and Dar. He studied the way they shoved their hats back off their faces in a rakish manner. Then he shoved his own hat back and leaned on his elbows.

"Have you mastered the multiplication tables?" Barc asked.

Nathaniel shrugged. "I don't think so. We're just doing sums." He held up two fingers on each hand. "Two plus two is four."

"Didn't you already know that?" Dar asked.

"Sure. But Starlight says that's learning sums. I can do both my fingers and my toes now. Right up to ten plus ten. 'Course," he added, "I guess I wouldn't be so good with my shoes on."

Barc choked back a laugh. "Don't you intend to go any higher? How about eleven plus eleven? Or fifteen plus fifteen?"

Again Nathaniel shrugged. "Starlight says fingers and toes are as much as she knows. She's a really fine teacher," he insisted. "And she makes the learning fun."

"That's important." Barc was grinning, but he was aware that his younger brother had gone very quiet.

"Here we are," Cal said over his shoulder.

He reined in the team and everyone jumped down. Within an hour Nathaniel had sorted out the things the others wanted him to do. The four of them fell into an easy rhythm of hard but satisfying work.

"Time to eat," Cal called.

"Let's see what Robert packed for us," Barc said as the others set aside their tools and dropped to the ground.

Nathaniel sat beside Cal, resting his back against the trunk of a giant oak. Cal lifted a jug of water to his mouth, then passed it to the boy, who followed suit.

"Tired?" he asked.

"No, sir."

Cal grinned. "You're a better man than I. I'm grateful for the break."

"Well, I guess I am a little tired. And I sure am hungry," the boy admitted. "But I don't need to take a nap. Naps are for babies. And girls," he added with disdain.

"Nobody said you had to nap." Cal replaced the stopper in the jug and set it aside. "Still, a little rest after we eat might be welcome. I do it myself sometimes," he assured the boy, who looked as though he might argue the point.

Barc passed around thick slices of turkey and buttered biscuits, and the four of them ate their fill before helping themselves to a jug of buttermilk and cookies wrapped in a square of linen.

"Those are just about the best cookies I've ever tasted," Barc said as he polished off his third.

"My ma made the best cookies in the world," Nathaniel boasted.

"What kind?" Cal leaned back, crossing one foot over the other. It was the first time Nathaniel had ever volunteered anything about his family. To Cal, it was an encouraging sign that perhaps some of the wounds were healing.

"Ma called them sweet-tooth Sammies. They were real sweet, with pecans on top. And I remember they used to melt in my mouth."

"How long since you lost your ma?"

Nathaniel shrugged. "I guess it must be two years or more, 'cause I've been with Dulcie now for over a year."

"How did you come to live with her? Was she your aunt or cousin?"

"I didn't know her. But when she found me sleeping in her shed one morning, she took me in to live with her and Fiona."

The brothers exchanged a look.

"Why were you in her shed?" Barc asked gently.

"After Ma died, I tried to stay on in the house." Nathaniel's voice lowered. "In case my pa came back. I knew he'd be worried about me and wouldn't know where to look if I left. I tried to keep up the fields, but without a horse or plow, I couldn't do much. But I did my best. At least I had a little to eat. One night, while I was sleeping, I heard the windows being broken, and I saw some men stealing everything they could carry. I slipped out an upstairs window and hid in the woods. And a little while later, they set fire to the house.

"I wanted to stay in the woods in case Pa came home. But I saw those same men heading toward me with torches, and I knew I'd better get going. So I started running and kept on until I couldn't run anymore." He looked away, afraid to meet their eyes. They probably thought he was a coward for running. "And that's when I hid in Dulcie's shed."

"So you were alone after your mother died." Barc glanced at his brothers and knew they were also wondering how a boy so young had survived. "And your father? Did he ever return?"

Nathaniel shook his head and stared down at his hands. "Dulcie says there are lots of orphans since the war. And I'm luckier than some. At least I'm not alone anymore."

The men were silent, moved as much by his story as by his bravery in the face of such overwhelming odds.

"I guess you were lucky to find someone like Miss Trenton." Barc studied the bowed head. "Have she and Fiona always lived together?"

"Oh, no." Nathaniel met his questioning gaze. "The plantation was Dulcie's. When I came to live there, Fiona wasn't even strong enough to get out of bed. Something bad had happened to her, something she never talked about, and Dulcie took her in and took care of her, just like she took care of me and Clara and Belle and Emily and Starlight."

"So none of you knew each other until Dulcie took you in?"

"No, sir."

Again there was a silence, as the men mulled over what the boy had said. This time it was Cal who spoke. "You say Dulcie lived on a plantation?" He felt a wave of guilt for having harbored the suspicion that she was lying.

"Yes, sir." He brightened, remembering his relief at having finally found a haven. "At first it was even bigger than yours."

At first. A puzzling phrase. "Why did she leave it?"

Like a shot the boy was on his feet. Tears flooded his eyes. How could he have been so careless? He'd promised. He'd taken a solemn oath. And here he was, jabbering like a parrot. "Dulcie didn't do anything wrong."

Cal stood up and reached a hand to the boy, but Nathaniel drew away in obvious distress. "I didn't suggest that she did, son. I just wondered why she would leave her home and take all of you with her."

"She just . . . left. And we left with her. Can we get back to work now?" Nathaniel asked. His lips were trembling.

"That's a good idea. Let's all get back to work." Cal spun away and reached for his ax. While the blade bit into the wood, he contemplated all he'd heard. Nathaniel was absolutely terrified of something. Something that had affected Dulcie in the recent past.

He should have known her tale of simple theft was only that. A tale. A fabrication. A damnable lie.

He lifted his ax and brought it down with such force it completely severed the trunk of the tree. There was something much more dark and dangerous here than stealing. Something Nathaniel and the others had witnessed. Or had been a party to. And, so help him, this time he would uncover the truth.

"Nathaniel," Emily called excitedly, running alongside the wagon, "did you get to chop down a tree?"

The boy was perched atop a log in the back of the wagon, his hat pushed dashingly back from his face, his sleeves rolled above the elbows. He was feeling better about himself than he could ever remember. He'd spent the entire day with three men he admired, who had treated him like one of them. Even that little slip of the tongue hadn't cost him too dearly. None of the Jermain men had pursued it further, and he was certain by now they'd forgotten all about it.

"Don't call me Nathaniel," the boy announced airily. "From now on, I want to be called Nat."

Shielding the sun from her eyes, Dulcie looked from Nathaniel to Cal, who seemed as surprised as she was by the boy's statement.

"And why in heaven's name should we call you that?" she asked.

"I think, since Calhoun is Cal and Barclay is Barc and Darwin is Dar, I'm old enough to be called Nat."

"I see."

"That's just plain silly," Clara said.

When the team came to a complete halt, Nathaniel jumped down beside Barc and began helping the women and girls into the wagon. Within minutes they were rolling over the green fields. In the back of the wagon, Nathaniel answered the girls' questions and regaled them with tales of his first day as a logger. Dulcie, in the seat up front beside Cal, had gone very quiet.

"Something wrong?" he asked her.

"Just yesterday he was a boy," she murmured.

"Don't look so sad," Cal said as he deftly handled the team. "It happens to all of us."

"But he never had a chance to be young and carefree, to play like other children."

"Neither did a lot of lads. But at least he's alive. And, for the moment, safe. I should think that counts for a great deal, especially with you, Miss Trenton. Isn't that what you told Nathaniel when you took him in?"

Dulcie turned to glance at the man beside her. His voice was low, his face expressionless. But there was something about his words that caused a little shiver of alarm. It was obvious that the boy had spoken freely in front of these men.

A new thought intruded with the force of a physical blow. Had Nathaniel broken their vow of silence?

She would have to tread carefully. "What do you mean by that, Mr. Jermain?"

"It's apparent that you are very concerned for the safety of your little band. Wouldn't you agree?"

"Of course. But—"

"And you would say or do anything necessary to keep them safe."

She saw where this was heading.

"Wouldn't you, Miss Trenton?" he prodded.

"Yes." Her chin came up in that infuriating way he had come to recognize.

"So, that little story you concocted about stealing food was merely a ploy to convince me that you and the others were worthy of my trust."

"I didn't ask you to trust me. You need us, Mr. Jermain. Every bit as much as we need you."

He kept his voice low so the others wouldn't overhear. "For now maybe. But remember this, Miss Trenton. The crops will soon be harvested. And when they are, when your work is finished, my family and I will remain here where it is safe. And you and your little band will have to go back and face whatever it is you're running from. Unless..."

"Unless what?"

He noted the way she'd jumped on his words. "Unless you're willing to trust me with the truth."

"I've told you the—"

"The truth, Miss Trenton," he whispered savagely. "Not another one of your clever lies."

She turned her face away, but not before he saw the color that flooded her cheeks. And the anguish in her eyes.

"There was a mama raccoon in the tree we chopped down this afternoon," Nathaniel related as they sat around the parlor after dinner. "You should have seen how mad she was when we started chopping."

Across the room, Cal refused to join in the conversation. He'd been brooding all evening. Now he sipped his whiskey and silently watched and listened.

Dulcie, keeping her distance, did the same. And felt the coldness of his stare whenever she looked his way.

"Why did you choose the raccoon's tree?" Clara asked in obvious distress. "That's where she lived. Why didn't you leave her house alone?"

"We didn't do it to be mean, Clara. We didn't even know she was there, until after we got started," Nathaniel explained. "Then she stuck her head out and hissed at us. I got so scared I dropped my ax."

"Did she come after you?" Little Emily's eyes were as wide as saucers.

"No. She was afraid to leave her babies. But when Barc and Dar kept right on sawing, she had no choice but to leave. She finally climbed out of her nest, with the little ones following, and ran off into the woods."

"Poor raccoons," Clara said softly. "Now they have no home."

Barc, sensing that the little girl was identifying with the animals, said with a gentle smile, "She's found another hollow log for her babies by now, Clara. There's nothing stronger or smarter than a mother raccoon. I'll lay a wager that right now her babies are all curled up around her, content after a big dinner of catfish from a nearby pond."

Clara relaxed, smiling at his vivid description.

"You missed your lessons today, Nathaniel," Starlight said.

"It's Nat," the boy said. "Remember?"

She wouldn't have to be reminded again. After all, hadn't she chosen her name? He had the right to do the same. "Nat, would you like to go over our new words?"

"I guess so. I don't want to fall behind the others." He crossed the room and sat down beside her on the small love seat where she was sewing.

Across the room Dar frowned and turned away, busying himself with a cup of tea from Robert's tray.

"We learned to spell two new words today," Starlight explained gently. "Clara was helping me, since she could remember a few words she'd learned before—" she paused a moment, then forced herself to say "—before her mama died."

"What are the words?" Nathaniel asked.

With great effort Starlight pulled herself back from the edge of that place in her mind where she often went at the very mention of death or war. She'd been trying, for the sake of the children, to grow stronger each day.

"Home," she said proudly. "H-o-m-e."

Nathaniel repeated the letters.

"Good. The next word is love." She relaxed, lulled by the sound of this word. It created such beautiful images in her mind. Memories of parents, sisters, happy times. "L-o-v-e."

Again he said the letters aloud.

"That's very good, Nat. I suppose," she said to the other children, "we ought to learn raccoon, in honor of Nat's special day."

They clapped their hands and gathered around, while the little boy sat beside her, looking proud and pleased that she would include his word in their lesson for the day.

"Raccoon," Starlight said clearly. "R-a-k..." She squeezed her eyes shut and tried as hard as she could to concentrate, then finished, "...u-n."

In clear voices the children repeated the letters after her.

"No. That isn't right." As the harsh words slipped from his lips, Dar glanced around to see everyone staring at him in surprise.

Flustered, he tried to cover up by sipping his tea, only to discover that he'd dropped four or five spoonfuls of sugar into it without even realizing what he'd done. Disgusted, he set it down on the tray with a clatter.

"It isn't right?" Starlight asked in dismay. "What letter did I get wrong?"

"Most of them." His hands clenched and unclenched at his sides. He saw the anguish in the girl's eyes, and the look of disappointment in the eyes of her trusting young pupils, and immediately despised himself for his outburst.

"Then how do you spell raccoon?" Starlight asked.

"I can't...It doesn't...You'll have to ask one of my brothers." With that, Dar strode from the room, slamming the door behind him.

Aunt Bessie watched in tight-lipped silence. And wondered how much longer her youngest nephew would continue to keep his demons locked tightly away in his heart.

Chapter Fourteen

Starlight went through her nightly ritual. After slipping into her nightgown and brushing her hair, she knelt beside the bed and whispered her prayers, taking care to mention everyone who had ever mattered to her. The names always brought a tear to her eye, but she refused to avoid the pain. The dead must be remembered, even if it brought suffering to the living. And so she enumerated them, one after the other, asking for God's blessing on them, trusting they had at last found their eternal reward.

That done, she began a careful examination of the room, checking the doors and windows, to be certain they were securely locked, tying back her curtains so that the room was flooded with moonlight. Satisfied, she turned down the covers and blew out the candle, then gathered up her locket and knife and turned her face for a last glimpse of the sky.

"Oh!" Seeing Dar's face at her balcony door, her hand flew to her throat. A fleeting moment of sheer terror ripped through her. When it passed, she struggled for breath. She felt as though all the air had been forced from her lungs, and for a long moment she could do nothing more than stare helplessly while she took in great gulps of air.

He lifted a hand and tapped at the glass pane. Very carefully she set her knife and locket on her pillow, then crossed the room and opened the door a fraction.

"You frightened me," she whispered furiously. She was still stung by his behavior in the parlor and more than a little afraid he was here to continue his tirade against her.

"Yes. I can see that. I'm truly sorry. I . . . need to speak with you."

"Can't it wait until morning?"

"No. I must speak with you now. Please," he added.

Starlight glanced around her room. "It wouldn't be proper to invite you in."

"Of course." He seemed as flustered as she. "Could we talk out here on the balcony?"

She seemed about to refuse, but there was something about this shy man that touched her. She sensed he was as troubled in his mind as she.

"I'll have to find a wrap." She left Dar standing outside while she went in search of a shawl, which she draped around her shoulders. Then she stepped out onto the balcony and automatically lifted her face to the sky. The presence of the moon and stars was reassuring.

She joined him at the railing. "What is it you wished to say to me?"

He stood beside her but kept his gaze averted, choosing to stare off into the distance. "I wanted to apologize for my boorish behavior this evening."

"It's all right," she said softly, though she wasn't quite certain what boorish meant. She supposed it described his sudden flare of temper. "I never was very good with spelling."

"That isn't the point." He gripped the railing so tightly his knuckles were white. "I had no right to be so angry."

"Please don't blame yourself. I guess, for someone as smart as you, it must be just plain awful to watch someone as dumb as me trying to teach the children."

"Don't say that." His voice sounded strangled as he turned to her. "You're not dumb, Starlight." He brought his hands to her arms as if to shake her, then caught himself in time to gentle his touch. His hands rested lightly on her upper arms, and he allowed his gaze to roam her sweet face. "You're just about the finest woman I've ever met."

Starlight's eyes widened in surprise. She thought about backing away from him, but the touch of his hands on her arms had her paralyzed. "Then why were you mad at me?"

"It wasn't you. Don't you see? I was angry with myself."

Now she was even more confused. "Mad at yourself? But that's silly. Why would you be mad at yourself?"

Instead of answering, Dar said, "Tell me something. Why are you trying to teach the children?"

She paused for a moment, struggling to gather her thoughts. "I guess because I realized how little I know. I don't want them to be like me. They have a right to learn. Everyone has the right to learn."

She heard a sound escape his lips and looked up in time to see a tear slip from the corner of his eye and roll down his cheek. Stunned, she lifted her hand, but he shook off her touch and turned away in shame.

She watched as he leaned against the railing, his head lowered, his body shaking with silent sobs. Gathering her courage, she reached out a hand to touch his shoulder. She felt him flinch, but he didn't pull away.

When at last he'd composed himself, he accepted the offer of her handkerchief. They stood side by side at the balcony for long silent moments.

"I wish I had met you sooner," he said softly. "Perhaps then I could have become a better person."

"I think you're a fine person," she said, bewildered by his words.

Silence again stretched between them. But it was not an uncomfortable silence. Instead, it seemed a comfortable, easy thing.

She waited patiently, knowing he needed time.

He began to speak, haltingly at first, as though the words had been locked inside him for a lifetime. "Before the war, I...was a teacher."

Starlight was thunderstruck. "How wonderful!"

There was no answering warmth in his voice. "I was employed at the Charleston Academy for Young Men. Within two years, I became the youngest headmaster in the history of the academy."

"Your family must have been so proud of you."

"They were. And I was filled with pride." His voice lowered. "So much pride. False pride. I held myself above all the others. I told myself that my God-given talent must be used for great good. And so I pushed my pupils mercilessly and berated them for the least little error. Looking back, I realize that many of my young pupils must have felt like failures, not because of any lack on their part, but because of my vanity."

"Don't you think you're being too hard on yourself?" she asked.

He shook his head. "Not nearly hard enough. When I think of what I did to those tender young hearts, I realize what a monster I was. I believed in the rod. They were punished most severely for the slightest infraction of the rules. And I became the most gleeful of avengers, forcing them to accept their punishment in front of the entire assembly, so that they would be even more humiliated."

He twisted his hands together, lost in thought. Starlight could read the anguish in his features.

"There was one young man I especially taunted. He was rather slow-witted, though he tried harder than any other pupil in my class. Instead of praising him for his effort, I constantly berated him for his lack of comprehension of Greek and Latin. I ridiculed him endlessly in front of the others. At last, because of me, he was forced to leave the academy, even though his father and his father's father had been two of our most esteemed alumni."

"It...must have meant a great deal to you," Starlight whispered, "that you can still not forget it."

"Forget it?" Dar's voice was harsh with self-loathing. "How I wish I could. But I shall never forget what I did to that boy. I shall see him in my mind until my dying day. For you see, when I left the academy to join the fighting, I came across that same dull-witted lad at Gettysburg."

Starlight fell into shocked silence. The death and destruction at Gettysburg was well-known. The place was spoken of only in whispers, because of the carnage there.

When Dar spoke of it, his voice was lifeless, as though he was again living that far-off battle in his mind.

"I became separated from my troops. I thought I'd descended into hell itself. You cannot imagine the horror of that place. All around me men were dying. It was impossible to see through the dust and the horses, and the crush of men and weapons. And suddenly a man in blue appeared before me wielding a bayonet, and I knew in that instant that I must prepare to die."

Starlight gasped, and Dar looked at her a moment before he continued, "And then, out of the confusion, loomed that boy from the academy. He called my name, and I was never more grateful to see anyone in my life."

He fell silent for a moment, and Starlight waited, knowing something of the agony he felt by forcing himself to say aloud what was in his heart.

"I had never seen such courage. While I awaited my fate at the hands of a Federalist, that boy, whom I had so cruelly treated, attacked with only his fists—and took the bayonet meant for me."

A cry was torn from Starlight's lips, but Dar continued with his narrative, compelled to confess his guilt.

"Even then, mortally wounded, he led me through the mass of tangled bodies, through the screams and cries and wild confusion, back to my troops. Only then, when I was safe, did he drop to his knees and allow me to see how serious his wound was. While I cradled him in my arms, I thanked him for saving my life and begged him to forgive my arrogance. Yet his only concern was that he bring honor to his old academy. And that I convey his love to his mother. And then he died in my arms."

Dar turned away, but not before Starlight saw another tear roll down his cheek.

It took him several minutes to compose himself. When he did, he said, "Now you see why I cannot allow myself to teach the children."

Starlight wished she had the education to put into words all the things in her heart. But though she felt woefully inadequate, she had to try. She laid a hand on his sleeve and said simply, "You have what we can only yearn for. Knowledge. It is such a wondrous thing. And it ought to be shared."

He swung around to face her. "Haven't you heard me? I am unfit to be called a teacher. I abused that fine young man. I humiliated him and caused him to leave the school he loved. And in return he gave his life for me."

"Because he thought you were worth it," she said softly. "He forgave you. Now you must forgive yourself. Don't you see, Dar? The man you were before the war is dead. The man you have become is kind and gentle and sweet. Now you must become even more. You must become worthy of this heroic boy's sacrifice. You must share your knowledge with those who are hungry for it.''

Dar was so moved by her passionate plea he could hardly speak. He caught her hand in both of his and stared down into her eyes. ''Will you help me, Starlight?''

''I cannot even write the name I chose for myself.''

''Then I will teach you. And you, in turn, can teach me. Teach me how to inspire the children as you have. Teach me how to be humble. Teach me how to love and accept them just for themselves. Will you, Starlight?''

This time it was her eyes that filled. She blinked rapidly and gave him a timid smile. ''I would be honored.''

He lifted her hand to his lips and pressed a kiss to the palm. ''Thank you, Starlight. You are my first—my only— friend. If you are willing, we will begin tomorrow.''

She nodded. ''Tomorrow, friend.''

They stood together, unmoving, unwilling to end this fragile bond they had just forged.

At last Starlight stepped back, drawing her shawl around her. ''I will say good-night now.''

He waited until she returned to her room and secured the balcony door. Then, with a light heart, he made his way to his own room. Starlight's words continued playing through his mind. *The man you were before the war is dead.*

He truly hoped so. He would not mourn his passing. If Starlight was right, if this was truly a chance to begin anew, he would grasp life with both hands and make of himself a man worthy to be called a Jermain.

The sweet, languorous days seemed to be rushing by in a blur. The crops, lovingly tended by the women and children, waved, strong and healthy, in the summer breezes.

Already the early crops of corn and beans had come in, along with several fruits. Robert's peach cobbler was the highlight of many an evening in the parlor, where the conversation became increasingly spirited as they discussed religion, politics and the introduction of the latest farming implements. Aunt Bessie even encouraged the children to join in, explaining that her parents had always insisted that she and her brother remain current in world affairs.

For their part, the children blossomed, not only because of the abundance of fine food and loving care, but because of Dar's excellent tutoring.

With so much of the farm chores winding down, the children were allowed two hours every morning with their teachers, Dar and Starlight. Classes were conducted in the restored ballroom, which was now filled with books and slates and the sound of music and laughter.

The new barn that was quickly taking shape would be twice the size of the old one, with an upper floor, beneath the rafters, to be used for the storage of crops and the drying of seeds for the next planting.

Dulcie stood on the balcony in the early-morning mist. Despite all that had been accomplished, her thoughts were troubled.

Cal had become increasingly cold and distant, and she knew it was because she would not confide in him. She wanted badly to trust him with her secret. But if she did, she was afraid they would all be banished immediately.

What did it matter? she asked herself. Very soon now, their usefulness to the Jermains would end, and they would have to face the daunting journey, anyway. They would return to Charleston. Their dilemma would be the same as before. No money to travel. No place to hide. And no way to escape the danger. Their future was indeed bleak.

She had bought some time. For that she would be eternally grateful. They had all been given a chance to eat, to rest and recover, to grow strong for the perils ahead. But was it enough to defeat the enemy?

"A penny for them."

At the sound of Cal's voice, she whirled. The frown of concern was still etched on her forehead.

"Why must you always sneak up on me?"

He ignored her comment and concentrated on what he'd read in her eyes before she'd spotted him. She was deeply troubled. "Is life really all that bad, Miss Trenton?"

Despite her dark thoughts, she forced herself to assume a bland look. "How could anything seem troubling on a day like this?"

"How indeed?" He remained where he was, reluctant to step closer. To be close to her was to tempt fate. She looked entirely too fetching in her nightgown, with only a tattered shawl around her shoulders for modesty. And since he'd spent the better part of the night fighting the urge to storm her room and satisfy a very raw ache, he thought he'd better keep his distance.

Seeing the way he looked at her, she turned toward her room. "It's time I got dressed."

"Just a moment, Miss Trenton." He removed a small pistol from his pocket. "From now on I'd like you to carry this with you while you and the others are working in the fields."

She stiffened, instantly alert to the subtle change in him. "Why? What has happened?"

"My aunt saw a boatload of men near shore yesterday."

He recognized the stark terror in her eyes.

"Why didn't she mention it?"

"After seeing the children's reaction to her last sighting, we thought it best if they were spared."

Dulcie let out the breath she'd been holding. "Thank you." She looked up, meeting his direct gaze. "That was very kind."

When he offered her the pistol, she prayed he wouldn't notice the trembling of her hand.

"Do you know how to use this?"

She nodded and looked away quickly. Too quickly.

"Then you've used a gun before?"

It took her a moment to find her voice. "Once or twice. Have you?"

"Growing up on this island, we learned to shoot a gun at the same time we learned to ride. Hunting and fishing were a part of my childhood." He waited, knowing she had once again deflected his question with one of her own.

When she offered nothing more, he said, "Just so you are assured that Nathaniel is safe while he works with us, I have a rifle I'll take along when we go to the forest. And I've instructed Robert to keep one at the ready here in the house."

"You think those men will return?"

He could hear the tension humming through each word. Though he hadn't intended to, he stepped closer and dropped a hand to her arm as if to comfort her. "Don't you, Miss Trenton?"

She glanced toward shore, where the tiny craft that had brought them to this island was slowly sinking. By summer's end it would most likely be completely submerged.

She struggled to keep her voice from wavering. "Let them have their boat."

He cupped her chin in his hand, forcing her to look at him. It was the first time he'd allowed himself to touch her in weeks, and they both felt the jolt. "You and I know it isn't the boat they're after, don't we, Miss Trenton?"

She swallowed, knowing he was waiting.

His thumb traced the outline of her lips, and she felt a flare of heat that left her weak. His voice was low, seductive. "Trust me, Dulcie."

"I . . . want to." It was time to admit the truth.

He rested his hand gently along the side of her face, loving the feel of her flesh beneath his fingertips. He felt a flicker of hope. He would move slowly, patiently, so as not to frighten her again. "I can help you, Dulcie. Just tell me everything."

Her body strained toward his and, without realizing it, she lifted her face to him, hungry for the taste of his lips.

He stood very still, staring down into her eyes. But he made no move to kiss her.

She felt a wave of bitter disappointment. She had hoped to be able to lose herself in the mindless pleasure of passion. But what he wanted from her was trust.

Though she yearned to be free of her burden of guilt, she discovered she couldn't speak over the lump in her throat. It wasn't just fear of being exiled that stopped her. It was the censure she knew she would see in Cal's eyes. It was the one thing she couldn't bear. For she knew with certainty that once he learned the truth, he would turn away from her forever.

The shadow of doubt was back in her eyes. "No one can help me."

The moment for honesty passed. His hand dropped to his side.

She turned away and walked into her room.

Behind her, Cal clenched his fist. He wanted her so desperately he was shaking. But he wanted her trust even more.

Standing very still, he muttered a few rich, ripe curses at her stubbornness.

Chapter Fifteen

"Excuse me, Aunt Bessie. It's time to teach the children."

As Dar dashed out of the room, with Starlight and the children in his wake, his aunt blinked away the mist in her eyes.

"The Lord works in mysterious ways," Robert muttered as he set her tea beside her at the breakfast table.

"So it would seem." She stared at the little party as they took their leave.

It was becoming more and more evident to everyone that Dar was undergoing an amazing transformation. Though he was still reluctant to speak in the midst of adults, he had no such problem with Starlight and the children.

His deep, cultured voice could be heard beyond the closed doors of the ballroom, leading them in their lessons, coaxing, praising. And his laughter was a joyous thing to hear. Rich and warm, it filled the house as he regaled his pupils with stories from his childhood spent on the island.

Sometimes he would press Aunt Bessie into service, encouraging her to speak to them about her travels. She was surprised and flattered, and soon threw herself into her lectures with great relish, reliving, as she spoke, the wonderful experiences of her youth. Her tales of trips to Europe and Asia held them spellbound.

"Are you sorry to be here instead of France or England?" Clara asked one morning as the older woman finished her story.

"There is no place I'd rather be than right here," she replied emphatically, and realized she meant every word. "It is indeed satisfying to see the world. But the heart is happiest at home."

Across the room, Fiona grew pensive. Watching her expression, Dulcie knew that her friend had returned, in her mind, to her beloved Ireland, which she had sworn never to see again.

Sometimes Dulcie worried about Fiona. Though she was restored physically, she had never fully recovered from her emotional injuries. Perhaps, Dulcie mused, she never would. Though she was wise and witty and worldly, the Irishwoman preferred the safety of Robert's kitchen or the dullness of farm chores to the challenges of life beyond these shores.

Perhaps it was true of all of them, Dulcie thought suddenly. They were all hiding. And pretending that the peril could not penetrate this snug harbor.

Dulcie was pulled from her reverie when Dar invited Barc to tell the children about law and politics. It was the first this charming young man had spoken of his legal training and his years spent as counsel to some very distinguished men.

"Of course," Barc said with a rare display of humility, "I am merely following in my father's footsteps. He was a very well-respected judge, who expected great things of me." For several moments his words stilled. Then he went on with his familiar self-deprecating humor, "And now it would seem I am following, instead, in the footsteps of my great-grandfather, Big John Jermain. Big John was a notorious

gambler who, according to family history, won this island
in a game of high-stakes poker that lasted for three days. His
wife, Matilda Livingston Jermain, never referred to it by
name, insisting on calling it John's Folly.''

The women and children were properly amused by the
story, though Dulcie sensed an underlying sadness in his
telling. She found herself wondering what important things
his father had expected of his middle son. And what goals
Barc had once had for himself.

"With your education and background," Fiona said to
him, "I should think you would consider a future in politics for yourself."

Barc's usually charming smile failed him. For a moment
his quick wit seemed to falter before he managed to gather
his thoughts. Then he said gravely, "I assure you, my only
future is in a deck of cards. I consider a glass of fine whiskey and a challenging game of poker the most satisfying
things a man can have in life."

Fiona looked properly horrified. Her brogue thickened as
her anger deepened. "I should think your father would be
bitterly disappointed in you. 'Tis a waste of a fine life."

He lifted his tumbler in a salute and drained it in one
quick swallow. When he set down the empty glass, he turned
to her with a grand bow. "I will remind you that it is my life
to waste as I please, Miss O'Neil. And now, I will bid you
all good-night."

With that he made his way to his room.

The next morning, he left again for Charleston.

The evening was hot and airless. The draperies had been
tied back from the open windows to allow as much air as
possible into the parlor.

Aunt Bessie sat in her chair, fanning herself. Cal and Dar
sat together, heads bent close, discussing a blight that had

been discovered in the corn. At least half the crop was damaged and would not even be salvageable as feed for the animals. It was a terrible blow, but they were counting on the other crops to more than make up for the damage to the corn.

As the evening wore on, Cal moved to the other side of the room, and the women and children gathered around Dar, who had chosen a book on science and biology. As usual, he gave them a thorough explanation of the subject matter before he began to read. But after only a couple of pages, he suddenly glanced up.

"What am I thinking of? Cal, you are far better equipped than I to enlighten my pupils on this subject. Perhaps you could read this text and—" A withering look from his brother cut him off in midsentence.

For a moment everyone went very still as Cal and Dar stared at each other.

"Forgive me. I wasn't thinking..." Dar began, but Cal was already on his feet and walking toward the open parlor doors.

Without a word he took his leave.

Puzzled, Dulcie watched as Dar quickly composed himself and resumed reading.

Aunt Bessie sat in silence, her gaze fixed on the stiff figure of her eldest nephew as he stalked up the stairs.

Later that night, Dulcie lay in her bed, pondering the strange scene in the parlor.

What had Dar said that had set his brother so on edge? It had seemed such an innocent request. Yet Cal's reaction had been thunderous.

She rolled to her side, trying to get comfortable. Trying to push these troubling thoughts from her mind. But they wouldn't let go of her. She couldn't dispel the image of Cal, shocked, angry, hurt.

What was he hiding? Could it be that the man who constantly berated her for her lack of honesty had been less than honest himself?

After an interminable length of time tossing and turning, she gave up the notion of sleep and slipped from the bed. Wrapping a shawl around her shoulders, she made her way to the balcony and breathed in the night air. Even now, with darkness covering the land, there was little relief from the heat.

She draped the shawl over the railing and lifted her heavy hair from her neck and shoulders. Looking up, she watched clouds scudding across the moon. Heat lightning cut a jagged path across the sky. And in that one brief moment of illumination, she had a quick impression of a figure moving along the shore.

Was it one man or many? Had there been a boat, as well? With the countryside shrouded in darkness, she had no way of knowing.

Heart pounding, blood heating, she raced to her room and retrieved the pistol Cal had given her. Then she tore down the stairs and out into the night.

She had no clear plan, but as she ran toward shore, her mind was working feverishly. If the boatload of men had returned, she must stop them before they reached the house. The darkness and the element of surprise were in her favor. She prayed the clouds would hold; the reappearance of moonlight would be her enemy.

Her foot encountered the jagged edge of a stone, and she gasped at the pain, cursing herself for not taking the time to pull on her boots. She forced herself to ignore the pain and the sticky warmth of blood and continued running, darting behind trees whenever possible, peering into the darkness for any sign of the intruders.

At last she reached the shore and dropped to her knees behind a boulder. Her breath was coming in short bursts, and her heart was pounding so loudly she feared the sound would give her away.

Ever so cautiously she got to her feet and studied the expanse of shoreline. At first she saw nothing. But then she thought she detected a figure moving toward her.

Knowing her white nightgown would make her an easy target, she ducked behind the rock and waited, straining for the sound of footfall.

After what seemed endless minutes, she chanced another peek. And froze. A tall figure loomed directly in front of her.

She knew he had seen her. There was no longer any point in trying to hide. With her heart lodged in her throat, she took aim with the pistol and stepped from her place of concealment.

"Stay where you are." She prayed her voice wouldn't reveal her fear.

Just then the clouds parted, allowing enough moonlight to reveal the man before her.

"Cal." His name tumbled from her lips on a sigh of relief. But her relief was short-lived when his hand swung out, knocking the pistol to the ground.

"Little fool. What are you doing out here?" he demanded. "Have you been following me?"

"Following you?" Her voice took on a note of contempt. "Certainly not."

"Then why are you here?"

"I...I saw something from my balcony and thought I should investigate, in case it was those men returning."

"Why didn't you bother to wake the others?"

"I didn't want to cause undue alarm."

His tone was heavy with sarcasm. "You don't think we'd be alarmed if you were found dead in the morning, Miss Trenton? Or worse, if you were missing with no explanation?"

Stung by his derision, she started to turn away, but he caught her by the shoulder. When she looked up at him, she was frightened by the scowl of contempt on face.

"What is the real reason you came out here alone, Miss Trenton? Was it, perhaps, your intention to see to it that intruders on this island should be eliminated as quickly, as silently, as possible before they had a chance to reveal why they were searching for you?"

She squirmed at the taunt that was dangerously close to the truth. "I will not listen to..."

"Oh, but you will. You will listen. And you will explain."

She tried to push away from him, but his fingers tightened their grasp on her, holding her still.

She knew better than to struggle against such strength. Especially when Cal was in such a foul temper. Instead, she would do her fighting with words.

"All right. I'll explain..."

She felt a slight relaxing of his fingers.

"...as soon as you explain that little scene in the parlor tonight." Her words rang out with cutting mockery.

She heard his sudden intake of breath and knew she'd hit a nerve. That only made her grow bolder. "Why were you so upset by your brother's request to discuss science and biology with the children?"

"That is none of your concern, Miss Trenton."

"Indeed?" She tossed her head, her confidence growing with every passing moment. She had wounded him, and she was determined to drive home the final blow. "You are wrong, Mr. Jermain. Anything that affects those in my care

is my concern. Tell me. What is it in your past that has you
pacing at night, instead of sleeping?"

He lowered his hand and took a step back, as though re-
pelled by the mere touch of her. His tone was low with anger. "My past is just that. Past. It has no bearing on now or
on the future."

"You once called yourself a simple farmer," Dulcie
whispered. "I did not believe it then, nor do I believe it
now."

He started to step around her. "Believe what you wish,
Miss Trenton. But see that you never again ask me about
anything so personal."

Anger made her careless. Without thinking she grasped
his maimed arm, stopping him in midstride. At once she realized her mistake, but it was too late. To release him now
would be to admit defeat. It simply wasn't her nature to be
the one to back down.

Nor, unfortunately, was it his.

He turned on her in black fury. "You go too far,
woman." He reached for her. His hand closed over her upper arm, and he found, to his dismay, that her nightgown
had slipped from her shoulder, revealing pale naked flesh.
Heat raced through him and he dragged her close.

She saw the passion, the fire, in his eyes and braced for an
angry tirade. Instead, she was taken by complete surprise
when he lowered his head and claimed her mouth with a
kiss.

Anger dissolved. Questions were forgotten. Flames of
desire rose up between them, fueling an already raging fire.
The lingering kiss alternately drained them and filled them,
until their bodies ached with unspoken need.

He moved his hand up along her shoulder, his fingers
tracing her nape before fisting in her hair. He took the kiss
deeper and thrilled to the little moan that escaped her lips.

In a daze he realized his mistake. He'd kissed her merely to silence her questions. Now, with his lips on hers and the fire building deep inside, he wanted more. He wanted her. Only her. And until he had her, there would be no relief from this burning need.

With a groan he crushed her to him and dropped to his knees, dragging her down with him. Neither of them took notice of the damp sand shifting beneath them as the kiss deepened. Desire clawed at him, begging for release. He had never known a need so demanding. It clouded his mind and stripped him of reason.

As suddenly as it had begun, the kiss ended. He lifted his head, dragging in great gulps of air. God in heaven, what had come over him? He had tempted himself far too many times. And with each temptation, he'd learned a painful lesson. Though he possessed great strength of will, he was, after all, just a man. A man who felt his common sense deserting him every time he touched this damnable female.

With a sigh of regret he struggled to his feet and hauled her with him.

Dulcie was afraid to move. The trembling in her hands and legs would surely reveal how deeply she'd been affected by his kiss.

He bent and handed her the pistol that lay at their feet.

"Next time, Miss Trenton, take care to ask more questions before you aim this."

Sparks leaped from her eyes. "Maybe next time I'll shoot first, Mr. Jermain, and then I won't have to ask any questions at all."

She turned and flounced away.

He watched as her nightgown fluttered in the darkness like a delicate white moth. At his side, his hand gradually unclenched as his temper, and his ardor, cooled by degrees.

Miss Dulcie Trenton never ceased to amaze him. And impress him. Once again, it would seem, she had caused him to lose his temper and his control. And once again, by turning the tables and demanding that her questions be answered, she had managed to distract him from his charted course. Once more she had deflected his attention away from the dark secrets harbored in her devious little heart. And forced him to look into his own.

Chapter Sixteen

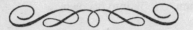

"I am deeply concerned about Barclay," Aunt Bessie whispered.

It was barely dawn, but she had come downstairs to find Cal alone and brooding in the dining room. From the dark scowl on his face, it was plain that his sleep had been as disturbed as hers.

"He'll come home when he's ready." Cal lifted a steaming cup of coffee to his lips. He'd given up on the hope of finding any rest as long as Miss Dulcie Trenton was asleep under the same roof. Maybe he ought to try his brother's remedy and set sail for Charleston. He doubted even whiskey and poker could cure what ailed him.

"But it's been five days now. He's never stayed away this long before. And you saw the look on his face the night before he left," his aunt said wearily. "He was so wounded. So bitter. I'm truly frightened."

It was true that Cal had seen his brother's face. But he would have described the look as one of self-loathing, though he kept this thought to himself. Perhaps all of them were disillusioned with what they'd become.

He looked up as a familiar figure came into the room.

"My, but you're up early," Aunt Bessie said.

Dulcie gave a start, as though surprised to see anyone else up at this hour, then quickly composed herself. "I might say the same for you."

She took her place at the table and kept her gaze averted. It galled her to feel Cal's probing look. This irritating man was the reason she had slept so badly. She'd hoped to slip downstairs and have some time alone. Now she would have to endure his scrutiny until it was time to work in the fields.

Aunt Bessie studied the pale blue shadows beneath Dulcie's eyes. "Have you had trouble sleeping, my dear?"

"No. Yes." She glanced up and caught the mockery in Cal's eyes. "A little."

"Well, I'm sorry you didn't sleep well, but I'm glad for the company," the older woman said as she buttered a biscuit. "The thought of my nephew, Barclay, in that wicked place has me terribly unnerved."

That wicked place. Did Aunt Bessie mean Nellie Simpson's sporting house, or the ruins that had once been the city of Charleston? Dulcie wondered. Since the war, it was difficult to decide which was the more dangerous.

Dulcie placed her hand over Aunt Bessie's. "Then don't allow yourself to dwell on it. Turn your thoughts, instead, to Dar and the wonderful knowledge he is sharing with the children."

The older woman's eyes lit with pleasure. "It is wonderful, isn't it? I've never seen my youngest nephew so animated. Why, it is as though someone breathed new life into his soul."

"It has changed Starlight and the children, as well," Dulcie remarked. "I've never seen them so happy, or so eager for knowledge. The more Dar shares with them, the more they crave."

"Life is funny that way," Cal said, pinning her with a dark look. "The more we know, the more we want to know.

Take your strange odyssey to our shores as an example, Miss Trenton. I'm sure my aunt agrees with me that there are many fascinating details you've probably not shared with us as yet.''

She heard the sarcasm in his tone and felt her hackles rise. "I might say the same for your life before the war, Mr. Jermain. I, for one, would be delighted to hear about it."

His smile faded. He lifted his cup in a salute. She was indeed a worthy opponent.

They all looked up when the door opened. Fiona, looking wan and tired, entered. "Good morning," she called. "'Tis happy I am that I'm not the only one who couldn't sleep. It must be the heat," she lied. The truth was, she'd been concerned about the fact that it was her words that had caused Barc to leave in such a state of agitation. That knowledge had robbed her of sleep now for several nights. "I even heard the children up and about earlier than usual."

As Robert entered carrying a tray, the Irishwoman said, "I spotted blueberries near a bog yesterday, Robert. Would you like me to pick some this morning before I start my chores?" It would be one way to keep her mind off her problems.

The servant beamed his pleasure. "Miss Bessie is especially fond of blueberry tarts. I shall bake them for supper this very afternoon." He turned away. "When you've finished your breakfast, I'll have a bucket ready."

Aunt Bessie felt the last of her worries fade away. She sipped her tea and smiled at those gathered around the table, delighted at the prospect of Robert's blueberry tarts. How could anything possibly go wrong on a day such as this?

Fiona strode across the fields, swinging the empty bucket at her side. There was much about this island that reminded her of her beloved Ireland. The green fields. The tang of ocean on the breeze. The sudden squalls. But she'd never seen such brilliant sunshine. Despite the long sleeves of her gown and the bonnet that shaded her face, she could feel the sun's rays burning clear through to her tender skin. She glanced at her sunburned hands. Her mother would be scandalized by the look of her.

Her mother. The mere thought of that genteel woman and her untimely death in childbirth made her heart ache. For the fourteen-year-old Fiona, life in their luxurious manor house had never been the same after that terrible day. There had been no one to turn to. No one to shield her. No one to protect her from . . .

She pushed the thoughts aside and concentrated on maneuvering the bog. It was cooler here, shaded from the sun, dampened by the dark, still water that pooled around fallen logs. It was a perfect breeding ground for leeches and mosquitoes, but she paid them no heed. She set the bucket on a stump and began picking berries.

The temptation to eat was too great, and she found herself pausing every so often to eat a handful. Soon her hands and lips were stained the color of the blue-black fruit.

As she worked, she hummed a little tune from her childhood. It eased her fears. Here in this cool, quiet place, it was hard to imagine that there were any troubles. But they were always there just below the surface. She'd come to this land to be free of troubles. Freedom, she thought bitterly. At first, she'd been intoxicated by the heady sense of freedom on these shores. Freedom from the past. Freedom to think beyond now to the future. Freedom to do as she pleased, to be what she pleased. But very quickly she'd learned that freedom came with a price.

So be it. She would work at any job, no matter how menial, live in any hovel, no matter how shabby. But she would

be master of her own fate. Never again would she be en-
slaved, forced to endure another's cruelty.

When the bucket was filled to overflowing, she picked
another handful and ate it, then turned away and started
toward the house.

"Well. Miss O'Neil."

At the sound of Barc's voice, she whirled. Her first in-
stinct was relief that he'd returned. But as she studied him,
her relief turned to despair.

Several days' growth of beard darkened his chin. His eyes
were red-rimmed and bloodshot. The sleeves of his wrinkled white shirt were rolled above the elbows. He carried his
jacket over his shoulder with a jaunty air.

"Picking berries, I see." He hastened his steps to catch up
with her.

"Aye. And you're drunk, I see. I can't abide a drunk."
She didn't stop or even slow down. In fact, as soon as he
reached her side, she wrinkled her nose and quickened her
steps. He reeked of cigar smoke and stale whiskey.

"Did you miss me?" he asked.

She lifted her head. "Not a whit."

"That's too bad, Miss O'Neil. Because I missed you.
Terribly."

At that she made a sound of disgust and continued on.
"'Tis only the whiskey talking. When you sober up, you'll
regret that slip of your tongue."

Stung by her rejection, he reached into his pocket and dug
out a handful of bills. "I want you to see what I did in
Charleston." His words were slurred. "I got rich, Miss
O'Neil. Very rich." He waved his fist in her face, and the
breeze caught several bills, swirling them about. He took no
notice. Nor did she. "So rich, in fact, that I'll be able to buy
all the seed we need for next year's crops, as well as those
new farm implements Cal talked about. There may even be

enough left over to buy you and Aunt Bessie and Starlight and Miss Trenton some lovely new gowns. You'd like that, wouldn't you?"

When she didn't respond, he went on, "So you see, Miss O'Neil, you were wrong the other night. I am not wasting my life. I can make far more money gambling than I ever could being respectable."

She rounded on him and, in a mixture of Gaelic and English, began viciously cursing him. "Getting drunk is never respectable," she snarled. "It is contemptible."

At that, Barc threw back his head and roared with laughter, which only made her more furious. Jaw clenched, she swooped past him and continued toward the house.

For a minute he studied her back, stiff and unyielding, and the proud, haughty lift of her chin. Then, when he realized she had no intention of stopping, he raced to catch up with her.

"Dammit, woman. Look at me." He caught her by the arm and spun her around more roughly than he'd intended.

Caught by surprise, she swung the bucket at his head. Despite his befuddled state, he managed to duck. The bucket went flying, sending blueberries raining down on everything.

That only made him laugh again. He dragged her against him and said, "By heaven, I wouldn't have believed it possible. But you're even more beautiful when you're angry."

Fiona wasn't listening. She knew only that his rough hands were on her, and the stench of whiskey was strong on his breath. With rising panic she pushed frantically against him. The more she struggled, the tighter he grasped her and the harder he laughed.

"Please, Miss O'Neil. Please don't be angry with me," he muttered against her temple. "Because I could never, ever be angry with you. You mean too much to—"

With a cry she shoved him away.

Seeing her eyes widen, he misunderstood her fear for anger. "Please believe me, I'm not really laughing at you. But I can't seem to help myself. It's the liquor, you see. It just makes everything seem so funny. You. Me. The whole crazy world. It's just so damned funny. But I don't want to fight with you. And I don't want you angry with me."

But Fiona was beyond hearing. She pummeled him with her fists until he lifted his arms in defense and took several steps backward.

"What in the . . . ? Woman, what's wrong with you?"

With screams that rivaled a banshee and hot tears streaming down her cheeks, she fled across the field, leaving him to stare after her in stunned surprise.

Cal and Dar hitched the team to the wagon and drove around to the back porch. Inside, the women and children had just finished breakfast and were helping Robert with the kitchen chores. That done, they emerged, ready for a ride to the fields.

"Don't forget to pick up Fiona," Aunt Bessie called. "My mouth is already watering at the thought of those blueberry tarts."

"We won't forget," Dulcie said as Robert handed her the linen-wrapped food he'd prepared for their noon meal.

They all looked up at the sound of screams piercing the morning air.

"God in heaven!" Dulcie cried. She dropped her bundle in her haste to leap down from the porch. She lifted her skirts and began running. Over her shoulder she shouted, "Get the rifles. It's Fiona."

The young Irishwoman raced across the open field and, sobbing, fell into Dulcie's arms. The others gathered around, helpless to do more than watch as the two women clung together, Dulcie whispering words of comfort, Fiona sobbing hysterically and mumbling incoherently.

Cal and Robert arrived, out of breath, each holding rifles at the ready. But they could see no enemy.

"Barclay," Aunt Bessie called as a familiar figure stumbled toward them. "Thank heaven you're home. Have you seen any strangers approaching?"

As he drew near, Fiona gave a shriek of alarm and pulled herself free of Dulcie's arms. While the others watched in bewilderment, she fled into the house.

"What in the hell did you do to her?" Cal demanded. He handed the rifle to Robert and looked as though he'd throttle his brother with his bare hands.

Barc seemed genuinely confused. "I don't know. Perhaps I was too bold." He didn't feel nearly as drunk, or as happy, as he had a few minutes ago. In fact, he felt thoroughly ashamed of himself. And thoroughly mystified.

"Too bold?" Aunt Bessie looked horrified. "What did you do to that poor girl?"

"Nothing, I tell you. I showed her the money I'd won in Charleston, but she wasn't interested in anything except that I'd been drinking." He stopped, exasperated. "I laughed at her. I guess she didn't like it. She started sobbing and hitting me with her fists. But you must believe me. I did nothing to cause such behavior."

"That young woman was absolutely terrified," Cal said. "You must be ly—"

Dulcie placed a hand on his arm to stop him before he wrongly accused his brother. "I think I had better explain."

The children huddled around her, clinging to her skirts. Even Nathaniel, whose time spent with the men had begun to give him a sense of independence, clutched her arm. His lower lip trembled and his eyes were clouded with fear. They were, after all, family. When one of them was hurt, they all suffered.

Dulcie said softly, "Fiona's father was a wealthy landowner. In Ireland, that made him a law unto himself. There was no one to challenge his authority. He was also a cruel drunkard, who regularly beat Fiona's mother whenever he'd had too much to drink."

"No wonder the poor child was so upset," Aunt Bessie breathed.

Barc lowered his head in shame.

"There is more," Dulcie continued. "After her mother died, Fiona became the object of his cruel beatings. As soon as she was able, she ran away and arranged passage to this country, for she'd heard that here a person could be free."

"Praise heaven," Aunt Bessie murmured.

Dulcie nodded. "When Fiona arrived in this country, she was introduced to a wealthy gentleman who made an offer for her hand in marriage and sent her passage to Charleston. By the time she arrived, however, he'd been killed in the war. And his family, instead of taking her in as one of them, kept her on as an unpaid servant, since they had lost all their slaves."

"But that is abominable," Aunt Bessie said vehemently. "I cannot believe one of our fine Charleston families would behave in such a barbaric fashion."

Beside her, Robert watched and listened in silence, his face revealing no emotion.

"What happened next?" Cal asked.

"Fiona persevered, willing to work in exchange for a place to sleep," Dulcie said in subdued tones. "Until the night the master of the house arrived home drunk and took a horsewhip to her when she resisted his advances.''

Aunt Bessie let out a cry and covered her mouth with her hand. The children were whimpering. Starlight had gone strangely quiet.

"How do you happen to know all this?" Cal asked. He recalled the scars he'd seen on Fiona's back when she'd first arrived. He'd wondered then about the beatings she'd obviously endured.

"I found Fiona, bloody and dazed and incoherent, drinking from my well," Dulcie explained. "I took her in and nursed her back to health. And during the long days and nights when she hovered between life and death, she told me everything."

At her recitation, Barc's eyes filled with tears. He hung his head in abject misery and whispered, "How could I have been so unfeeling?"

"You couldn't possibly have known," Dulcie said.

"But now that I do, I must find a way to make amends." He glanced down at himself. His clothes were dirty and wrinkled; his shoes mud-spattered. His pockets bulged with crumpled bills. He ran a hand over his unshaven face and closed his eyes on a wave of revulsion. What had he done? What had he become?

"Excuse me," Dulcie said. "I must go to Fiona. She needs me."

"The children will come with me," Starlight said, pulling herself together with great effort and herding them toward the wagon. "Come. The work in the fields will keep our minds off our troubles."

Cal and Dar followed the children, while Aunt Bessie and Robert made their way back to the house.

Barc stood alone, wishing he had never heard of Nellie Simpson's sporting house. Wishing, more than anything in the world, that he could turn back the clock and take away all of Fiona's pain.

The house felt strangely silent and empty. Barc had closed himself in his room and had not been seen or heard from since the unfortunate incident with Fiona. In the heat of late afternoon, Aunt Bessie retired for a nap. Robert strolled off with a bucket in the hopes of retrieving any blueberries that might be left in the thicket. There would be, he surmised, a special need for a soothing dessert at the end of this long, difficult day.

After remaining in her friend's room until Fiona had fallen into an exhausted sleep, Dulcie had walked out to the fields to join Starlight and the children.

In Fiona's room, the draperies had been drawn against the sunlight, leaving the room cool and shadowed. The young woman, clad in camisole and petticoat, lay sprawled across the bed. At Dulcie's urging, she had washed herself, picking off the leeches from the bog that clung to her legs, removing all stain of berries, and at the same time, all remnants of tears. Her eyes were closed, her breathing slow and steady.

Suddenly she sat up, shoving her heavy red hair from her eyes. For a moment she felt disoriented. Then it all came rushing back. Barc's disheveled state, his drunken laughter, the stench of liquor on his breath. She closed her eyes a moment, trying to erase the memory of those other times, other men who had hurt her. But it was impossible. All the memories ran together into one blurred image of a figure looming over her inflicting pain.

It didn't matter that Barc hadn't been like the others. He had done her no harm. In fact, even drunk, he was nothing more than his laughing, charming self. But though her mind could accept that fact, her heart could not.

Summoning her strength, she crossed the room and opened the draperies, flooding the room with sunlight. For a moment she looked away, unable to bear the pain. Then, as her tear-swollen eyes adjusted, she looked out over the fields and caught sight of Dulcie and the others bent to their task of hoeing and weeding. She felt a momentary stab of guilt for not being there with them. Then she sighed and returned to her bed, feeling drained and listless.

Fiona ignored the timid knock on her door, praying Aunt Bessie would go away. She lacked the strength to see anyone yet. But when the knock became more insistent, she tossed a shawl around her shoulders and opened the door.

Barc's tall figure filled the doorway.

He was clean-shaven, his hair freshly combed, his clothes immaculate. Only his eyes showed the effect of his dissolute living. And his usually charming manner was now hesitant and contrite.

"Please, Miss O'Neil. I must speak with you."

"No." She tried to close the door, but he was too quick. When he stepped inside her room, she backed away.

The look of fear in her eyes was like a knife in his heart.

"Please hear me," he said as he closed the door and leaned against it. "I've come here to apologize for my disgusting behavior this morning."

She stared at the floor.

"For so long now I have been thoughtless and vain, relying on wit and charm, instead of solid virtues like honesty, integrity, dependability."

She held her silence, and he feared that his words fell on deaf ears.

"I thought, by surrounding myself with careless, raucous people, I could become like them." He continued to lean against the door, watching her. She neither looked at him, nor acknowledged his presence. "I thought that if I drank enough and played enough and laughed enough, I could forget the pain of the damnable war that robbed us of our livelihood and our pride."

At last she looked up. "No one can take away your pride, Mr. Jermain." Her brogue was thick, her words formal. "It is yours to keep or to discard. Only you can choose to toss it aside or wear it like a mantle of respect, rising above any defeat."

"I know that now, Miss O'Neil." He felt a rush of relief that she had finally spoken. At least she was listening. And responding. Now if only he could find the way to reach her heart. "But I believed, when I returned from the war, that I had let my family down. My father had invested a great deal of time and money in my education, and his expectations of me were very high."

"What was it he expected of you?" she asked.

Barc stepped closer. Though she watched him warily, she didn't back up. Another good sign, he hoped.

"With my knowledge of the law and my connections with those in power in the government, he was grooming me to lead the country."

"As president?" For the first time she met his gaze directly.

It was his turn to look away. It shamed him to have her look at him in such a probing fashion and to know that he was found lacking in her eyes. How he wished she had known him before, before the war, before he had allowed himself to become sullied.

"If not president," he said haltingly, "then at least someone in a position of power within the government."

Her curiosity was piqued. She had grown up with a rich and powerful father. She understood power and the way it could be used to build. Or to destroy.

"But why have you abandoned the dream? Could it be that it was not your dream at all, but only your father's?"

He shook his head. "I shared the dream. But it is useless now, don't you see? The South has been defeated. The power lies in Washington. And a politician from South Carolina, the first state to secede from the Union, will not be warmly welcomed into the halls of government."

"I see." She moved restlessly to the window, her mind working. This was something she understood, perhaps better than he. For he'd been born in this land, while she was still trying to absorb all the delightful surprises offered by a free and democratic society. Therefore, she questioned things he took for granted.

"It would seem to me that your countrymen would be eager for someone to represent them in those sacred halls. Someone who shared their pain, their sorrow, their shame at having been defeated." She turned to study him. "Someone who was handsome and charming, and had the ability to persuade without forcing his will. Someone who wouldn't back down in an argument. But of course," she said, as if to herself, "it would have to be a man who knew how to use power without abusing it. Someone who would not use such power for his own gain. And especially someone strong enough to resist the temptations that come with such power. Temptations such as whiskey, women, gambling."

His heart skipped a beat. Was she opening the door to accepting his apology? Or was she about to close the door? He had no way of knowing, but he had to try.

He took in a deep breath and crossed to her side. Getting down on his knees, he said, "Miss O'Neil. I humbly beg your forgiveness for the pain I've caused you. Not only this day, but all the days since you have been under this roof. I would do anything to erase all sorrow from your heart. And if you will but give me another chance, I will make it up to you."

"How, Mr. Jermain?" she asked softly.

He looked up to meet her eyes. He longed to take her hand, but he knew he had no right. "I swear to you on my parents' graves that I will never touch whiskey or cards again."

"That may prove a difficult promise to live up to," she said. "It would seem that spirits are a way of life for the Jermains."

"Indeed they are. My Aunt Bessie likes nothing better than a sip of spirits each night before retiring. And we do have a stock of some of the finest whiskey in the land. But a promise is a promise, Miss O'Neil. And I take mine very seriously. I swear to you that whiskey will never again pass my lips."

"Will that not make some of the women at Nellie Simpson's very unhappy?" she said.

She was not about to let him off easily.

"For me there were no women, Miss O'Neil. My weakness has always been whiskey and gambling, though some of Nellie's girls are tempting. But I thought I would save myself for a fine, decent woman. Though I must admit, I am no longer worthy of a good woman."

"Aye, most unworthy," she agreed. "But I suppose there may be . . . one or two who would find you appealing."

He heard the lilt of laughter in her tone and felt his heart begin to lift. "And I swear one more thing. I will rekindle my father's dream. If the people of the Carolinas will have me, I will represent them in Washington and work for their good. Of course, a politician's life can be difficult. It would take a very special woman to share it. A woman who could set a fine table and converse with common men and kings. A woman—"

"Are you mocking me, Mr. Jermain?" she asked sharply.

"Not at all, Miss O'Neil. I am merely wondering aloud if such a paragon exists."

She shrugged and turned away, but not before he caught the spark of fire in her eyes and the flush on her cheeks. "Only time will tell," she murmured as she pretended to study a colorful bird that had landed on the balcony railing outside her window.

"Time is something I have in abundance, Miss O'Neil." He got to his feet, daring for the first time to touch a hand to her hair. His palm tingled at the encounter, and he longed to plunge his fingers into the wild red tangles, to draw her close and taste her lips. But it was too soon. Much too soon. He must first earn her respect, her trust, by proving himself worthy. "I have all the time and patience in the world when the goal is a noble one," he muttered thickly before turning away.

At the door he paused and glanced back. She remained staring out the window. Despite the fact that she wore only a chemise and petticoat, a shawl over her shoulders for modesty, she was as regal as any queen. A queen who owned his heart. For he knew now that he was hopelessly in love with her.

Chapter Seventeen

The hot, humid days of late summer took on a slow, lazy rhythm. There were still crops to be tended and harvested, and timber to be cut for the last wall of the barn. But the hottest part of the day forced everyone to seek shelter indoors, where they engaged in quiet activities.

Dar and Starlight took advantage of this to add to the children's lessons. Aunt Bessie continued to share her experience and knowledge of foreign countries. She added lessons on manners, which she thought essential to the survival of mankind.

"Ever since those terrible Yankees muddied our waters, good manners have fallen by the wayside. Only a true Southern gentleman knows how to treat his fellow man," she was fond of saying, as she taught them how to sit and stand, how to shake hands, how to set a proper table.

Dulcie winced at such statements, but left it to Dar to tactfully correct his strong-willed aunt's comments. They were, after all, guests in this house. It was not her place to remind their hostess that the war was over, and that the land that had been bitterly divided was now struggling to become unified.

She glanced at the stern profile of Cal Jermain as he passed by the window and felt a band tighten around her heart. How could there be healing when so many of its citizens carried permanent reminders of the turmoil?

After days of coaxing, Dulcie finally persuaded a reluctant Robert to allow the children into his kitchen to learn his secrets of good cooking. Though he tried to remain distant and aloof, he seemed to warm to the three little girls, who were eager to test their skills. But he found the presence of fun-loving Nathaniel annoying and scolded him for the least infraction. When he saw the boy dip his finger into a peach preserve, he lost his last thread of patience.

"Why did you do such a thing?" he demanded.

"I was hungry. And it smelled so good."

"You do not belong in my clean, orderly kitchen, young man. You belong out in the fields!" Robert shouted. "Go and annoy Mr. Cal, but do not waste my time again. Go. Now."

Behind Robert, Clara stuck out her tongue at the boy, enjoying his humiliation.

Nathaniel was mortified by the banishment and furious at Clara's reaction. He trudged all the way to the forest, where he found Cal working alone in the heat of the afternoon.

Of all the Jermain men, this solemn, silent man was Nathaniel's favorite. It was not just Cal's physical strength the boy admired. Despite the loss of his hand, Cal managed to do everything the others did, only better. It was as though he drove himself to prove, over and over, that he was unaffected by his loss. But it was also his inner strength, his integrity, that drew the boy to him. Of the three brothers, Cal was the acknowledged leader. Though Cal could be abrupt and demanding, Nathaniel was eager to please him. With the wisdom of a child, he sensed this man's inner wounds were much deeper than the obvious physical wound.

Cal looked up from the log he was hewing. "What are you doing here, Nat?"

Cal's use of his new name pleased him more than he cared to admit. Though the others merely indulged him, Cal seemed to understand his need for respect. "I thought I could help."

"The truth, boy," Cal said sharply.

Nathaniel ducked his head and wondered how Cal had seen through him so easily. "Robert ordered me out of his kitchen."

"Did you break one of his cherished crystals?"

"No, sir. I dipped my finger in the peach preserve."

"Is that all?" Cal grinned. "When I was nine, he threw me out for licking the frosting off Aunt Bessie's birthday cake."

"He did?" Nathaniel's eyes grew wide. It was impossible for him to imagine this stern man as a mischievous little boy. "How long did it take before you were allowed back in his kitchen?"

"Two or three days. I hauled all Robert's water from the well. I picked squash, peeled potatoes and even scrubbed the big black pots and kettles. And he finally allowed me to come back, but only under his watchful eye. And only if I promised to eat all my greens."

"I guess I'd better offer to do some chores for him after dinner," the boy mused aloud.

"That might be a fine idea." Cal erased his grin. "Now, how would you like to finish this log while I start on another tree?"

"Yes, sir." Nathaniel's mood brightened. He picked up a saw and began removing branches.

Cal walked some distance away and studied the trees until he found one that was straight and sturdy. With quick, efficient strokes of his ax, he carved a deep notch in the wood.

Nathaniel paused to watch. Cal had removed his shirt, and the muscles of his back rippled with each movement. Despite having only one hand, Cal managed to swing the ax with deadly accuracy.

As Nathaniel returned to his chore, he found himself thinking about his father. He'd been a big man, or at least he'd seemed big to the little boy who had kissed him good-bye before he'd ridden off to war. He could vaguely remember arms corded with muscles, hair dark and curly, and a voice low and deep, whispering words of endearment to the woman and child who had stood beside his horse, weeping inconsolably.

Sometimes, in the dark of the night, Nathaniel could no longer remember his face. It filled him with secret shame.

"Dreaming, boy?"

Cal's words brought his head up sharply. "No, sir."

"Let's get to work, then. It'll soon be time for dinner."

"Yes, sir." Nathaniel bent to his work with a vengeance.

The two worked in companionable silence until the sun had made its graceful arc to the western sky.

"Time to go," Cal announced.

Nathaniel climbed up beside him on the wagon. With a crack of the whip, they took off. The trees they had managed to cut and trim remained behind to be loaded into the wagon when Barc and Dar could lend their assistance. With the back of the wagon empty, the team pranced smartly, pulling the rig easily across the fields toward the big house.

"Aunt Bessie said that you're like your father." Nathaniel pushed his hat back from his forehead and chewed on the stem of a yellow jessamine as he'd seen Cal do.

"I guess that's true. I know I look like him."

"You're lucky to have that portrait in the parlor. You'll never forget what he looked like."

Something in the boy's wistful tone caused Cal to glance at him. What he saw made his heart turn over. "I suppose it's hard to hold on to a picture when it's only in your mind."

Nathaniel looked away. "Yes, sir."

Cal stared out over the fields of green. "It's funny how the images of those we love can fade with time. But that's just nature's way of healing the pain in our hearts. The important thing to remember is how much we loved them. And how much they loved us. That will never fade as the years go by, son. The heart will remember."

Beside him, Nathaniel fell silent. But his heart felt lighter than it had in a long time. He realized he wasn't a bad son for forgetting the face of his father. For the truth was, he would never forget the love they had shared. It would sustain him and warm him for all the years to come.

As they rolled nearer the house, Nathaniel could see someone taking clothes from the line. His face creased into a smile.

"There's Dulcie."

"You think the world of her, don't you, son?"

"Yes, sir. I guess I love her almost as much as my ma and pa." He glanced over at Cal, embarrassed by his admission. "Do you think they would mind?"

"I think your parents would be pleased that there was someone to look out for you. Loving her is a natural enough feeling. She took you in when you were lost. She continues to take good care of you and the others. I think she's earned your love."

And mine, Cal thought, though he acknowledged it grudgingly and refused to give in to it.

When they drew alongside Dulcie, he brought the wagon to a halt.

Nathaniel leaped down, suddenly infused with energy. "I guess I'll fetch a bucket of water for Robert. And maybe I can do a few chores for him before supper."

"It wouldn't hurt." Cal pulled his hat from his head and said formally, "Good afternoon, Miss Trenton."

She returned the studied formality. "Mr. Jermain."

Nathaniel glanced from Cal to Dulcie, then back again. Why did these two people, who meant so much to him, have to be so distant with each other? Cal's smile had vanished. Dulcie was actually glaring at Cal. Yet he'd seen the way Cal watched Dulcie, when he thought no one was looking. And the way her gaze softened sometimes whenever it was fixed on Cal.

Grown-ups. He'd never understand them.

Cal flicked the reins and brought the wagon to the rear of the house. As he unhitched the team, he glanced back at the woman folding the clothes. Her skirts billowed in the breeze. The basket, when she lifted it, was nearly as big as she. He was tempted to offer to help, but he resisted. He was determined to stay as far away from Dulcie Trenton as possible.

His glance strayed to the little boy struggling beneath the weight of the overflowing bucket.

Cal smiled to himself. Robert would exact a price for his forgiveness. And in the process, he would teach Nathaniel important lessons that would serve him well throughout his life.

"I filled the buckets." Nathaniel stood just outside the door to the kitchen. It had been three days since his banishment from Robert's domain, and he had yet to redeem himself.

Each day he had arisen before dawn to begin his extra chores to impress Robert, and each night he had worked long after dark, while the others enjoyed refreshments in the parlor.

"I shucked the corn and shelled the peas. And if you'd like, there's still time for me to scrub the pots and kettles before I leave for the woods."

Robert held the door open. "That would be fine, young man." He stood aside as the boy entered. It was the first time he had permitted him entrance since the transgression.

Without a word the lad filled a basin with warm water from the stove and began to scrub at the blackened pots. An hour later, as the wagon rolled toward the back door, he stood back to admire his handiwork.

"I've finished, Robert. Is there anything else I can do for you?"

"No, thank you. That is sufficient."

When Robert had examined each pot and kettle, Nathaniel started toward the door.

"One moment," Robert called. "Tomorrow, if you wish, you may join the others in a cooking lesson."

A slow smile of appreciation lit the boy's face. "Thank you."

Robert crossed the room and handed him a linen-wrapped parcel.

Mystified, Nathaniel stared at it. "What is this?"

"A little treat, to thank you for the tasks you performed so admirably," Robert said sternly. "Lest you forget, though, I remind you that a task well-done is its own reward."

When Nathaniel climbed onto the wagon beside Cal, he unwrapped the linen and stared at Robert's gift.

"He gave me biscuits." He added in awe, "Smothered with fruit preserve."

"The same fruit preserve that got you banished in the first place?"

The boy nodded. "The same. What do you think I should do with these?"

Cal grinned, wondering if the boy had any idea that Robert was teaching him a meaningful lesson. "I'd eat them quickly, son. Before Barc and Dar get their hands on them."

He watched as the little boy wolfed down the sweet treats. By the time they reached the forest, Nathaniel's head was bobbing, his breathing slow and easy. Knowing the extra hours he'd put in the past few days, Cal left him asleep in the wagon, where he remained until the sound of ax and saw awakened him nearly an hour later.

"Think you can handle the team, son?" Cal and his brothers struggled under the weight of the log while Nathaniel sat on the wagon seat, keeping a firm grasp on the reins.

"Yes, sir."

"Hold 'em steady," Cal cautioned as the horses fidgeted and the wagon began to roll.

The boy used all his strength to pull back on the leather until the team settled down. The men gave a final push, and the log was stowed with the others in the back of the wagon.

"That's enough for today," Barc said. "Let's head for the barn."

Cal glanced skyward. "There's time to cut one more tree before dark."

"But there's no more room in the wagon," his younger brother argued.

"There's no point in wasting valuable time. I'll cut it and leave it until tomorrow." Cal lifted the ax and started toward the row of trees. "Why don't you and Dar take this load back to the house and then bring the wagon for me before you pick up the women and children in the fields."

Barc shook his head. Leave it to his older brother to fill every hour of the day with work, work and more work. "Come on," he said to Dar and Nathaniel. "Let's unload this timber at the house." He glanced at Nathaniel, who had climbed up to the seat beside him. "Want to drive, Nat?"

"You mean it?"

"Sure. Why not?" Barc moved over, making room for the boy to take the reins.

Nathaniel flicked the whip and the team moved out at a slow, plodding pace, straining against the heavy load.

In the back of the wagon, Dar straddled the logs and kept up a running conversation with the boy.

"Ever drive a team before?"

"Yes, sir. After my pa left to fight, there was just me and my ma. I had to take the team into town every week for supplies. But after my ma died, I had to sell the team to Mr. Smithfield at the mercantile to pay for food."

"I guess you had to learn to do a man's job when you were still a little boy," Barc said.

"I didn't mind. And I'm not a little boy anymore," Nathaniel declared.

Barc lifted his hat and glanced at the boy beside him. Despite the thin, angular frame, he had begun to fill out, thanks to Robert's fine cooking. There were traces of muscles developing along his arms, the result of a summer of farm chores. "I can see that, Nat. You've grown an inch just since you arrived here." Barc shot him a wink, and the boy's smile bloomed.

As the wagon rolled across the fields, Barc pulled his hat down over his face. "You're doing fine, Nat. I'll just rest my eyes until we get home."

The boy was flushed with pride at such a compliment.

When they arrived at the almost finished barn, Nathaniel held the team steady while the two men pushed and shoved and struggled until the logs were unloaded.

Exhausted from their efforts, Barc and Dar headed for the well, where they took turns drawing up the bucket and splashing water over their heads. Then they flopped down on the grass.

Nathaniel nudged the team into a slow walk, halting the wagon a few feet from the brothers. From the back door wafted the most intoxicating smells as Robert prepared supper.

"Chicken and dumplings," Barc said with a sigh.

"And peaches," Dar added. "I bet Robert is making peach cobbler."

Barc propped himself up on his elbows. "I can't believe we have to go all the way back to the woods for Cal."

"I could go," Nathaniel offered. "And you two could stay here and wash up for supper."

"Cal would have my hide if I let you go alone," Barc said.

"And mine," his younger brother put in.

Nathaniel shrugged. "Suit yourselves. But I don't mind. And I'd be real careful with the team."

Barc looked longingly at the rain barrel, filled to the brim with cool water. The thought of a bath before the women and children returned from the fields was too tempting. "I think I'll stay here," he said to Dar. "Maybe you and Nat can go without me."

"I was hoping to prepare a lesson on the constellations for tonight," Dar said quickly. "There won't be time if I don't do it now."

Barc glanced from his brother to the boy who sat on the wagon seat. "I guess that settles it, Nat. You're elected to drive the team and pick up the others."

The boy was clearly delighted to have earned such trust. "I won't be long."

"Hold on now," Barc said as the boy gathered the reins. "You take your time, you hear?"

"Yes, sir." Nathaniel flicked the reins.

Grateful to be free of this burdensome task, the two brothers watched until the wagon dipped below a rise. Then they turned away, intent upon their own interests.

The horses, free of their heavy burden, pranced easily across the fields.

Nathaniel wasn't bothered by the bouncing of the hard wooden seat. He felt a rush of exhilaration as a stiff wind ruffled his hair.

He smiled to himself, wondering what Dulcie and the others would think when they saw him driving the team. Just seeing the look on Clara's face would make up for all the times she had acted so smart.

Dark clouds began rolling in, obscuring the fading sunlight. The boy breathed in the tang of ocean carried on the wind. Rain. He could smell it, taste it. He flicked the reins and urged the team to move a little faster.

Thunder rumbled across the sky, followed by a jagged slash of lightning. Within minutes the sky turned an ominous black. A clap of thunder caused the horses to skitter nervously, and they strained against the harness.

"Whoa, boys," Nathaniel called, but the animals' ears were laid back and they charged ahead, veering off the path and tearing across neatly planted rows of beans. The horses' hooves churned up the earth, while the wagon wheels flattened the plants.

Frantic to stop the destruction, Nathaniel pulled on the reins, but the horses, spooked by another clap of thunder, veered once more and continued racing at crazy angles. The reins were jerked from the boy's hands. Now all he could do was grip the wooden seat and struggle to keep from being thrown.

The wagon rattled along behind the erratic team, bouncing over ruts and crops, at times traveling so fast it seemed airborne.

Nathaniel's fear was replaced by sheer panic. The team was completely out of control and racing too fast to allow him to jump to safety.

Up ahead was a solid wall of palmetto trees. Lightning danced across the sky and streaked down the tallest spire, sending a shower of sparks that seemed to light up the forest. Seeing it, the wild-eyed horses reared in terror, twisting in the harness until it snapped, freeing them. While they galloped off, the wagon flipped end over end, sending its driver sailing through the air. He landed with a thud in the dirt moments before the vehicle came to rest upside down on top of him.

Great waves of pain crashed through him. He struggled to free himself, but found, to his horror, that his body would not respond. And as the first patters of rain began, he realized he was hopelessly trapped beneath the wagon.

The pain grew and grew until he let out a series of piercing screams. But there was no one to hear. Only the rain and the wide, empty fields. His voice faded to a croak, and then to a whimper.

At last, just when he thought he could bear the pain no longer, a wide, yawning chasm opened up and enveloped him. Nathaniel slipped into a deep, black pool of unconsciousness.

Chapter Eighteen

At the first rumble of thunder, Dulcie gathered the others around her to begin the long trek back to the house.

"I'm tired!" five-year-old Emily cried. "Why can't we wait here for the wagon?"

"I know you're tired," Dulcie said, trying to soothe. Though her body ached from the work in the fields, she crouched down to piggyback the little girl. "But the men aren't here yet, and I don't see them coming. They're probably still loading logs on the wagon. We'll start out on foot and meet them along the way."

"I'm afraid of the storm," six-year-old Belle whimpered.

"Nonsense. It's just a little thunder and lightning." Dulcie struggled beneath her burden and caught the second little girl's hand. "The rain will be good for the crops."

Fiona gathered Clara close and peered around in dismay, trying to put on a good face, despite her own fear. "The men should be coming any minute now."

"I don't see them," Starlight shouted above the rumble of thunder.

"Just keep walking," Dulcie commanded. "We're bound to run into them before long."

The sky grew darker by the minute, and the thunder and lightning intensified until it seemed one continuous rumble of deafening noise and flash of fire. Far ahead, sparks danced along a row of palmetto trees, sending fireworks high in the sky. And then, to add to their misery, the rain began.

Cal felt a moment of satisfaction as the giant oak fell to earth, causing the ground beneath his feet to vibrate. It took him a moment to notice that, while he'd been distracted, the sky had grown dark.

At the first streak of lightning, he set aside his tools and started walking toward home. Any minute now, he surmised, the wagon would come rolling over the fields.

The wind picked up, ruffling the crops, causing the branches of trees to sway and dip. With every step he took, he saw the sky grow darker. Jagged ribbons of lightning made blinding slashes across the darkness, and thunder drowned out all other sounds. Once or twice Cal thought he heard a human voice crying, but brushed aside such thoughts. It was merely the cry of birds as they sought shelter from the storm.

When the rain began, he muttered a few ripe obscenities and hoped his brothers had sense enough to at least rescue the women before the fields turned into a sea of mud.

As for himself, he'd been through worse. The thought of dry clothes and Robert's good cooking had him setting a steady pace toward home.

Robert set a kettle of water over the fire to boil and looked up at the thunder of horses' hooves. Mr. Cal must be in quite a state to run the team at such a speed. But at least he'd managed to outrun the storm.

Robert walked to the back door, intent upon greeting the women and children. To his consternation, the yard was empty. No women and children. No Mr. Cal. And no wagon.

His heart stopped. All he could see were two snorting, stomping horses. Still tangled in their torn harness.

Dulcie hovered between fear and anger. The lightning seemed close enough to touch, and the shudder of thunder was fierce enough to be felt deep in her chest.

Where was Cal with the wagon? It simply wasn't in his nature to leave them out here at the mercy of the storm.

Could there have been a logging accident? Even as her heart lurched, she dismissed such a thought. One of the men would have come for them. Wouldn't they?

Now the rain began in earnest. The sky opened up, flattening the rows of corn, plastering hair and clothes against the little band of women and children as they moved doggedly forward.

"I think we should seek shelter!" Starlight shouted above the roar of the wind.

"No!" Dulcie shouted back. "Did you see the way the lightning hit those palmetto trees? We're safer out in the open."

They bent low and continued walking. The fields were rapidly turning to muck, which sucked at their ankles, holding them fast with every step.

With a cry, Starlight fell in a deep rut between two rows of corn and struggled to get up. With Fiona on one side and Dulcie on the other, she was helped to her feet. Just then a flash of lightning illuminated the sky, and Dulcie caught sight of a familiar figure.

"Cal!" she yelled. "Over here!"

Cal strode swiftly toward them, his face registering surprise. "You're still out here? You mean the wagon never came for you?"

His surprise turned to anger as he saw the exhaustion etched on the women's faces. Without a word he lifted Emily from Dulcie's back and placed her on his own shoulders, then took Belle by the hand.

"Follow me," he said tersely. "We'll be home in no time."

He looked up as two horsemen galloped toward them. Barc and Dar were astride the plow horses. Their faces mirrored their concern. Even before the horses came to a halt the two men were sliding to the ground and racing toward their older brother.

"We sent Nathaniel to fetch you in the wagon . . ." Barc began.

". . . but the horses returned alone," Dar finished.

"We thought maybe you'd come upon the boy and the wagon—" Barc stopped when he saw the look on Cal's face.

"My God. I heard someone crying out," Cal muttered in alarm. "By the palmetto trees. I thought it was birds. But it had to be Nathaniel."

He swung himself up on the broad back of one of the horses and dug in his heels.

With a choked sob Dulcie began to race after him. Then, realizing she couldn't catch him, she turned back and pulled herself onto the back of the second horse. Despite Dar's protest, she wheeled her mount and followed Cal into the darkness.

It took only a moment for the others to gather their wits about them. Then they began running toward the line of trees in the distance.

Cal spotted the overturned wagon and slid to the ground. Behind him Dulcie let out a cry and reined in her mount.

The two of them knelt beside the boy. Rain and blood pooled around him. So much blood.

Cal touched his hand to Nathaniel's throat. A quick examination revealed a pulse. Thready, feeble, but at least a sign of life.

"Is he . . . ?" Dulcie swallowed, unable to form the word.

"He's alive. Barely." Cal stood and leaned a shoulder to the wagon frame. "We have to get this off him."

Though he shoved and strained, it was impossible to budge the massive load.

Within minutes the others came rushing up. Seeing Nathaniel buried beneath the shattered wagon, everyone, including the children, pitched in to help. When the broken slats and wheels had been tossed aside, the three men leaned their shoulders to the frame. While they managed to hold it up a few inches, Dulcie and Fiona caught the unconscious boy by the shoulders and dragged him free.

The rain fell in torrents as the women and children formed a protective circle around the still, silent form.

Barc and Dar, riddled with guilt, began arguing over which one would be allowed to carry the boy back to the house.

"Barc, you're the strongest," Cal said firmly. "You'll carry him. Dar, you'll stay with the others and accompany them home."

There was no voice raised in dissent. At this time of crisis, Cal was the acknowledged leader. Calmly, authoritatively, he instructed his two brothers how to tie a tourniquet. That done, Dar tenderly lifted the boy in his arms while Barc mounted one of the horses and Cal the other.

Dar handed Nathaniel's still form up to Barc, then stepped back. As the two men wheeled their mounts, Dulcie suddenly let out a cry of torment.

"You can't leave me. I have to be with him. Don't you see?"

Catching sight of her anguished face, Cal drew back on the reins. "Come on. You can ride with me."

He helped her up onto the back of the horse, and she wrapped her arms around his waist. As the horse broke into a gallop, she pressed her cheek against Cal's strong, muscled shoulder and choked back the sobs that threatened to destroy the last thread of her composure.

Aunt Bessie and Robert stood waiting at the back door, faces pressed to the glass, eyes straining against the darkness. Long before the somber little party reached the porch, the door was thrown open, and Robert, lantern in hand, led the way inside.

"What is it? Oh, Lord, what's happened?" Aunt Bessie cried as she spied the boy in Barc's arms.

"Nathaniel is badly hurt. I'll need my bag, Aunt Bessie." Cal's voice was unusually calm. "And boiling water and fresh linens. Bring that lantern, Robert, and any other lanterns and candles you can find."

"Yes, Mr. Cal."

"Where do you want him?" Barc asked.

"Take him up to my room."

While Robert turned to the kettle that bubbled over the fire, Aunt Bessie hastened up the stairs behind her nephew.

"What can I do?" Dulcie asked.

Cal studied her a moment. Though her fear was evident, she had it under control.

"I'll need you to assist me."

"Assist you?"

"I'm a surgeon," he said brusquely. "Or was, before this." He glanced at his maimed arm, then back at her.

"And though I wish it weren't so, I'm the best hope Nathaniel has right now."

Dulcie's mouth dropped open, then closed. Anything she'd been about to say could wait.

He started up the stairs and she followed him.

Barc had placed the boy on the bed. Cal cut away what was left of Nathaniel's clothes and bent to examine his patient. What he saw sent shock waves through him. For a moment his face contorted with many emotions. Fear. Pain. Deep, abiding rage. Then he reverted to his professional manner.

"Barc, bring that table over here," he commanded. "And that lantern."

His brother did as he was told, and Aunt Bessie lifted a scuffed black leather bag down from a shelf. The moment Robert arrived with a steaming kettle, Cal ordered him to unpack the bag and deposit the contents in the kettle. Next he ordered Aunt Bessie to lay out a linen towel, before removing a series of instruments from the kettle and placing them in precise order on the towel.

"Barc and Robert, I'll ask you to lift him gently onto the table. Then position two lanterns as I need them," Cal instructed.

The two men complied.

"Dulcie," Cal said softly, "you will be my second hand. You must do everything I say without hesitation. Can you do that?"

She forced herself not to look away from the small, still form of the little boy she loved, and the blood from the mangled leg that had already begun to soak the blanket beneath him.

She swallowed. "I'll do whatever you say."

"Without question." His tone was challenging.

She nodded. "Without question."

"We'll get started, then."

"What about me?" Aunt Bessie asked.

Cal turned. He'd forgotten about his aunt. But one look at her pale face, and he had no doubt that she couldn't be allowed to remain in the room.

"I'd like you to wait downstairs for Dar and the others, Aunt Bessie. They will need dry clothes and a great deal of comfort."

She started toward the door.

"And, Aunt Bessie?" It was Dulcie's voice, thin, strained.

The older woman turned.

"I'd like you to pray," Dulcie said.

Aunt Bessie barely made it out the door before the tears began to fall. It took her several minutes to compose herself before she was able to descend the stairs. With each step, the words of a long-forgotten childhood prayer tumbled from her lips.

"Hold this." Cal's voice was strong and sure.

Dulcie grasped the long-handled instrument that gripped a flap of torn flesh, while Cal tied off several bleeders.

"Mop that blood."

She did as she was told and was shocked to see remnants of jagged bone poking through the wound.

"There's bone—"

"I know. Hold this." He worked quickly, skillfully, cutting, tying, suturing. "The broken bones are the least of our worries," he muttered.

Dulcie glanced at him. He had been working now for more than two hours, and sweat poured down his face. She lifted a damp cloth from the table and brushed it across his forehead. He shot her a quick look of gratitude before bending once more to his work.

Nathaniel moaned and began to fidget.

Cal whispered, "Give him a little more chloroform."

Dulcie placed a cloth over the boy's nose and mouth until he fell silent and still once more.

"I need your hand, Dulcie." At Cal's command she moved quickly into position beside him and did as he ordered. Working in unison, they mended the torn flesh and set the broken bones, then finished the job with disinfectant and clean linen bandages.

When at last Cal looked up, the lanterns had burned low, and those around the table were pale and exhausted.

"You may lift him onto the bed now," Cal said to Barc and Robert.

As they did so, Barc asked, "What do you think? Is the worst over?"

Cal shook his head and turned stiffly away. "The worst is yet to come."

The house was quiet. Still as death, thought Dulcie as she made her way unerringly in the midnight darkness to the kitchen.

Robert's special dinner of chicken and dumplings had congealed, untouched, in a blackened pot. His peach cobbler had grown cold on a sideboard, beside a forgotten pot of coffee.

Dulcie needed no candle to locate the stash of tea or the kettle that remained hot over the coals. Filling two cups, she returned to Cal's bedroom, where she had kept vigil since the surgery.

The storm had blown over, leaving the night cool and clear. As she opened the door to his room, she could see Cal silhouetted against the window.

He turned and accepted the cup. "Are the children asleep?"

She nodded. "They couldn't be alone, so Clara is in Fiona's room, and Emily and Belle are with Starlight."

"What about my aunt?"

"She is taking this very hard. But Robert fixed her a drink of honey, warm water and whiskey, and she took to her bed."

"And my brothers?"

Dulcie shook her head. "They are riddled with guilt, each taking blame. I doubt they'll even try to sleep. Barc is walking the shore. Dar is locked away in his room."

"I'd like to throttle—"

"Don't," she said. "It was a mistake. An error in judgment. We've all made them. But this time..." Her words trailed off. There had been so many errors made. So many times they should have paid a dear price for their mistakes but hadn't. This time, as her papa would have said, luck had not been with them.

She turned to the still form in the bed. He looked so small. So helpless. "What do you think?"

Cal set down the cup of tea and rubbed at his stiff shoulder. There was no point in giving her the bad news yet. Besides, he could be wrong. He hoped he was. Prayed he was.

"I'll know more in the morning. Why don't you get some sleep?"

"I can't leave him. I have to be here in case he wakes up." She pulled a chair close to the bed. "If you'd like to rest, you can use my room. Or Nathaniel's."

He shook his head. She wasn't the only stubborn one. "I expect he'll be facing a crisis in the next few hours. I'll need to be here."

He turned and walked to the window. In the moonlight he could see his brother pacing the shore like a caged panther. This island had always been their refuge. And their prison.

He rubbed at his gritty eyes and thought briefly about washing and changing his clothes. His pants and shirt were stained with dried blood. His boots were stiff and caked with mud. He glanced at Dulcie. She was no better, with her blood-soaked gown and wet, matted hair.

And yet, for all the dirt and blood, she had never looked more beautiful in his eyes. She was... magnificent. It was the only word that came to mind. Throughout the entire ordeal, she had been extraordinary. He'd never seen such determination. Not once had she flinched, even when he'd ordered her to do things that trained surgeons would have found difficult. She had mopped, tied, sutured. And even now, when she must be exhausted beyond belief, she was prepared to remain by Nathaniel's side.

How could he do less? He pulled up a chair on the other side of the bed and sank into it gratefully.

"We'll wait together," he said as he lifted the cup of tea to his lips.

The crisis came shortly before dawn. One minute Nathaniel was still and silent, the next he was sitting bolt upright in bed. The moan that issued from his lips was wild and primal.

Dulcie, who had been dozing, felt her blood chill at the sound. Gathering her wits, she caught the little boy's hands. They were as hot as coals.

"Dear heaven," she whispered. "He's burning up."

"Get water to sponge him," Cal said as he began to unwrap the boy's leg.

When she returned from the well with a bucket of water, she was shocked to see Cal once again laying out his instruments. Lanterns burned at either side of the bed. Nathaniel lay, pale and still again, his dressings cut away, his leg swollen and mottled with purples and blacks. The odor of chloroform was strong.

As she watched, Cal withdrew a small saw from his black bag.

Dulcie's heart stopped. "What do you think you're doing with that?" Her voice was thick.

Cal didn't look at her. Instead, he turned away and said, "I want you to leave now."

"I will not." Water sloshed over the rim of the bucket as she set it down and hurried to stand beside the bed like an outraged mother bear protecting her cub. "And I will not allow you to . . . to do what you're planning."

"You won't allow?" He turned on her with a look of fury. "You won't allow?"

"That's what I said. I know what you're planning. I won't allow it."

"For God's sake, woman. Do you think I would do this if I had any other choice?"

"How can you?" she demanded. "How can you even think about such a horrible thing? Do you know what it will do to him?"

"You would dare ask me such a thing?" Cal held up his maimed arm, forcing her to look at it. "Don't you think I know, better than anyone, what it will do to him? Don't you think I wake up every morning, wishing I'd been given any other choice?"

Dulcie was shocked into silence. But when he turned away and picked up the saw, she fought back the sob that threatened to choke her. She must not cry. Not now. Not when it was so important for her to be strong.

"Please," she whispered. "Can't you at least wait a little longer?"

He kept his back to her. His words were gruff, as though he, too, might be fighting an overpowering emotion. "The wound is badly infected. For every hour we hesitate, that infection is spreading through his body. Soon, it won't be just his leg, Dulcie. It will be his life.''

She digested that, then said softly, ''Just another hour. Please. I'm begging you.''

Ever so slowly he nodded his head and returned the saw to the table.

She closed her hand over his. And felt the tremors he couldn't hide.

Chapter Nineteen

"**Y**ou can't keep this up, Dulcie. You need to rest."

Cal stood by the window watching as she bathed Nathaniel's fevered body.

"How can I rest when he's fighting for his life?" She dipped a cloth in the bucket of water, then draped it across the little boy's brow. His chest rose and fell with each shallow, unsteady breath.

"I know how terrible this is for you, Dulcie. But give it up." Cal came around the bed and caught her by the arm, hauling her to her feet. "Look at you. You're ready to drop. Go to bed. Stop trying to play God."

"How dare you!" She pushed him away. "I am not trying to play God. I am simply refusing to give up. Unlike you, Dr. Jermain."

Her sarcastic use of his title wasn't lost on Cal, but he refused to take the bait. Instead, his tone softened. "That's the hardest part of being a doctor, Dulcie. Sometimes we're forced to make difficult decisions. Decisions that will change a patient's life forever."

"I suppose you never made a mistake?"

Again her sarcasm rolled off him. In a voice that betrayed his weariness, he said, "Too many to count. But in the heat of battle, decisions had to be made quickly. In order to save a man's life, I was forced to sever limbs that, in peacetime, in a well-equipped infirmary, might have been saved."

"Your own hand included?"

"Yes."

She heard pain, layer upon layer of pain, in that single word. All the anger drained out of her. Before she had time to think she cried, "Oh, Cal. How did it happen?"

As soon as the words were out of her mouth, she regretted them. But it was too late. The question had been asked, and it hung between them.

He turned away, busying himself by peering closely at Nathaniel's leg. But she knew he was struggling to compose himself. As the silence stretched out between them, she hung her head, expecting no response.

Instead, he surprised her by saying, "I had volunteered as field physician for Lieutenant General Thomas J. Jackson."

"Stonewall Jackson?"

He nodded. "When he led the troops at Chancellorsville, I attended to their medical needs."

He ran a hand over the instruments laid out on the linen towel, and Dulcie had a sense of the esteem he had once felt for his noble profession. A profession he had abandoned since the loss of his hand.

"At first our casualties were few. General Jackson was a brilliant leader, and though our number was less than half that of our enemy, our troops were sending the Yankees on a wild rout. But as more and more Federals were brought in, the fighting became fierce. I was ordered to retreat so that I would be spared the danger."

"Where did you go?" Dulcie asked softly.

"I refused to retreat. I stayed with my men. How could I leave them? They were being cut down at the rate of hundreds every day."

"But how could you attend them under fire?" she asked with a trace of awe.

"The situation was...less than ideal. But at least I managed to save some lives." His tone lowered, and again she heard the thread of deep emotion. "During an especially fierce battle, I was attending a group of wounded soldiers in the field when I took a musket ball in the hand."

She gasped, and he paused a moment, before continuing, "I realized at once the seriousness of the wound. Most of the fingers and the larger bones in the hand were shattered or missing. I had no choice."

"Are you saying...?" She covered her mouth with her hand to stifle the cry that threatened.

He nodded. "I had to amputate immediately."

The knowledge left her stunned and reeling.

He turned toward the window, unknowingly rubbing his arm, feeling, once again, the agony he'd endured. An agony of both mind and body, as he'd been forced to cut off his own hand with whatever crude instruments were available.

"Chancellorsville was General Lee's most brilliant victory," he said. "But it came with a heavy cost."

Dear heaven. What a cost, Dulcie thought as tears sprang to her eyes.

And then she recalled Barc's dry remark one night at the dinner table. *Cal stayed a little too long at Chancellorsville.* He could have retreated to safety. But he refused to leave his men. And this was the price he paid.

Without thinking she crossed to him and touched a hand to his shoulder. There were no words to convey her feelings. She had never known a finer, braver man. Or a more tormented one.

And then she turned away. For she dared not allow him to see the tears that streamed down her cheeks. Tears that she shed for a hero and the terrible toll he had paid for his act of courage.

"I must sleep," Cal announced, "before I...see to Nathaniel. I'll need to be alert for what is to come." He glanced at Dulcie, who had refused all offers to rest. Her eyes were red-rimmed and darkly shadowed. "You must do the same, Dulcie. He will require a great deal of care after..." His voice trailed off, but Dulcie had no doubt as to his meaning.

At a tap on the door, Cal opened it to admit his aunt. To Dulcie he said, "I've asked Aunt Bessie to sit with Nathaniel while we sleep. She will wake us if there is any change." To his aunt he said, "I'll be in Nathaniel's room if you need me."

Dulcie followed him from the room. But when he closed the door to Nathaniel's room, she walked past her own room and knocked on Fiona's.

"What is it?" the young woman asked as Dulcie entered. "Has he...?"

"No. Nothing yet." Dulcie sank onto the edge of the bed and buried her face in her hands.

At once the little girls gathered around her, patting her shoulder, offering what comfort they could.

"Don't cry, Dulcie. Please don't cry," Emily murmured.

"Cal thinks there is no hope left. In order to save Nathaniel's life, he feels he must..." Dulcie knew she mustn't speak the words in front of the children.

Catching her meaning, Starlight and Fiona sucked in their breaths. And though the little girls had no idea what was going on, they sensed the urgency of the situation and began to weep.

Now it was Dulcie's turn to try to comfort them. "Here, here now. Hope is not gone yet."

Suddenly Dulcie whispered, "I just thought of something."

Fiona's head came up. "What is it, Dulcie?"

The young woman ducked her head. It was probably foolish. And certainly unworthy of consideration. Except that she was desperate. Papa used to say that desperate situations called for desperate measures. "Fiona, do you remember that blueberry bog?"

Fiona blushed until her cheeks were as red as her hair, recalling the scene with the young man who made her heart pound each time he came near. Barc had been true to his word, refusing to drink a drop of spirits since that fateful day. "Of course I do."

"This is what I'd like you to do."

After a whispered conversation, Dulcie returned to her room for a much-needed rest, while Starlight, Fiona and the girls hurried away.

Cal sat up and rubbed his stiff neck. His muscles protested even that small movement. A glance out the window told him that the sun was already high in the sky. He felt a rush of anger that his aunt had allowed him to sleep so long. He'd meant only to catch thirty minutes or so in order to be fresh for the coming ordeal. Instead, he'd fallen into a deep, dreamless sleep.

He would take this as a good omen. The fact that Aunt Bessie had not disturbed him for several hours must mean that the boy was no worse. But of course, that was not nearly enough to save the leg. Cal had seen the signs of infection. Once it traveled through the blood, it would invade every part of the boy's body. And so, although he had tried his best, it simply hadn't been good enough.

He crossed the room and opened the door. It was time. It tore at his gut and wrenched his heart, but he knew he was the only one who could perform this hideous task.

With a heavy heart Cal stepped into his room and leaned against the closed door until his eyes adjusted to the gloom. The draperies had been drawn against the sunlight.

Aunt Bessie's chair was empty.

As Cal stepped closer, he realized that someone lay sleeping beside Nathaniel.

Dulcie! Her eyes were closed. Her arm rested protectively across Nathaniel's shoulders. Her breathing was as soft and rhythmic as that of the boy beside her.

It took a moment for the fact to register.

Nathaniel's breathing was no longer tortured and shallow.

Cal moved closer, listening. When he had confirmed that the boy was indeed breathing easily, he crossed the room and tore open the draperies.

As sunlight flooded the room, Dulcie sat up, startled and confused, and watched in horror as Cal advanced upon the figure beside her on the bed.

He touched a hand to the boy's forehead, then placed his fingers on Nathaniel's throat to check his heartbeat.

"How can this be?" His frown deepened as his glance flew to the exposed leg.

He was shocked to see the wound covered with fat leeches. For a moment he was taken aback. Then, as he recovered his composure, he sat down and peered closely at the wound. Though it was still raw and puckered, the stench of infection was gone. And the flesh around the wound was pink and healthy.

Cal arched a brow in stunned disbelief. "You did this?"

Dulcie nodded fearfully. "Papa said he did such a thing before my mother died. It...did not help. Her infection was too severe. But I thought—at least I'd hoped—that it would not be too late for Nathaniel."

"Not too late! God in heaven, not too late!" Cal closed his eyes and pressed the back of his hand over his face as though in terrible pain.

Dulcie jumped up and rounded the bed to stand at his side. Seeing the depth of his emotion, she began wringing her hands.

"Forgive me, Cal. I was desperate. I would do anything to save Nathaniel. I'm sorry if I've only made things worse."

"Worse?" He lifted his hand, and for a moment she thought he would strike her. Instead, he clamped his fingers on her shoulder, dragging her roughly against him. "Do you mean you don't know what you've done?"

Tears flooded her eyes as she looked up at him. Unable to speak over the constriction in her throat, she could only shake her head.

"My God, woman. You saved him. You saved, not only his life, but his leg."

The words didn't seem to register. She was weeping openly now, murmuring, "I didn't mean to make things worse. I'm sorry. I'm so sorry."

"Didn't you hear me, Dulcie?" He caught her by the chin and forced her to look at him. "I said you saved him. Your desperate measures saved Nathaniel."

"Saved him?" She could hardly see for the tears that blurred her vision. But as she lifted a hand to his face, she could feel the moisture there. And she knew that Cal Jermain, the cold, calculating, unfeeling doctor, was weeping with her.

Her heart nearly exploded with the love she felt for this man. Love. Sweet heaven, how she loved him! As the wonder of it dawned on her, she knew she could no longer deny what her heart had known all along. She loved this angry, wounded, heroic man as she had never loved anyone.

He drew her close. And for what seemed an eternity, the two of them clung together, crying openly. At last they stepped apart and called to the others to share their joyous news that Nathaniel would recover.

Dulcie stood on the balcony and felt the cool night breeze whisper across her skin and flutter the hem of her night-gown. She drew the shawl more firmly around her and breathed deeply.

She had spent the afternoon catching up on her sleep, while Fiona and Starlight took turns sitting with Nathaniel, who had been returned to his own room. Though the little boy had awakened for several brief moments, he was un-aware of the crisis through which he'd passed.

After a long, refreshing bath, Dulcie had joined the others below for a festive dinner. And had been dealt a crush-ing disappointment when Cal hadn't joined them.

She needed to see him. Needed desperately to see him, to calm her own raging fever and still the demons that stirred her blood.

Now, as the rest of the household retired, she felt a rest-lessness stirring within her, as though she, too, was passing through some sort of crisis.

What she felt for Cal Jermain was love. She knew that now. It was not mere gratitude, though she would be for-ever grateful for what he'd done. Nor was it pity for the sacrifice he'd made for the men entrusted to his care. It was, plainly, simply, love. She loved him. Loved him with a depth that made her chest ache and her heart swell with longing.

She moved quickly along the darkened balcony until she was standing outside Cal's room. Through the window she could see him seated at his desk leafing through a medical textbook. Smoke from his cigar curled over his head.

She took a deep breath and, before she could lose her nerve, pushed open the door to his room.

Like her, he'd finally shed his blood-soaked clothing. He was barefoot and naked to the waist, wearing only clean, slim-fitting black trousers. She could tell, by the droplets of water that still clung to his dark hair, that he had just finished washing. He appeared refreshed and well rested. And startled to see her standing boldly in his room.

She leaned against the door and hoped he wouldn't notice the way her legs were trembling.

"A penny for them," she said.

"What...?" He managed to close his mouth before his jaw dropped any farther. "Dulcie, what are you doing here?"

"I didn't see you at dinner."

"I slept through it."

"I could fix you something to eat," she offered.

He shook his head and drew on his cigar. "I'm not that hungry." He released a cloud of smoke and watched as it drifted toward the ceiling. It was better than looking at her, because, when he did, he felt a tightness in his chest that made it hard to breathe. "I can wait till morning."

"I can't." She started across the room, and he got to his feet as though he'd been prodded by a hot poker. If she touched him, he'd be lost.

"I looked in on Nathaniel a little while ago." He wanted to keep the conversation safe, neutral. He backed away from her, but she kept on coming.

"So did I. We must have just missed each other." She clasped her hands, and a radiant smile seemed to touch all her features with light. "He was sleeping so peacefully I wanted to hug him." She waited the space of a heartbeat and added, "Of course, that's what I'd like to do to you, too."

For a moment he wasn't sure he'd heard her. Had she said what he thought she had? He stared down into those gleaming cat's eyes of hers and saw a look he'd never seen before. Or had it always been there and he just hadn't noticed?

"You're having fun with me, aren't you, Miss Dulcie Trenton?"

"Not yet. But I hope to." She reached out and took the cigar from his hand and stubbed it into the crystal ashtray on his desk.Then she turned back to him and spread her hands across his naked chest.

He hadn't absorbed this many tremors when he'd sent a hundred-year-old oak crashing to the ground. His muscles bunched and tightened. His nerves jangled and screamed until he thought they'd snap.

"I want to kiss you," she murmured against his lips.

He couldn't stop himself. When her lips moved over his, his reaction was the same as any man's would be. He kissed her back. The rush of heat was so intense they both stepped back for a moment, each studying the other through narrowed eyes.

Cal's mind was working feverishly. He had to stop this before it went any further. At least he had to try. Dear God, he had to try.

With a studied casualness he pushed her away. "If you're through, I have some medical books I'd like to read. To prepare for Nathaniel's recovery." He saw the hurt in her eyes and drove home the final blow. After all, he was doing this for her own good. "You remember Nathaniel, don't you?"

She closed her eyes a moment against the pain and thought about crawling back to her room where she could hide and nurse her bruised heart. But just then she happened to look up. And saw the regret in his eyes.

"You're not a very good liar, Cal."

"Unlike you, Dulcie?"

"That's right. I'm the best. Now," she whispered, backing him into the corner, "let's try that kiss again. I haven't had much experience, but I'm told I'm a quick study." She brushed her body against his and heard his sudden intake of breath. That was all she needed to give her confidence.

His blood hammered in his temples, and he felt a quick rush of desire that left him dazed. Still, he had to fight her. "You're an innocent, for God's sake."

"I'm certain you can change that," she murmured against his lips.

He struggled to catch his breath. But with every bit of air that filled his lungs, he tasted her. Only her. And wanted her as he'd never wanted anything, anyone, in his life.

"Stop it, Dulcie." He tried to pull her head back and found his hand fisted in her hair. Before he knew what he was doing, he lifted a handful and watched as it sifted through his fingers.

"You don't understand what you're doing." He watched the way the candlelight cast her lovely face into light and shadow. "I'm not one of your strays begging for a crumb of kindness." He hardened his tone, hoping to dissuade her from this dangerous course she'd charted. "I'm a man, Dulcie. And not a very nice one. If you don't leave now, I'll do things to you that aren't pretty. And afterward, you'll hate me."

"I could never hate you, Cal. Not after the way you fought for Nathaniel."

He shoved her away, intentionally rough, so that she would have no further cause to argue. If he dared to touch her one more time, he'd be lost. "There you are. Confusing gratitude with love. I did what I did, not for any noble reason, but because I was the only one available. But tomorrow I'll go back to being a farmer. Nothing more. Now get out of here before you completely embarrass yourself.''

To add the final note of insult he turned away from her and picked up his cigar. Jamming it into his mouth, he lifted a candle, and held the flame to the tip.

She started to turn away, humiliated and defeated. What had ever possessed her to think she could hold the interest of a world-weary man like Cal Jermain? She'd been nothing more than a passing fancy. An amusement for a man who had been too long without a woman on this godforsaken island. But just as she glanced up, she saw that his hand was shaking. And in that instant she knew that her presence here affected him far more than he cared to admit.

She prayed her tone wouldn't betray her. ''You're right, Cal. I'll go now and leave you to your medical books. But could I . . .'' She swung around and kept her gaze lowered. ''Could I ask a favor?''

He took a deep drag of the cigar, relief flooding through him. A minute more and he would have been lost.

''You want me to look in on Nathaniel tonight while you stay in your room,'' he said smugly. ''Of course I'll be happy t—''

She let her shawl drop to the floor, then lifted a hand to the buttons that ran from throat to hem on her nightgown. As she unbuttoned the first ones, he crushed out his cigar and crossed the room to take her hands in his. His voice was thick with anger. ''Good God, woman. Have you no shame?''

''None,'' she whispered as she freed her hands to wind them around his neck. ''None at all.''

''Dulcie—''

"Don't send me away, Cal. I couldn't bear it. I want to be here with you."

He closed his eyes and muttered, "Then God help me. God help us both."

His anger was gone. Drained away as quickly as it had surfaced. As was his last shred of resistance. He lifted his hand to stroke the gentle curve of her cheek. "If you stay, there'll be no going back," he murmured. "Tomorrow, you won't be the same person you are right now."

"I know."

"You don't know anything, Dulcie. Not yet. But you're about to learn," he whispered as he claimed her mouth.

Chapter Twenty

His mouth crushed hers with a fierceness that left her gasping. His fingers dug into the tender flesh of her upper arm as he dragged her close.

If he intended to frighten her, to give her one last chance to change her mind, it didn't work. She offered her lips willingly.

He took them, feasting on her like a starving man. Later he would take the time to taste, to savor. For now, he was a glutton, devouring.

With his lips still on hers he drove her back against the wall and lifted her until her legs were wrapped around him. She'd been prepared to surrender, but that wasn't what he wanted. He wanted, he demanded, complete participation. There would be no soft words or whispered promises. No tender entreaties. Instead, she found herself in the eye of a storm. Riding the wind and waves, tossed about without a ship, without a compass.

His lips left hers to nuzzle her throat. Impatiently he tore aside her opened nightgown. As his mouth closed over her breast, she gasped and clutched his head. But he gave her no time to recover as he moved from one taut, throbbing nipple to the other, nibbling, suckling, until she moaned and writhed and cried out in a fever of need.

Never had she felt like this. Her body was alive. A million tiny nerve endings begging to be touched.

He shoved aside the billowing skirt and found her hot and moist and ready. Though she gasped at this invasion, his lips covered hers, swallowing her moan of protest. His work-roughened fingers excited her, bringing her to a first breathless peak that left her dazed and trembling. But before she could even catch her breath, he was taking her on an even faster ride; she was swimming against the tide and swept away by rolling, tumbling surf. One minute she was riding the crest, the next she was being dashed against the shore, drained and spent.

She wanted him to give her a moment to get her bearings, to think this through. Too late she realized that she hadn't known, hadn't even had the vaguest idea, what it was she had set into motion. Yet she knew that if he stopped now, she would have to beg him to go on. She wanted more. Wanted all.

His hand tangled in her hair, drawing her head back while with his lips he explored her neck, her throat, her shoulder. With a sigh of impatience he tore her nightgown from her, and she heard the buttons snap, the seams rip, as the fabric fell away. With quick impatient motions he shrugged out of his trousers and kicked them aside.

He fell to his knees, dragging her down with him. The heat rose up between them, making their breathing labored, their heartbeats erratic.

The world beyond this room had slipped away. The wind outside the window still sighed, but they no longer heard. A night bird cried, but they were unaware. They knew only the seductive touch, the heady taste, the dark, musky scent of passion. It clouded their vision, clogged their throats. It drove them to the brink of insanity. And still, there was no relief.

Cal felt himself slipping over the edge. He wanted desperately to slow down, to stop the madness. But it was too late. This need for her was a tidal wave, carrying him along, dragging him down, down. And Dulcie with him.

"I've wanted you for so long, so long," he breathed against her lips, inside her mouth, as he tasted and nibbled and devoured.

His admission only fueled her own hunger. How long had he wanted her? It seemed too much effort to ask. Hungry for more of him, she wrapped herself around him, eager to give and take and give until they were both sated.

With a moan he took her on a ride of dizzying delights, as with fingers, teeth and tongue he drove her until she cried out, "Cal. Please..."

She was lying on the floor, though she couldn't remember how she'd come to be there. Only their discarded tangle of clothes cushioned her body. As he levered himself above her, all she could see was herself reflected in those dark, dangerous eyes. And in his eyes she felt beautiful, desirable. All she could feel was pleasure. So intense it bordered on pain. And she wanted, more than anything, to give him the same pleasure she was experiencing. All she could taste was desire, so deep, so urgent, she knew if he didn't take her, here, now, she would go mad.

"I need...I need..." The words were wrenched from her lips.

"Say it, Dulcie. Say you need me. You want me."

"I do, Cal. I need you. I want you. Oh, Cal, I love you."

Love. The word unlocked all the doors. Threw off all the shackles. His heart. His mind. His soul. All were torn free. There were no more restrictions. No more doubts or fears.

This was what he had wanted, dreamed of, all those long, dark nights. His woman. Only his.

He took her then, with all the frenzy of a hurricane. He heard her cry out. Knew that he'd hurt her, was hurting her still. Dear God, she was an innocent. And he was taking her like a savage. Calling on every ounce of willpower, he hesitated. For a moment he lifted his head and went deathly quiet. He felt a swift, terrible pain of remorse as he struggled to hold back the tide of passion.

"I'm sorry, Dulcie. I know I've hurt you. Forgive—"

"Shh."

With her fingers over his lips she stared up into his eyes. And what he saw shook him to his very core. Her eyes burned with a need, a passion, a desire that matched his own.

"I'll only forgive you if you promise not to stop," she whispered.

"Oh, Dulcie. Do you know how much I love you?"

His mouth closed over hers and they began to move together, faster, then faster still, until, breathless, they were swept into the maelstrom.

"God, Dulcie." Cal rested his forehead against hers and tried to calm his ragged breathing.

She lay still, absorbing the calmness of the shore after the frenzy of the storm they had just weathered. It had been like dying. Or being born.

"Is it . . ." She tried again. "Is it always like that?"

"No," he said quickly. He still couldn't believe it himself. It had been the most incredible experience of his life. "I mean, I've never known anything like it before. I didn't mean to be so rough." He pressed soft kisses across her face until he suddenly encountered the saltiness of her tears. "Dear God, I've hurt you. How could I be so thoughtless?"

He started to roll aside, but she stopped him. "You didn't hurt me. I'm crying because... I'm not sure why. I guess because I'm overwhelmed. You took my breath away." She gave a choked little laugh. "But I must admit, you are a little heavy. And the floor is a little hard."

He rolled to his side and gathered her close, cushioning her against his chest. "Is that better?"

"Mmm. Much. But the bed would be even better."

As tempting as it was, neither of them made a move to get up. It seemed too much effort. And the thought of separating for even a moment was far too painful.

"Have you really wanted me for a long time?" she asked.

"Mm-hmm." He twirled a strand of her hair around his finger, loving the feel of the silk against his callused skin. His heart still hadn't returned to its normal rhythm. He wasn't certain it ever would.

"How long?"

"My, my, Miss Trenton. How many questions am I supposed to answer?"

"As many as I ask."

"And how about me? Am I allowed to ask any of you?"

"I suppose so." She thought a minute. "For every answer you give me, I'll give one in return."

"Fair enough."

"All right." She sighed as he began to move his fingers idly down her back in long, even strokes. If she were a kitten, she'd be purring. "How long have you wanted me?"

"Since that first night I saw you, more dead than alive, ready to stand toe-to-toe with me and fight for your band of strays."

She snuggled closer. "You called me Sarah."

"What?" He pulled back to look into her eyes.

"I said you called me—"

"I heard what you said." He grinned. "I think that's the last time I ever gave her a thought. You've managed to wipe her completely from my mind."

"Barc said you loved her. And she left you for someone else."

"Thank heaven for small favors."

"You mean you aren't sorry?"

He threw back his head and laughed. "I was at the time. Now I realize she would have been the worst thing that ever happened to me. She was very prim and very proper. And very dull. And by now we would have learned to hate each other."

As Dulcie opened her mouth to speak, he stopped her. "My turn to ask a question." He felt her tense and knew she was bracing for the inevitable. So. It would seem that even now, after what they had just shared, she was afraid to trust him with the truth. He swallowed his disappointment. He couldn't bear to spoil the moment. Her secret could wait another day or two, until she felt more secure in his love.

Love. It was a strange and wonderful feeling, and it filled him with the kind of peace he'd come to believe he would never experience again.

He surprised her by asking, "How did you happen to take in all these strays?"

He heard the deep sigh that welled up inside her and knew he'd made the right choice. For now he would keep his questions simple and give her time to trust.

She relaxed in his embrace. He loved the way she fit against him as though made just for him.

"Papa said I was always taking in strays. I guess it's just my nature. Before the war it was puppies and foxes and baby raccoons. But then there was Fiona. And then Nathaniel. And before I knew it, I had a whole houseful of people depending on me." She pressed her lips to his throat.

"If you keep that up," he muttered thickly, "you'll have another stray on your hands. I have a definite weakness for little butterfly kisses. Especially along my throat."

"You mean like this?" She ran moist, openmouthed kisses across his sensitive flesh until he growled low and deep.

"Miss Dulcie Trenton, you are shameless."

"I know." She continued raining kisses across his chest and down his stomach, then lower, until he reacted in exactly the way she'd expected.

"Why, Cal Jermain, I do believe I've found another weakness of yours."

"Absolutely shameless," he said as he dragged her upward and captured her mouth with his. "I can't believe what you do to me."

How was it possible that he wanted her again so soon? But he did. God in heaven, how he wanted her!

As he rolled over and gathered her against him, she whispered, "Just one more question."

He groaned with impatience before saying, "What is it?"

"If you're thinking of doing what I think you're thinking of doing, could we use the bed this time?"

With a laugh he scooped her up and carried her across the room. As they tumbled onto the covers, he promised himself that this time he would take her on a slow, lazy journey. Even if it took all night. Especially if it took all night.

It did.

Though they managed to doze, the two lovers were too excited to waste the night in sleep. At times their lovemaking was as easy and gentle as the lapping of the water along the shore on a hot summer day. At other times it was as frenzied as a hurricane, gathering momentum as they fed each other's passions and learned each other's most secret desires.

"Why did you give up medicine?" She was snuggled against his chest, her fingertip idly tracing the line of one dark eyebrow.

"In case you didn't notice, surgery requires two hands. Without your help, I couldn't have done anything for Nathaniel."

"But you're wrong," she said, sitting up.

He could see that her temper was starting to surface. A temper that always fascinated and amused him. "Am I? If I recall, it was your hands that tied off the bleeders. Your hands that pulled through the sutures."

"But don't you see, Cal? It was your knowledge that saved Nathaniel. Not my hands. And that knowledge is such a precious thing. The war couldn't take that from you. Your knowledge of medicine shouldn't be squandered any more than Dar's knowledge of history and literature should be, or Barc's knowledge of the law. Papa used to say—"

He pressed his hand to her lips to silence her, and Dulcie wondered if he was angry or just thoughtful. Was he considering her words or rejecting them?

At length he said, "You quote your father a lot. Tell me about him."

"Papa had the smoothest tongue I've ever heard. People just naturally took to him. Men wanted to buy anything he wanted to sell. And women..." She shook her head, remembering. "Women just wanted to take care of him. And his motherless little girl." She glanced at Cal. "Did I tell you that my mama died when I was a baby?"

He twirled a lock of her hair around his finger and shook his head. "You neglected to mention that."

"Well, she did. But Papa took care of me, and I took care of Papa. We didn't need anyone else taking care of us."

"I can see that you're very good at taking care of yourself." Cal found himself grinning. "I can see, also, that you take after your father."

She nodded, unaware of the humor in his voice. "I was always Papa's girl. Everyone said so."

"Was there any other family? Brothers or sisters?" Cal asked.

She shook her head. "Only Papa. Until Belinda."

"Belinda?" Cal's hand stilled.

"Papa married her when I was thirteen. Belinda said after just one look at Papa, she knew he was the man she wanted to marry."

Cal's grin widened. He knew just how Belinda had felt.

"Belinda's papa was a horse-breeder in Charleston who didn't want to lose his only daughter. So, he gave Papa one hundred acres of his prime land on which to build his own plantation. It was Grandpa's way of keeping his daughter close."

"So you grew up close to your grandfather," Cal remarked.

"I liked him well enough, but—" Dulcie's voice warmed "—Papa was all I needed. He was so colorful, so..." Her voice trailed off, and Cal could hear the love in her voice.

"I'm tired of talking," she murmured as she began to run little kisses across his chest. "Is there something else we could do, instead?"

"Miss Trenton," he drawled, and felt his heartbeat quicken, "I do believe you are a cunning, devious little witch."

"That would make my papa proud," she muttered as they came together in a swell of passion.

Later, as they lay spent, Cal realized he had really learned very little about Dulcie's father. Except for his words, which she quoted constantly, the man remained a shadowy figure from her past.

Cal lay quietly watching Dulcie sleep. Outside the window, the first faint ribbons of light colored the horizon. The tang of the ocean was carried on the fresh morning breeze. Everything on this small island was as it had always been. And yet, because of this woman, everything seemed new and wonderful.

He felt clean and fresh. Reborn. For the first time since the war, he felt at peace. And all because this bold, fiery little woman loved him.

Love. It blossomed in his heart, filling him with such joy he felt like waking the household and shouting out the truth for all to hear.

Dulcie's eyes flickered, then opened. She lifted a hand to his lips. "What are you grinning about?"

He pressed a kiss to her palm. "Am I grinning?"

"You are."

"You have only yourself to blame. You're the reason for my smile, Dulcie. You make me feel like a whole man again."

She sat up and shoved a tangle of hair from her eyes. And he saw the flash of fire even before the words of anger and outrage came tumbling out. "That's a perfectly horrible thing to say. When are you going to realize that the loss of a hand doesn't make you less of a man?"

If he'd been aroused by her attempts at seduction, he was even more aroused by her temper. He swallowed back his grin and decided it might be fun to goad her into a fight. "Are you saying you love me, anyway? Even though I don't have a hand?"

She poked a finger in his chest and lectured him like a stubborn child. "Cal Jermain, your hand, or the lack of it, doesn't even enter into it. I just love you. It's that plain."

And that complicated, she realized with a sudden pang of conscience. If she truly loved him, why couldn't she be honest with him? Why couldn't she trust him with her secret?

He pulled her down on top of him and kissed her long and hard. Against her lips he muttered, "Say that again."

"What?" She blinked, pulling herself back from the edge of dark thoughts.

"You know."

She smiled. "I love you."

"Again."

"I love—" The rest died in her throat as he rolled her over. And took her once more to that secret place where only lovers can go.

"Do we have to get up?" Dulcie snuggled close and buried her lips against Cal's throat.

He sighed, deep and long, and wondered how he had lived before now. It hadn't been living, he realized. He'd been barely surviving. Hanging on to his sanity by a thread.

And now he felt gloriously alive. Filled with hope. And so content he wanted this same feeling of contentment for everyone.

"I'd like nothing better than to bar the door and hide away in here forever," he murmured against her temple. "But there's a heap of chores waiting for us."

"Not to mention your family, who would probably break down the door if we didn't show our faces for a whole day."

He kissed the tip of her nose and said, "It's time to wash up and face the world. If you'd like, I'll let you go first."

She shook her head and slipped out of bed. "I didn't bring anything with me. I'll have to go back to my own room to wash and dress."

When she pulled the tattered remnants of her nightgown around her, she remarked dryly, "Appears I'll have to do some fancy mending, as well."

Just looking at her, he felt again the tug of desire that had driven him to such desperation. "Don't bother, Dulcie." He dragged her close and gave her a long, lingering kiss. "I'd just have to tear it off you again tonight."

"And what makes you think I'll be back tonight, Mr. Jermain?"

He caught a handful of her hair and kissed her again. When he released her, he muttered, "Because, Miss Trenton, you'll have all day to miss me."

She wrapped the shawl around her shoulders and started toward the balcony door. Suddenly changing directions, she crossed the room and twined both arms around his neck. With her lips pressed to his she murmured, "Just a little something to remind you of what *you'll* be missing all day."

But as she started to let go, his arms came around her so firmly she was lifted off her feet. Before she knew what was happening, she was lying on the bed with Cal beside her. The nightgown and shawl were in a heap on the floor.

"You shouldn't have done that, Dulcie," he whispered against her throat. "Now I'm afraid we're going to be late for breakfast."

"Are we going to cut timber today, Cal?" Barc asked.

Before Cal could answer, Dulcie swept into the room, skirts swishing around her ankles. Her hair had been carefully arranged with ribbons. Her eyes sparkled with secrets. Her smile was radiant.

"Isn't it a glorious day?" she asked no one in particular.

Cal watched in silence while she filled her plate and took her place beside him at table.

"Tea, missy?" Robert asked.

"Yes, thank you."

"Jam, missy?"

"I'd love some."

Cal's food lay forgotten as he finished his coffee. He breathed in the fresh, clean scent of her, filling his lungs like a drowning man, and wished with all his heart that he could carry her off to his room and stay there forever.

"Well?" Barc demanded. "Are we?"

Cal blinked. "Are we what?"

His brother couldn't hide his exasperation. "Going to cut timber today."

Cal forced himself to concentrate. "We've cut enough. I've been thinking we ought to spend the day putting up the last wall of the barn. That way, it'll be ready for harvest. And if Nathaniel should need me, I'll be close by."

"Good idea," Dar said. "I looked in on him this morning. He's sleeping like a baby."

"Dulcie, did you stay with him through the night?" Starlight asked innocently.

Dulcie's head came up sharply. "Why do you ask?"

"I knocked on your door. I—" Starlight looked down at her hands "—was having a bad night, and I wanted to talk to you. But when you didn't answer, I figured you were sitting with Nathaniel. So I stayed with Fiona, instead."

Dulcie felt a wave of guilt. Her breakfast forgotten, she reached across the table to catch Starlight's hand. "Are you all right now?"

The girl gave her a shy smile. "I'm fine. I guess it was Nathaniel's accident and the fact that it was so dark and cloudy last night."

"Really? I hadn't noticed," Dulcie said.

She glanced up and caught Cal's eye. At once she looked away, but not before she saw the hint of a smile that tugged at the corners of his mouth.

"Are you sure you're feeling up to a lesson this morning, Starlight?" Dar asked with a trace of concern.

"Oh, yes. I wouldn't miss it." Her face bloomed in a smile. "You said we could read some of Shakespeare's sonnets."

"Shakespeare's sonnets?" Across the table, Barc studied his younger brother with interest.

"So I did." Flushed and embarrassed, the young man pushed away from the table to avoid the grin he knew he would see on Barc's face. "Let's hurry then, if we're going to hold class before we begin work on the barn."

At the head of the table, Aunt Bessie watched and listened. So much had happened in such a short time it made her head spin. Dar was a new man, finding delight once again in teaching. Barc hadn't once mentioned Charleston or gambling since the incident with the Irishwoman.

But it was her oldest nephew who had her the most puzzled. He was definitely a changed man this morning. And she would like to think it was Nathaniel's accident that had triggered the change. Cal had, after all, finally acknowledged that he was a doctor. Her gaze traveled from Cal to the young woman beside him. There was a glow on her cheeks, a sparkle in her eyes, that had not been there before.

Just then Cal muttered something, and Dulcie turned to him with a smile. Aunt Bessie's heart stopped. Dear heaven. She knew instinctively that her nephew and Dulcie Trenton had become lovers. Knew by the look that passed between them. A look that only lovers can share.

Chapter Twenty-One

"He's awake." Clara's voice rang through the hallways. "Hurry, everybody. Nathaniel's awake."

Solemn little Clara had surprised everyone by appointing herself guardian, keeping vigil by Nathaniel's bedside while he lay, heavily sedated.

Because Cal had anticipated the little boy's pain, he had administered sleeping powders for several days and nights, until the worst of the crisis had passed.

"So," Cal said, pulling up a chair beside the bed, "you've finally decided to join the living."

"I thought I was going to die." Nathaniel's voice was little more than a whisper as he recalled the desperation he'd felt when his cries had gone unanswered.

"You had us pretty scared." Dulcie caught his hand and squeezed it hard, feeling a great welling of love for this tough little boy. "But Cal says you're going to be just fine."

Nathaniel glanced around at the smiling faces and wondered why everyone was so happy when he felt so miserably ashamed.

"I'm sorry about the team," he whispered. "Did the horses hurt themselves?"

"They're fine," Barc assured him.

"And the wagon," the little boy added. "I know it got smashed."

"Barc and I have already repaired it," Dar said gently.

"I guess I let you down." Nathaniel couldn't meet Cal's eyes. "I let the team go too fast, and the next thing I knew, I was flying through the air. I was just showing off. I deserved to get hurt."

"You listen to me, son," Cal said sternly. "What happened to you was an accident. Accidents don't happen because we deserve some kind of punishment. They just happen. In your case, you had no way of knowing about the storm that was blowing up somewhere over the ocean. And no way of knowing the wind would shift and bring it to our shore. We're just thankful you survived. And now that you have, you have a bigger chore ahead of you."

"What is it?" Nathaniel was ready to do anything to make amends.

"You're going to have to be very brave. Your leg was badly injured. It's going to take a great deal of pain and a great deal of courage to make it work the way it once did. It will mean walking even when you think you can't take another step. And flexing your knee when every movement makes you want to cry. And it means watching the others outrun you, even when you're running as fast as you can. Think you're up to all that?"

Nathaniel swallowed. Right now he would walk through burning coals, rather than risk losing Cal's respect. "Yes, sir."

"Good boy. For a few more days you'll have to rest. As soon as you're able to leave that bed, we'll get started." Cal squeezed his shoulder, then stepped back and allowed the women and children to surge closer.

They pounced on the opportunity, clutching Nathaniel's hand, kissing his cheek, just to assure themselves he was really back with them and ready to resume his life. And though he pretended to merely tolerate such behavior, he was secretly delighted by the show of affection. Especially when it came from Clara.

"This is excellent venison, Robert." Aunt Bessie touched her linen napkin to her lips.

"Thank you, Miss Bessie." He poured tea and placed the china cup beside her plate, then did the same for Fiona and Dulcie. "If there's nothing more you need, I shall see to young Nathaniel's dinner."

In the kitchen he carved two slabs of juicy venison and set them on a plate with a mound of whipped potatoes, pouring rich gravy over all. He added biscuits, filled a crystal tumbler with milk and included a smaller plate with three large cookies. Placing everything on a silver tray, he climbed the stairs to Nathaniel's room.

As he paused outside the door, he recognized the sound of crying. Great choking sobs that signaled pain. He waited, knowing the boy's pride would be hurt if he should be caught giving in to any weakness.

When the sobbing subsided, Robert made a great show of rattling his tray before knocking.

"Who...who is it?" called Nathaniel.

"I have your dinner." Robert pushed open the door and busied himself lowering the tray to the bedside table, taking care not to glance at the boy who was wiping his tears on his sleeve. That done, Robert removed a linen napkin and handed it to the boy.

"It...looks good, Robert. But I'm not very hungry."

"I know it is difficult to work up an appetite when you are forced to lie in bed all day," the man said as he folded down the covers and smoothed them. "But you must build up your strength for what is to come."

He cut the meat into small pieces and broke open a steaming biscuit. Setting the plate in front of the boy, he crossed to the window and peered out, deliberately keeping his back to Nathaniel. He hoped the boy would at least try a few bites. Perhaps if he stayed and engaged him in conversation . . .

"The crops are looking very healthy. I have an idea the harvest will be successful enough to show a profit for the first time since the war."

Nathaniel said nothing as he picked at his food.

"I remember the first year I arrived." Robert looked out over fields arranged in perfect symmetry. "Mr. Cal's father, God rest his soul, offered me a refuge when my small boat arrived on his shore. He suggested I might like to work in the kitchens so that I could be with my wife and young sons. I was grateful of course, because the field hands had to walk such distances—"

"Sons?" Nathaniel interrupted. "You have sons?"

Robert was pleased he'd found a way to spark Nathaniel's interest. It was the first he'd seen in the boy in days. He turned slowly.

"I had three sons. Robert, Thomas and Joseph."

"Where are they now? How come I've never seen them?"

Robert's voice trembled for just a moment, before he brought it under control. "Robert and Thomas died in the war. Joseph would be thirteen, almost a man now. He is . . . safe somewhere in the North, according to his last message."

"But why? Why doesn't he live here with you?" Nathaniel thought about his own father and how much he missed him. "If I knew where my father was living, nothing could keep me from him. Not even the fact that I can't walk."

Robert smiled, but the sadness showed in his eyes. "It was not safe for Joseph to remain here."

"But why? The war is finally over."

"Yes, but there are still many who cannot accept the fact that my son is a free man. Free to live and work as he pleases." Robert took a seat beside the bed. "There are a lot of reasons the war was fought. But that is the only reason that matters to me. You see, I was born a free man on a small island in the Caribbean. But when I came to this land, I lost my heart to the daughter of a slave. It was her greatest shame, and when our first son was born, she made me promise he would be free, as I had been."

"Did she run away with you?"

Robert nodded. "We ran. There were many who would have killed us. But the Jermains took us in and made us welcome. And gave us back our dignity. They made it clear I could remain here for as long as I chose, sharing the work and the rewards, or I was free to leave."

"You work here for a wage?"

Robert nodded.

"Then why don't you take your money and go North to live with your son?"

"This is my home. My wife and two sons are buried here, along with the Jermains and their ancestors. This island reminds me of the childhood home I left. I can no more leave it than I can leave this skin. I would shrivel and die in the snow and cold of the North."

"Will Joseph ever come home to live with you?" Without realizing it, Nathaniel bit into the biscuit and began to eat the meat and potatoes.

Robert watched approvingly. "Joseph will return when I decide, along with Miss Bessie and Mr. Cal, that it is safe."

"Do they know where he is?"

Robert nodded and took the empty plate from the little boy's hands. He placed the smaller plate of cookies before him and handed him the glass of milk.

"It was Mr. Cal who found a safe place for Joseph. A place where he can receive an education while he is shielded from the violence. Had it not been for Mr. Cal's kindness, I would surely have lost him, too, for though he is very brave, he is also very young and foolish, and was determined to follow his brothers to war." Robert sighed. "Very soon now he will be back where he belongs. With a father who loves him. And a family that will welcome him as an equal, with affection and respect."

"I'm glad." Nathaniel bit into the first cookie and his eyes rounded. "Robert, these are just like my mama's sweettooth Sammies."

"Are they?" Robert chuckled, a rich, warm sound unlike anything Nathaniel had ever heard before.

"I never knew what to call them. But they were Joseph's favorites. That was why I made them for you."

Outside the door, Dulcie tiptoed away. She hadn't meant to eavesdrop. But now that she had, she knew one more reason that she loved Cal Jermain. Though he would never admit it, he shared her weakness for strays.

"He's coming," both Emily and Belle said excitedly.

They took their places at the table and joined the others in watching the door.

Aunt Bessie sat at the head of the table, wearing one of her best gowns for the occasion. The men wore their black suits and white shirts, while the women and children were in brightly colored, freshly ironed gowns. Robert stood stiffly in the doorway, his black pants and crisp white shirt starched and pressed to perfection.

The footfalls were so faint they would not have heard them if they hadn't been listening for them.

Robert's face was wreathed in smiles as he held open the door and intoned, "Good evening, Nat. We're so happy you could join us."

Nathaniel removed his arm from around Clara's shoulders and stood alone. Sensing his need to walk the last few steps by himself, the little girl made her way to the table and waited with the others.

He moved slowly, painfully, to his chair. On his face was a look of extreme concentration. By the time he was seated, sweat beaded his forehead and he was gritting his teeth. He sank down gratefully and allowed Robert to slide his chair closer to the table. Beside him, Clara squeezed his hand.

"Oh, Nat." Dulcie's smile was positively radiant. "It feels so good to have our whole family together again. Doesn't it, Cal?"

Cal nodded, wondering if she knew what she'd just said. Somehow this widely divergent group had become family. "You've made great progress, Nat," he said gravely.

Despite his pain, the boy smiled and felt a surge of pride. He was walking. Maybe more like a baby than a man, but he was walking. And every day he grew a little bit stronger. Now if only he could find a way to convince the Jermains and Dulcie that all of them ought to stay here forever.

"In honor of this happy occasion," Robert announced as he carried in the first tray, "I prepared duck with peach glaze and sweet potatoes and garden vegetables."

Aunt Bessie murmured her appreciation as she took the first helping and spooned it onto Nathaniel's plate.

"So much," Dulcie protested. "Are you sure you can eat all that, Nat?"

"Nonsense. He's a growing boy," Aunt Bessie insisted as she took a second portion for herself.

When all their plates were filled, Dulcie said, "I think Nat should lead us in prayer."

Aunt Bessie caught the little boy's hand in hers and reached her other hand to little Emily. Slowly the others followed suit around the table. Dulcie's hand was engulfed in Cal's, while her other hand closed around Belle's.

Dulcie studied the smiling faces, the glowing eyes, as Nathaniel began. "Father, I thank You for looking out for me when I forget to look out for myself. And for sending special people into my life to fill up all the empty places. And thank You for Robert's good cooking. Maybe You could send his son home soon to enjoy it with us."

For a moment no one spoke. Robert turned his face away, but not before Cal saw him wipe tears from his eyes.

As they began to eat, the little boy's words kept playing through Cal's mind. Special people, who fill up all the empty places. Wasn't that what Dulcie and her strange little band had done? It certainly hadn't been planned. Or had it? Though he, like his aunt, had stopped believing in divine intervention, this hardly seemed like an accident.

He glanced at his brothers and thought how drastically all their lives had changed. His lips curved, and he found himself wondering what words of wisdom Dulcie's father would have had for this occasion.

"That'll do it," Barc hollered as he and Dar set the last log in place.

Wiping sweat from their brows, the three brothers stood back to survey their handiwork. As planned, the barn was twice the size of the old one, with a second story for safe, dry storage of crops. The structure had been reinforced with thick beams to withstand the strongest of winds. The logs would be sealed with hot pitch to prevent leakage during rainstorms.

The women and children, returning from the fields in a wagon driven by Robert, stopped to admire it.

"Not bad," Dulcie declared, "for a doctor, a lawyer and a headmaster."

The three men threw back their heads and laughed, and she thought again how wonderful it was to see these three, formerly solemn, men be so happy and at ease with each other.

"And not a day too soon," Cal said, glancing at the clouds that billowed far out at sea. "We're going to need every available hand to harvest our crops before that storm reaches us."

The women and children jumped down from the wagon and walked into the cool barn, breathing in the fresh scent of newly scattered hay. Robert unhitched the team and led the horses to their stalls. Cal and his brothers set ladders in place to reach the upper level.

"You'd better prepare enough food for several days, Robert," Cal called from his perch high above them. "You won't have time to cook if you're going to lend a hand in the fields."

"I started this morning, Mr. Cal." The older man picked up an empty bucket and started toward the well.

"Who'll stay with Nathaniel?" Dulcie asked.

"Miss Bessie assured me she'll take good care of young Nat," Robert said before he strolled away.

At the mention of Nathaniel, Clara scampered off to see him.

"I don't know about the rest of you," Barc said, "but I'm looking forward to a cool bath before dinner." He arched a brow at Fiona. "Or better yet, how about taking a swim?"

He held out his hand and little Emily and Belle caught it, dragging a laughing Fiona with them.

"Dar?" he asked.

"Only if Starlight will accompany me."

"I'd like that," the girl answered shyly.

Dar waited until Starlight caught up with him.

"Cal?" they called.

Seated high in the rafters, Cal shook his head. "Not just yet. I have a little unfinished business to see to."

"How about you, Dulcie?" her friends asked.

She shook her head, disappointed that Cal seemed to be ignoring her. "Go ahead without me."

As soon as they scampered off toward the shore, she glanced upward, frowning.

"Well? What are you waiting for?" Cal patted the clean fresh hay strewn about the upper floor.

Dulcie stared at him, uncomprehending. Then, as his meaning dawned, she broke into peals of laughter. "Cal Jermain. I thought you had some unfinished business."

"I do, Miss Trenton." He joined in the laughter. "And the sooner you get up here and into my arms, the sooner I'll get to it."

"I suggest you retire early this evening," Aunt Bessie said as they assembled in the parlor after dinner. "The next few days in the fields will be long and tiring. As I recall, harvest time taxes the muscles far more than planting time."

Fiona groaned. "I'd thought the worst was behind us."

"We'll give you the easy crops," Barc assured her, "like the tomatoes and corn. And we'll take the harder ones, like potatoes and sorghum."

"You're much too good to us," Fiona said dryly.

Barc merely grinned. He seemed to be doing a lot of that lately whenever he looked at her. And his glances always brought an answering bloom to her cheeks.

Robert entered with a tray of coffee and desserts, and a tumbler of spirits for Aunt Bessie.

Dar gathered Starlight and the children around his chair in the corner. "Just one story," he announced as he drew the lantern close to the book, "and then it's off to bed. We'll have to be up by dawn and out in the fields if we hope to take a break during the hottest part of the day."

He adjusted the wire rims of his spectacles around each ear as he explained, "This is a fable. That means the story has a lesson to teach us. It's about a sailor who finds himself shipwrecked at sea and has only the stars to guide him. But one night the clouds block his view of the stars, and he becomes hopelessly lost. And so he journeys to a distant—"

He stopped in midsentence to stare at Starlight, who had bolted to her feet. From her mouth came an eerie, keening cry that bore no resemblance to anything human. Her eyes glazed over, and she seemed unaware of anything except the terror locked inside her.

While the Jermains looked on helplessly, Dulcie and Fiona hurried across the room to soothe and comfort the girl. Fiona calmed the children, while Dulcie gathered Starlight into her arms, holding her tightly until the terror passed.

When at last Starlight came out of her trance, she became aware of the others watching her in stunned silence. This had happened so many times before she would have chosen to ignore it as she always did, except for one thing. She could read the utter confusion in Dar's eyes.

She thought of his humble confession to her and how much it must have cost him that night.

"Come on, Starlight," Dulcie whispered. "I'll see you to your room."

The young woman shook her head. Turning toward Dar, she said in a halting voice, "You all have a right to know why I have spells."

Thunderstruck, Dulcie glanced at Fiona. The Irish-woman arched a brow in surprise, but held her silence. Dulcie squeezed Starlight's hand, prepared to help her through this terrifying narrative. But the young woman waved her away.

In a voice that trembled with emotion Starlight said, "My papa was a sharecropper. When he went off to join the attack on Fort Sumter, he left my mama and my two sisters and me to work the fields until he returned. I remember Papa kissing each of us and telling us the war wouldn't last a month." Her voice nearly broke, but she managed to say, "That was the last time I saw him.

"It was my birthday." Her voice was little more than a whisper now. "I had just turned thirteen the day the soldiers came. Mama took up Papa's rifle and ordered me to hide in the well. She said that no matter what I heard, I was not to show myself."

The others in the room had gone so quiet it was as if they were not even breathing. Robert stood by the door, the tray in his hand forgotten. Cal had gotten to his feet earlier and stood rooted to a spot by the window. Aunt Bessie sat stiffly in her chair.

"I heard the rifle fire and thought Mama had driven off the soldiers. But then I heard my mama's cries, and those of my two older sisters, and I knew..." She took a deep breath and forced herself to go on. "The cries went on all day. By nighttime, there were only a few moans, but I knew they were still alive. And by the sounds of the men's laughter, I knew they were still there... hurting them. Then I smelled fire, and the sky was lit by flames. And I knew the soldiers had burned our little house. I cried and cried, wondering if my mama and sisters were inside.

"I cried until I finally fell asleep. When I awoke, it was raining, and I couldn't tell if it was day or night. But then, when the rain stopped, I saw the stars and I knew it was night. And still I waited, hoping Mama would tell me it was safe to leave the well. But there was only silence. And I was afraid. So afraid. I stayed there two more days and nights, and each time the stars came out, I recited some words my papa had taught me." In a little-girl voice she recited, "'Star light, star bright, first star I see tonight. Wish I may, wish I might, have the wish I wish tonight...' And I wished for only one thing."

She swallowed several times, and the others in the room were certain her story was finished. But she surprised them, and herself, by lifting her head and saying, "Then one night, I heard Mama's voice calling me. Telling me there was something I had to do. So I climbed out of the well and found—" her face contorted, and they could see in her eyes the carnage she'd witnessed "—what was left of my mama and my sisters. I knew which one was my mama by this." She held up the locket she wore around her neck. "It was a wedding gift from Papa to Mama. Inside there's a picture of them."

Starlight twisted her hands together and looked down at the floor. "I knew why my mama called me. There was something I needed to do. I had no tools to bury my mama and sisters, so I lowered their bodies into the well. And then I saw the soldiers. Far across the fields, heading toward another cabin, to hurt more helpless women and children. And I knew I ought to go after them. But, instead, I ran. Like a coward. And I kept on running until Dulcie found me. But by then I couldn't remember my name. So I told her she could call me Starlight. Sometimes...sometimes I start to remember, but then that awful feeling comes over me again and...by the time I wake up, I can't remember anything, except the emptiness...and the starlight."

Tears streamed down Aunt Bessie's cheeks. Cal clenched his hand at his side and felt a terrible, wrenching fury. He watched helplessly as his younger brother made his way to the young woman's side.

"Don't try to remember," Dar said softly. "It's too painful. Just let it go. Let it all go."

"But don't you see?" she cried. Her face was twisted in anguish. "I was such a coward. I hid, while my mother and sisters were..."

Dar wrapped his arms around her and gathered her close, burying her face against his chest, awkwardly patting her hair. "Your mother was able to go to her death knowing one of her children survived. That was enough for her."

"But her voice..."

"She was calling you out of the well. But she wasn't calling you to vengeance. She was calling you to live, Starlight."

She lifted her tearstained face. "Do you really believe that?"

He framed her face with his hands and murmured, "I know it. She guided your feet to Dulcie's home. And then brought all of you to the shelter of our shores. It's what any mother would do."

"But I bring shame to my family. I don't even have a name."

"You have a beautiful name." He wiped her tears with his thumbs, then caught her hand and whispered, "Come on. I'll walk you to your room. And if you'd like, I'll sleep outside your door all night just so you'll feel safe."

"You'd do that?"

He led her toward the stairs. His voice drifted back to the others. "I'd do anything for you, Starlight. Anything."

* * *

It was a somber group that made its way upstairs a short time later. Starlight's recitation had brought back all the horrors of the war. Still, in a strange way, it had brought healing, as well. For no matter what each of them had been forced to endure, they realized they were not alone.

As Dulcie led the children to their rooms, she spotted a blanket-clad figure curled up outside Starlight's closed door. Dar was as good as his word. The wounded young woman had found a fierce protector.

Chapter Twenty-Two

A merciless sun blazed in a cloudless sky. Not even a breath of air stirred the palmetto fronds.

Dulcie straightened and swatted at the gnats that stuck to her skin. She removed her wide-brimmed hat and fanned herself with it, but it gave her no relief. Jamming the hat back on her head, she lifted the basket bulging with corn, straining under the weight as she hauled it to the wagon, which was already filled to overflowing with heaping baskets.

At that same moment Cal arrived from the other direction carrying a sack of sweet potatoes over his shoulder.

"There's no more room," Dulcie said.

He dropped the sack and studied the profusion of vegetables. Despite the heat, he managed a smile. "Looks like we won't go hungry this winter."

Clara, Emily and Belle staggered up, each grasping an edge of an overflowing basket of corn.

"Well done." Cal caught it, relieving them of their burden.

"I'm thirsty," Emily complained.

"There's water under the wagon," Cal told her.

The three little girls crawled gratefully into the shade beneath the wagon and passed a dipper of water around until they were satisfied.

Cal touched a hand to Dulcie's cheek, noting the pale blue smudges beneath her eyes. "I should have insisted you get more sleep last night."

She gave him a throaty laugh. "As I recall, Mr. Jermain, we had more important things to do."

He smiled at the memory. He'd told himself he had merely gone to her room to console her after Starlight's emotional revelation. But the truth was, he'd gone there as much for his own consolation as hers. Starlight's story had moved him, and he realized once again how little he really knew about these women and children.

Perhaps, too, he'd hoped that Starlight's words might give Dulcie the courage to trust him with her own story. But, though their lovemaking had been gentle and he had remained with her throughout the night, she had revealed nothing more to him. He cautioned himself to be patient, remembering how long it had taken him to learn to trust. He would give her as much time as she needed. Somehow they would work it out.

He nodded toward the team. "Why don't you drive this wagon load to the barn? And take Fiona and Starlight and the girls along with you. It will be cool there, and by the time you've finished unloading, the worst of the day's heat should be behind you."

She brightened. "All right. Maybe Nathaniel will want to ride back here with us."

"Good idea. He's probably sick of looking at four walls by now and will be eager to escape."

"Not a chance," Dulcie said with a laugh. "Can you imagine how much attention he's been getting from your aunt? He may learn to like it too much to ever give it up."

Not to mention Aunt Bessie, Cal thought as he walked away. He'd feared that his aunt might never again find purpose or happiness. But the arrival of the women and children on their island had given her new life. She had even brought her entire collection of crystal figurines to Nathaniel's room for his entertainment. Considering how jealously she had guarded that collection, it was an amazingly unselfish act.

He bent once more to his task, joining his brothers and Robert in the harvesting of sweet potatoes.

Dulcie climbed atop the wagon seat and waited with the three little girls until Fiona and Starlight made their way to the wagon, dragging baskets heaped with more ripe vegetables.

"Cal thought you might like to help me haul these to the barn," she said.

The two young women, eager to escape the broiling sun, climbed aboard.

"The first thing I'm going to do," Fiona said, fanning herself with her hat, "is pour a bucket of water over my head. I feel like I'm on fire."

"You are," Clara said, giggling and pointing to Fiona's red hair. "At least it looks like your hair is on fire. See?"

It was the first time anyone had ever heard the solemn little girl make a joke. They were so surprised they all burst into laughter.

"That reminds me of a song I learned in Ireland," Fiona said. "About a boy whose hair turned red after he set fires in the fields."

"Can you teach us?" Emily asked, clapping her hands.

Soon, with Fiona's coaching, they were all singing the funny lyrics at the top of their voices. By the time the wagon rolled into the yard and came to a halt at the well, they were laughing uproariously as they made up even sillier words to the song.

Dulcie felt her heart swell with love. Despite the hardships, these days spent on the Jermain island were among the happiest of her life. It had been a time of healing. A time of growing. And she had even begun to believe that all the bad things in their past were just that—in the past. She'd been wise to keep her own counsel and refuse to reveal her secret to Cal. It was beginning to look as though no one need ever know. Her future was indeed bright and shining.

She helped herself to a cool drink of water from the well, then climbed back onto the wagon seat. Lifting the reins, she looked down at the others, taking turns dumping buckets of water over their heads. "I'll drive the team to the barn," she said to them. "As soon as you've finished here, you can give me a hand unloading these baskets. Then we'll go inside and see if Nat would like to join us."

Fiona plunged her hands and face into a bucket of water and gave a long sigh of delight. "Aye. We'll be along in a minute, Dulcie."

Dulcie flicked the reins and the team headed toward the barn. Inside it was deliciously cool and dark. After the brilliance of the sunlight, it took her eyes a few moments to adjust.

As she climbed down from the wagon, she saw, too late, that she was not alone. She froze in terror. Before she could force herself into action, strong fingers closed around her throat, shutting off her breath. Though she clawed at the hands, she couldn't budge them. Stars danced in front of her eyes, and there was a strange buzzing in her head as she struggled for air. Just as she thought she would die, the hands loosened their grip. She stood, gasping, taking great gulps of air into her lungs.

The blunt muzzle of a rifle was rammed against her back.

A chilling voice from her past sliced like the blade of a knife. "I told you that you couldn't run far enough or fast enough to get away from me, woman. Now you and your little band are going to have to pay, and pay dearly, for what you did in Charleston."

Aunt Bessie sat in the chair beside Nathaniel's bed and watched with concern as he tried to make himself comfortable. He had insisted on climbing the stairs, saying Cal wanted him to exercise his injured leg. But the effort had cost him. Sweat beaded his brow. Pain etched his forehead, and he chewed his lower lip to keep from crying out.

In so many ways he reminded her of her oldest nephew. Cal had been a stubborn boy, determined to follow his own path. When her brother, Calhoun, had learned that his firstborn wanted to study medicine, he had been adamantly opposed, saying that, with Cal's fine mind, he ought to follow his father into the law. Being so close to both of them, she understood the real battle. Her brother didn't want anything to come between himself and his son. And he saw the long years of study at a prestigious Eastern medical school as divisive. Cal, on the other hand, reveled in the chance to put some distance between himself and his opinionated father. And more than anything, he wanted to be free of this tiny island, which had begun to feel like a prison to the headstrong young boy.

"Calhoun left some pain powders here in case you had need of them. Why don't I fix you one?" she coaxed.

Nathaniel shook his head. "I don't need one of those awful-tasting powders, Aunt Bessie. This will pass. I'll be fine."

Ignoring his protest, she stirred powder into a glass of water. That done, she held it to the boy's lips and said, "Just a couple of sips."

When the glass was half-empty, she picked up a fan and settled herself into the chair beside his bed. The boy was stubborn. Just like her nephew. But not nearly as stubborn as she.

Fiona, Starlight and the girls started toward the barn, still singing the silly lyrics of their song. They felt cooler now and much refreshed, ready to tackle the chore of unloading the wagon.

They shoved open the door and stepped inside the darkened barn, idly noting the empty wagon seat. As their eyes adjusted to the gloom, they glanced around for Dulcie.

Fiona tilted her head upward, peering toward the rafters. "Dulcie? Don't tell me you started without us."

"No," came a chilling voice from a nearby stall. "We waited for you."

A band of ragged men stepped out of the enclosure. In their midst was Dulcie, her hands pinned behind her, her lip bloody and beginning to swell.

"We wanted all of you to enjoy the little party we have planned," the man said as he gave Dulcie a vicious shove, propelling her forward where she landed sprawling on her hands and knees.

With a cry the women and children gathered around her and helped her to her feet. The men closed around them. In their hands were rifles, pointed at the children's heads.

The leader of this cruel band had long, dirty blond hair and an unkempt beard, and was wearing faded remnants of a Confederate uniform. His eyes glittered with a hatred that bordered on madness.

The other three men wore little more than rags. On their feet they'd tied strips of cloth.

"Looks like you found yourselves a rich plantation owner to take you in," the leader said as he studied the wagon loaded with the fruits of the harvest. He winked at his partners. "Now why should we have our fun out here in a barn when there's that fancy big house just waiting for us?"

He aimed the rifle menacingly. "Go on now, ladies. Show some manners. Invite us into your new home."

The children began to sob, and Starlight, unable to control her hysteria, fell into a trance. Fiona was busy trying to stem the blood from Dulcie's lip with the hem of her skirt, but Dulcie pushed her hand away, her mind racing. It was bad enough that they were in danger. But inside the house were an injured little boy and a helpless woman. They had to be shielded.

"You don't want to go in there," she said.

"And why not?"

"You'll . . . be seen. You're lucky you got this far without being spotted. If you leave this barn, someone on the island is bound to see you."

The leader threw back his head and roared with laughter. "This island is deserted except for the people who live in this house. And right now, all the men are out in the fields busy with the harvest. There's no one around to see us except an old woman."

"How would you know that?" Dulcie's heart nearly stopped.

"Because we're not stupid. We've been living by our wits for quite a while now," the leader boasted. "We've been watching ever since we spotted that boat you stole. We've sailed around the entire island just to make sure no one else lives here. And today, we saw all the men go out to the fields." His eyes glinted. "You couldn't have picked a better place for us to hide out for the winter. After we get rid of the men, we can take all the time in the world having our fun with the lot of you. And when we're tired of you, we'll just throw your bodies into the water. And no one will ever be the wiser.''

The children were sobbing hysterically now, and Fiona and Dulcie drew them close, trying in vain to comfort them.

"Hush now, Clara," Dulcie whispered. "Remember your faith. The Lord will provide."

The leader jammed his rifle into Dulcie's back. "That's right. He'll provide us with food and shelter for as long as it suits us. Now start moving toward the house. Anyone who doesn't move fast enough can die right here."

Dulcie and Fiona grabbed Starlight's and the little girls' hands and forced them to walk beside them toward the door. As they stepped into the brilliant sunshine, Dulcie swallowed back the tears that threatened. She must not allow herself to become paralyzed by fear. Not when so many depended on her.

Aunt Bessie's head came up, and she rubbed at her stiff shoulder. She must have been dreaming, for she thought she'd heard voices. She glanced at Nathaniel, sleeping fitfully on the bed. It was obvious his leg still pained him, but at least the powder had taken effect.

She eased herself from her chair and pressed a hand to the small of her back. Rain must be coming. The pain was always more pronounced before a storm.

She walked from the room and made her way along the hall toward the head of the stairs. As she descended, she heard the rumble of masculine voices. Unfamiliar masculine voices. One of them raised in anger.

She paused, experiencing a jumble of conflicting emotions. Her first thought was of the Yankees who had once violated this peaceful haven to burn and plunder. Though she was afraid, her sense of anger and outrage was even stronger. If she saw a Federal uniform, she would drive the scoundrels off, using nothing but her bare hands if necessary.

She strode down the last few steps and swept along the hallway toward the kitchen. As she rounded the corner, she caught sight of the women and children and, directly behind them, a rough-looking man in Confederate gray.

The fire in her eyes died and she gave a sigh of relief. "Oh, praise heaven. You are a Southern gentleman. I had feared for a moment you were one of those hated Yank—"

"Shut up, old woman." He waved the rifle and snarled, "First we want food. And damned plenty of it."

Aunt Bessie, seeing the tearful children and frightened women, stiffened her spine and glowered at him. "I will not permit such language in my home. Do you not see there are women and children present?"

"And don't you see who's holding the guns here?" He nodded toward one of his men, who moved forward and pressed the muzzle of his rifle against her throat.

Horrified, Dulcie stepped between them. "Don't hurt her. Can't you see she's confused?"

"Confused, am I?" Aunt Bessie went rigid with anger.

"Please, Aunt Bessie." Dulcie forced herself to turn away from the rifle, feeling the press of the cold steel against her back as she did. Bracing herself for a bullet that might come at any moment, she said softly, "Come and sit down, and don't argue with these men."

"Don't argue? In my own home?" Still protesting, the older woman allowed herself to be led to a straight-backed chair, where she gathered the children into her arms. The mere touch of them, frightened and trembling, filled her with a sense of quiet rage. No one had the right to harm these innocents. No one. But sensing the volatile hostility that might erupt at any moment, she swallowed back the angry words that rushed to her lips and became uncharacteristically silent.

"That's better." While his men held their rifles on the women and children, the leader began rummaging through the kitchen, helping himself to the slabs of turkey and biscuits that Robert had prepared before going to the fields.

"Food," he called as he tossed it to the others. The men were ravenous and gulped down the food without even tasting it.

"Get me something to drink!" the leader shouted at Dulcie.

When she didn't move quickly enough, he turned the rifle on the older woman and children. Fumbling nervously, she poured coffee from a pot that was sitting on the coals and brought it to him and his men.

"That's better," he muttered. "Don't forget who's giving the orders here. This gun says I am."

All the while, Starlight stood, her gaze fixed on the spots of light along one wall, caused by the sunlight pouring through the window.

"What's the matter with her?" one of the men asked.

"Probably touched in the head," the leader replied.

Aunt Bessie caught Starlight's hand and forced her into a chair beside her. The young woman sat without moving, her gaze still fixed on the light.

Without warning the leader suddenly threw his cup against the wall, where it shattered into a hundred pieces.

"I've had enough of this swill!" he shouted. "I want whiskey!"

He moved about the kitchen, tossing dishes out of his way in his haste to open drawers and cabinets. The sound of glass smashing on the floor made everyone wince, although Aunt Bessie sat very still. The only evidence of emotion was the glint in her eyes.

The leader strode to the pantry and began heaving crates and baskets, jars and bottles to the floor until he spied the crystal decanter of whiskey.

He returned to the kitchen and filled four glasses to the brim.

Seeing the look of outrage on Aunt Bessie's face, he grinned and slid the decanter across the table. "Help yourself, old woman. But don't take too much. It's been a long time since we've enjoyed fine whiskey. And such an assortment of women, if you get my meaning."

Forcing herself not to show the revulsion she felt, Aunt Bessie poured herself a stiff drink. "I have the feeling that you did not just happen upon our island. Why did you seek us out?"

The leader gave a cold, mirthless laugh. "Why don't you ask the pretty little lady here? Maybe she'd like to tell you how she shot our captain dead."

Aunt Bessie's hand paused in midair. "Dulcie? What is this man saying? Did you actually kill one of our fine Confederate officers?"

At once the children burst into renewed sobbing. They had carried the secret for so long. And now, hearing it spoken aloud, they understood clearly just how serious Dulcie's crime was. And theirs, as her accomplices.

Dulcie struggled to control the emotions that twisted inside her. Rage against the helplessness she felt at allowing these men to once again threaten all those she loved. Regret that these innocents would all be forced to pay for her crime. A slow, simmering fury at her carelessness. Hadn't she known, from the first time a boat was spotted offshore, that she would be hunted down and caught? But she had stayed. Stayed out of love for a man who would be forced to condemn her now that the truth was known.

At last she found her voice. It was strong and sure. "Yes. I shot his captain. And my only regret is that I didn't manage to kill the rest of his company, as well."

As soon as the words were out of her mouth, she felt the blow from a rifle. Jagged edges of pain crashed through her brain. A cry escaped her lips as she sank to the floor. And then she was swallowed up by merciful darkness.

Nathaniel awoke and struggled to remember where he was. The sleeping powder always had that effect. It was like swimming through layers of seaweed, always close to the water's surface but never able to break free. Each time he got close, he would sink beneath the slippery mass and begin the struggle again.

Sweat beaded his forehead, and he found himself fighting old demons. It was the powder, he told himself as he felt panic begin to slice through him. He imagined he was back in Dulcie's house, hearing again the voices of the cruel soldiers.

A man's laughter drifted up the stairs, and he shivered violently. His eyes opened and he tried to focus. This wasn't Dulcie's house. It was Cal's. He glanced at the chair beside the bed. Aunt Bessie had been sitting there when he'd fallen asleep. Her fan was still there on the bedside table. But just as he began to relax, he heard the rumble of men's voices, followed by a woman's cry, then a burst of raucous laughter. His blood chilled.

He wasn't imagining it. The soldiers were here. In Cal's house. And the cry had been Dulcie's.

He sat up and felt the room spin. He held on to the edge of the mattress until everything came into focus. Then, placing both feet on the floor, he forced himself to stand. Pain ripped through him, and he dropped to the floor.

Gripping the foot of the bed for support, he pulled himself up and began to walk, slowly, painfully, toward the door.

The voices sounded louder now, and he realized they were directly below him. Changing direction, he retreated and crossed his room to the balcony door. When he eased himself out, he stared at the ground far below. Such a long way to jump. But he had to. For Dulcie's sake.

He prayed he wouldn't faint when he landed.

Chapter Twenty-Three

Aunt Bessie and Fiona worked feverishly to revive Dulcie. The side of her face was badly swollen, and blood trickled from a cut over her eye. But after applying wet cloths to her face and throat, they managed to bring her around.

She sat stiffly in a chair, her eyes focused unblinkingly on the leader of these cutthroats.

Aunt Bessie watched shrewdly as the men gulped down huge quantities of liquor. It seemed a shame to waste some of the finest aged whiskey in the land. It was meant to be sipped, to be held on the tongue and savored before sliding down the throat. But it was, after all, being used for a purpose.

She knew she was taking a calculated risk by not smashing the decanter. They could become even more savage when drunk. Or they could, as she hoped, become careless, allowing their captives to overpower them.

"I want the red-haired woman," one of the men said as he downed his drink. He'd been watching Fiona as she tended her fallen friend.

She shivered at his words and shot him a look of fury.

"You can have her, with my compliments." The leader's words were slightly slurred. He nodded his head in Dulcie's direction. "I'm going to take the captain's killer first. But only for revenge. What I'm really going to enjoy is the little girls. I've always had a fondness for little girls."

Aunt Bessie covered her mouth with her hands, but not before her gasp of horror escaped her lips.

"What's the matter, old woman? Have we shocked you?"

"Since the war, I thought I was beyond shock." She brought her glass to her lips and realized her hand was trembling. She sipped the whiskey and felt it light a fire in her stomach. With every word out of this man's mouth, she felt her anger growing.

"Tell me." She kept her tone conversational. "What brought you to Miss Trenton's door?"

"Hunger. But when we got a look at all this fine flesh she was hiding, our captain suggested we stay awhile and indulge ourselves. After all, we'd given a lot of years to our country. The least our countrymen, and women," he added with a sneer, "can do is pay us back for the sacrifices we made."

Aunt Bessie's hand tightened around the glass until she feared it might shatter. Forcing herself to uncurl her fingers, she said, "And Miss Trenton refused to...give in to your demands?"

"The damned fool held a gun on us while the women and children ran. We torched her house and all her outbuildings, and then, when we found her and the others hiding in a shed, we thought we'd won. But when we forced open the door, she fired and the captain fell dead. The rest of us had to take cover. But I promised her then we'd keep on searching until we found her. And when we did, she'd pay for what she did." He puffed himself up and said, "She knew that if I turned her in to the army, they'd shoot her for killing a Confederate officer. So I'm just saving everybody time by doing it myself. And hell, why not get a little pleasure out of it before I kill her?''

"I hardly think your fellow soldiers would sanction your attack upon helpless women and children."

His eyes glittered with malice. "It would be her word against ours."

Aunt Bessie watched as he reached for the decanter and refilled his glass before sliding it toward the others. "Drink up," he said. "And then the fun will begin."

She turned to glance at Dulcie, dazed, bloody, but still ready to fight for those she loved. Dear heaven. How the young woman must have suffered. And suffered still.

She studied the dull-eyed men who sat at her table and drank her whiskey. "Have you not heard that the war is over? Why have you not returned to your homes?"

"What homes? While we were off fighting, our homes were burned, our families scattered. We have no homes to return to. And our captain said the war needn't ever be over. We'll keep it going as long as there's breath in us."

"Against your own helpless people?"

"Against anybody who has what we want."

Aunt Bessie lifted her glass and drained it, then set the glass down carefully. "I would like to know your name."

"Everel Bruel. But my men call me Evil." He laughed. "It suits me, don't you think?"

She got to her feet, standing straight and tall. In her most commanding tone she said, "Everel Bruel, you have managed to do what no one else could have ever done."

His mouth curved into a cruel smile of anticipation, but her next words had his jaw dropping.

"You have made me ashamed of my heritage. You bring shame to that once proud uniform you wear. And shame to the woman who bore you."

His face darkened at the vehemence of her words. "How dare—"

Her voice rose. "And you shame the land you pretend to love. If God is truly in His heaven, you shall not live to see the light of another day. For you are not a man, and even less than an animal. And you do not deserve the sweetness of life."

His arm swung out in an arc, and his palm connected with her cheek, sending her staggering to her knees. He lifted his rifle, intent upon silencing her forever.

In that instant Dulcie reached into her pocket and withdrew the pistol Cal had given her. Though it was only one weapon against many and she'd intended to save it as a last resort, she now had no choice.

As she took aim, Everel saw her out of the corner of his eye and swung toward her, firing as he did. The bullet would have slammed into her had she not dropped to the floor. She hit her head with such force she lay, stunned and reeling. Her pistol fell to the floor.

All his anger, all his pent-up vengeance, was now directed against the woman who had dared to draw a gun on him. He advanced on Dulcie as she lay bleeding. "No female threatens me."

"Stop!" Fiona shouted as she leaped at him. Though she had no weapon, she could not stand by helplessly and watch her friend die.

Surprised, the man swung his rifle at her and she latched on to his arm with both hands and sank her teeth into it. He let out a scream of pain, dropping his weapon.

The other three men rushed to his defense.

But they weren't counting on the children. Though their eyes were clouded with tears, the three little girls attacked with feet and fists and teeth, causing mass confusion.

Clara picked up the blackened coffeepot and hurled it at one of the men, causing him to shriek with pain as the scalding liquid momentarily blinded him. While he rubbed at his eyes, she tugged his rifle free and tossed it across the room.

Emily and Belle slipped between the legs of the scuffling men and managed to evade capture. Then, instead of retreating, they attacked with the only weapons they could find. Emily wielded the jagged neck of a broken jar like a knife, laying open one soldier's thigh. Belle grabbed the fire tongs and pulled a burning ember from the fire, dropping it on another soldier's rag-covered foot. His screams of pain and rage filled the kitchen.

Aunt Bessie managed to pick up one of the discarded rifles and charged into the wild melee like an avenging angel. She fired off two quick shots, both of which found their marks. Two of the soldiers dropped to the floor, mortally wounded. But as she looked around for another victim, she heard the report of a rifle and felt something hot sear her flesh. The gun slipped from her hand. She staggered backward, and as she fell to her knees, she pressed her fingers to her shoulder. They came away smeared with blood.

At the sound of her cry, the fighting ended as abruptly as it had begun. Fiona and the children raced to her side and watched helplessly as she sank onto the floor in a faint.

"Oh, no!" Clara cried. "Is she dead?"

Fiona felt for a pulse, then shook her head. "No. But she's losing a great deal of blood. We'll have to—"

"Get away from her," Everel snarled. In his hands was his rifle.

Shocked, the women and children backed away and watched as he tossed a rifle to his remaining companion.

"If any of them move," he commanded, "shoot them. As for me," he said through gritted teeth, "I'll do what I came here to do." He caught Dulcie by the front of her gown and dragged her to her feet. "And when I'm through with this one," he said to his grinning partner, "you can have what's left of her before I kill her."

Cal looked up to see the team heading toward him at breakneck speed. But instead of moving in a straight line between the rows of vegetables, they were hauling the loaded wagon at crazy angles, flattening crops as they thundered forward.

"What in the hell...?" There was no sign of the women. Only Nathaniel, doubled over on the hard wooden seat, whipping the team like a madman.

"Whoa there!" Cal shouted, grasping the reins as the team came abreast of him and his brothers. It took all his strength to settle the team and bring it to a halt.

The horses' mouths were flecked with foam, their ears flattened in fear.

He stared at the boy in anger and disbelief. "What do you think you're—"

"It's Dulcie and the others—" Nathaniel began, but Barc cut him off with an exclamation.

"My God, Cal! Look at his leg."

Blood oozed through the dressings, which were now dirty and missing in places, revealing torn flesh. It was a wonder the boy was still alert. The pain had to be excruciating.

"What happened?" Cal demanded.

"I had to jump from the balcony," the boy said, struggling to remain conscious. "The soldiers are there. And they're going to kill her and the others."

"Soldiers? What soldiers?"

"Confederate soldiers!" Nathaniel cried. "Hurry. Please."

"Why would Confederate soldiers want to harm one of their own?"

Nathaniel was crying now, as much in frustration as in pain. "Dulcie shot their captain. In Charleston. He was going to hurt us. And now they've come for revenge. Hurry, Cal, please, before it's too late."

Cal and his brothers climbed onto the wagon. Robert caught the little boy in his arms and lay him in the back amid the pile of vegetables, where he tore his shirt into strips to stem the flow of blood.

As the wagon moved out with all the speed the team could muster, Cal experienced a fear unlike anything he'd ever known. Even on the field of battle, with the sound of gunfire and the cries of the wounded all around him, he had been prepared to calmly accept death. But the thought of Dulcie at the hands of avenging deserters filled him with sheer terror.

These men would be desperate. And that made them doubly dangerous.

He whispered a prayer that he would make it in time.

Fiona and the children were herded into a corner of the kitchen, where the lone soldier could keep an eye on them and still watch the anticipated action.

Aunt Bessie lay on the floor, blood spilling from the wound to her shoulder.

Starlight had not moved. Even during the wild brawl, while the others had fought for their lives, she had remained in her trance, sinking deeper and deeper into that secret place in her mind.

Dulcie gritted her teeth against the fear and pain as her attacker dragged her close. The sound of her gown being torn from her shoulders was loud in the quiet room.

The remnants of tattered gown fell to the floor, and she stood before him in chemise and petticoat, head lowered, hands clenched at her sides in an attitude of defeat. The children began to whimper and cry. Their cries suddenly strengthened her resolve, and though her mind was still befuddled, she resumed her struggles.

Everel's fetid breath assaulted her nostrils as he laughed at her feeble attempts to defend herself. "I've been hardened by years of fighting, woman. Do you really think you can stop me?"

"I won't give up until I'm dead. So be warned. You'll have to kill me first. I will never let you take me." Without her pistol she was reduced to ineffective kicks and bites, which only inflamed her attacker more.

His laughter faded as her booted foot connected with his groin. Suddenly his eyes took on the feral gleam of a wild predator as he brought the butt of his rifle against her temple.

With a cry she dropped to her knees. As she shook her head to clear it, she felt the cold muzzle of his rifle pressed to her chest.

"I've changed my mind. I don't need you, woman. You've been nothing but trouble for me and my men from the first day we met you. Now you're going to pay for killing my captain. And for denying me my pleasure." He gave a smile of triumph as his finger closed over the trigger. "And when you're gone, I'll have all these sweet little things for my very own pleasure. I'll start with the youngest one there and work my way through the other two—"

The sound of a gunshot reverberated through the kitchen, startling everyone into sudden, shocked silence.

Dulcie watched as Everel's eyes went wide with surprise. His attention shifted from Dulcie to the figure facing him across the room, and he turned and aimed the rifle at Starlight, who was holding Dulcie's discarded pistol. The vacant look was gone from her eyes. In its place was a chilling look of determination.

"So," he said with mocking laughter. "The crazy one thinks she's found her courage. You'd better put that gun down before you hurt yourself, fool."

"My name…" Her voice trembled, not with fear but with righteous anger. "My name is Laura Garland. And I do this for my mother and my sisters, who died cruel deaths at the hands of a monster like you. You have harmed your last woman, Everel Bruel."

A second shot rang out. Everel's body seemed to jerk upward before it sagged. His look of surprise slowly changed to one of anger, then pain. Blood spurted from a gaping hole in his chest, spilling down his ragged uniform in ever-widening circles. His rifle slipped from his hands, and Dulcie managed to snatch it up before darting out of the way as he fell to the floor.

She saw the other soldier take aim at Starlight, who, unaware of the danger, was still staring at the body of the man she had shot. There was no time to call out a warning as Dulcie fired. The soldier fell, clutching his chest, just as Cal and his brothers burst through the door.

"Dear God!" Cal cried as he took in the scene. The kitchen resembled a battlefield, with bodies everywhere and broken dishes and overturned furniture.

The room erupted into bedlam.

The children were alternating between sobs and wild-eyed screams of terror. Cal recognized the signs of hysteria as they clung tightly to Fiona and Starlight.

Cal knelt beside each ragged soldier to check for a pulse. Finding none, he hurried to kneel beside his aunt's still figure. Barc and Dar were already on either side of her, working to stem the flow of blood.

"How serious is the wound?" Cal demanded.

"Her pulse is strong and steady," Barc assured him.

Cal examined the wound and located the torn flesh where the bullet had entered and exited. "It's clean," he announced. "We'll disinfect it and apply clean dressings. She should be as good as new in a few days. Let's carry her to her room."

"I'm not some helpless old woman. I can walk," she protested.

"Not this time," Cal said firmly.

With all three brothers helping, Aunt Bessie was taken upstairs and made comfortable.

Returning to the kitchen, Cal looked around for Dulcie, surprised that she was not in the middle of the confusion. Though the others were weeping and embracing, she continued standing stiffly, the rifle at her shoulder, all her attention focused on the bodies that littered the floor.

Cal approached her. "They're dead, Dulcie. You're safe now."

She backed away from him, her eyes wide with shock.

"They can't hurt you, Dulcie. Give me the rifle." He reached out, but she snatched it away and continued backing up.

"You don't understand," she said in a voice choked with emotion. "They'll come back. They always do. And I have to stay alert. I have to be strong..."

"Oh, my darling," he said softly. "You've had to be strong for such a long time now. But it's over. Truly over. They're dead. And they'll never hurt you or your loved ones again. I promise you."

"You... promise?" She blinked and seemed to be struggling with inner demons. "But why would you care about me?"

"Dulcie—" he began, but she cut him off.

"How can you ever forgive me? It was my fault that these monsters came here. I brought this destruction."

"Dulcie, there's nothing to forgive. It isn't your fault." He held out his hand and slowly, gently, removed the rifle from her grasp. He tossed it aside, then turned back to her.

"God, Dulcie, I thought we were too late. I don't know what I would have done if they had hurt you." He opened his arms and she went to him then, feeling the shudders that racked him as he pressed his lips to her temple.

Her own fear evaporated as she sought to comfort him. It was, after all, what she did best. "Shh. We're all right now."

"Yes, we are. We're just fine," he breathed as he gathered her close and felt her strong, steady heartbeat.

"Aunt Bessie . . ." She started to push away.

"She's fine. The bullet passed clear through, without doing any serious damage. Right now I'm more concerned about you."

She took a deep breath and closed her eyes. "I'm all right now. But I need to see to the others."

"I know you're used to taking care of everyone," Cal muttered, "but you can see for yourself they're all doing fine."

She pushed away from him slightly and turned. Starlight was in Dar's arms. Though they said not a word, the love in their eyes spoke volumes.

Fiona and Barc were locked in a fierce embrace. The words he was whispering caused her to weep. But she was smiling through her tears.

Nathaniel stood uncertainly in the doorway, leaning heavily on Robert. Surrounding them were the three little girls, still weeping and clutching hands.

"How did Nathaniel manage to be with you?" Dulcie asked.

Cal caught her hand and linked his fingers with hers, unwilling to let her go for even a moment. "He leaped from the balcony when he knew you were in danger."

"Leaped? With his injured leg?"

Cal nodded and gave her a smile. "Starlight isn't the only one you've inspired, Miss Dulcie Trenton. I guess there's just something about you that brings out the hero in all of us. Now if you don't mind..." He gathered her firmly to him again and wrapped her in his arms. "Why didn't you tell me about the soldiers?" he asked against her lips.

"I was...afraid to trust you. They were Confederate soldiers. I thought the murder of their captain would be an unforgivable crime."

"Dulcie. They have committed unspeakable acts against innocents. You had to defend yourself."

"Yes, but—"

"Mr. Cal," Robert called urgently from across the room. "Nathaniel has fainted." He lifted the boy in his arms and headed for the stairs.

Against Dulcie's lips Cal whispered, "I know it will be hours before we find any time to be alone. Though I wish it wasn't so, it looks like I have no choice but to apply my medical training to Nat once again. Would you mind being my assistant?"

"I'll get your bag."

As she hurried away, he felt a wave of frustration. Why was it, when it was most needed, there was never time to say the words? He made a vow to himself. When the wounded had been tended and order restored, he would make the time to share with Dulcie all the things he carried in his heart.

Chapter Twenty-four

The following morning, Cal washed and dressed quickly, then headed for the stairs. When he passed Dulcie's door, he paused. The urge to see her, to hold her, was driving him to distraction. All through the night he had waited, hoping she would come to him. But he had heard her voice in the children's rooms, murmuring soothing words, calming fears and, later, comforting Nathaniel when he cried out in pain. Cal knew he had no right to ask more of her. After what she'd been through, she had to be exhausted.

"So," Aunt Bessie said as he entered the dining room. "My nephew, the doctor." She nodded toward Dulcie, who sat beside her at the table. "I was just telling Miss Trenton that I hoped you would leave the farming to others and return to your first love, medicine. It is a shame to waste such talent when it is so desperately needed. I hope you don't mind, but I did a little boasting. After all, you were considered one of the finest surgeons in the country before the war."

Cal didn't say a word. He merely stared at Dulcie, hunger evident in his eyes.

She was wearing a simple gown of white cotton, with a high neck and long, tapered sleeves. Her dark hair fell in soft waves to her shoulders. She looked so incredibly young and lovely it was hard to imagine her holding a rifle and fighting like a she-bear for her cubs.

Aunt Bessie touched a hand to the clean linen dressings at her shoulder. "You haven't lost your touch, Calhoun. I feel almost human again. And that's more than I can say about the way you look."

Cal chuckled. "Is it that bad?" .

"Worse." She smiled as he took a seat. "Did you get any sleep at all?"

"Not much. And you, Dulcie? Did you manage to sleep?"

"I'm feeling ... well rested."

"Tell me about Nathaniel," Aunt Bessie ordered.

"I'm happy to report that Nathaniel's leg wasn't damaged too severely." Cal directed his words to his aunt, but he continued staring at Dulcie. There were dark circles beneath her eyes. "With his youthful energy, Nathaniel will be walking again in no time." Cal glanced around. "I thought Barc and Dar would be here. Their bedrooms were empty."

"The last I saw of them, they were walking along the shore with Fiona and Starlight. They seemed most eager to get away by themselves," Aunt Bessie said with a sigh. "I suppose it is to be expected, after all that has happened."

Robert entered carrying a steaming cup of tea, which he placed beside Dulcie's plate. "You must eat something, missy," he said firmly. Despite the fact that he had spent the night cleaning his kitchen and removing all evidence of yesterday's chaos, his white shirt and black pants were immaculate.

"I don't seem to be hungry." Dulcie glanced beyond him to the spotless kitchen and felt a wave of relief. She had wanted no reminder of their ordeal. It was bad enough that it had been replayed in her mind all through the night.

They looked up at the sound of footsteps on the stairs and were surprised to see the three little girls surrounding Nathaniel as he slowly made his way to the table.

"What's this?" Aunt Bessie exclaimed. "I wasn't expecting to see you up and around so soon."

"I didn't want to miss anything," the little boy said eagerly.

Emily held his chair while Nathaniel maneuvered himself into it. Clara filled his plate, and Belle tucked his napkin under his chin. Nathaniel seemed to be thriving on all the attention.

Barc and Fiona hurried into the room, faces flushed, eyes shining. A few minutes later Dar and Starlight entered. Her hair was mussed. His eyes danced.

Seeing them, Aunt Bessie said slyly, "You look as though you've been running in a race. The lot of you seem a bit out of breath." She lowered her gaze, hoping to hide the smile that tugged at her lips. "Now that we are all together—" she extended her hands to those on either side of her "—who would like to lead us in prayer?"

"I would," Starlight said softly.

When everyone clasped hands the young woman began, "Heavenly Father, thank You for delivering us from evil. I especially thank You for giving me back myself. And for giving me—" she chanced a look at the beaming young man seated beside her "—my heart's desire."

"Amen," the others intoned.

Barc moved his food restlessly around his plate without eating any of it. Finally he blurted, "I thought I'd take the boat to Charleston this morning."

Beside him, Fiona sipped her tea and stared pointedly at the table.

"I thought you'd given up drinking and gambling," his aunt protested.

"I did. But I need to fetch a preacher."

Everyone turned to stare at him.

"A preacher?" Aunt Bessie set down her fork with a clatter.

"We can't have a wedding without a preacher." The pent-up excitement was tugging at him, bursting to be free, and he could no longer hold it back. "I asked Fiona to be my wife, and she has agreed."

"Wife!" The children nearly bounded out of their chairs. But one look at Aunt Bessie and they stayed where they were, though with great difficulty.

"I thought you said you'd never be a farmer's wife," Clara said to Fiona.

"That I did, darlin'." Fiona squeezed the child's hand. "But Barc has promised me he will return to the practice of law. And he intends to follow his dream to lead his country."

"Only because Fiona has promised to be at my side every step of the way. I wouldn't even consider such lofty goals without her as my partner."

"Doesn't that mean you will have to leave our island?" Aunt Bessie's smile wavered as the realization dawned.

"Yes. But Fiona made me promise we'll return often."

"Aye," she said. "This wonderful island has given me back my life. How could I not want to come back here always?"

Dar, who had remained silent throughout this exchange, suddenly surprised everyone by shoving back his chair and jumping to his feet. "Perhaps, Barc, when you bring the preacher, we could have a double ceremony."

Everyone gasped.

"Starlight has agreed to be my wife," he announced proudly.

"Ah, no!" Aunt Bessie cried. "Am I to lose two of my nephews at once?"

Dar shook his head and caught Starlight's hand, bringing her to her feet beside him. "We thought we would remain here on the island. I would like to found a school for children made homeless by the war. Nathaniel and the three little girls would be our first pupils, along with Robert's son, Joseph, when he returns. Starlight and I believe that this place could become a haven of peace after the horrors the children have suffered across our land."

"Oh, how wonderful. I quite agree," Aunt Bessie said, obviously relieved that the children would remain. "In fact, I should be more than happy to teach a few classes myself. Perhaps in comportment and etiquette. And music and dance. And—"

Cal, seeing that his aunt was getting carried away, interrupted to stride forward and clasp first Barc's hand and then Dar's, before gathering his two brothers into a fierce hug. Next he bent to kiss Fiona's cheek and then Starlight's, saying, "Now I'll have two sisters. I bid you both welcome to our family."

Dulcie got up and kissed her two best friends, then warmly embraced their intended husbands. "I'm so happy for you."

When she turned away, Cal caught her arm and whispered, "Since they're bringing the preacher, I thought...I hoped we could add another wedding to his list."

Seeing the shocked look that came into her eyes, he murmured, "I'm sorry, Dulcie. That was clumsy. I'd hoped to court you with tender words and a more romantic setting. But there's been so little time, and I fear I lack your father's way with the turn of a phrase..."

At the mention of her father, she felt the sting of hot tears. In a choked voice she said, "I can't possibly marry you, Cal."

"Dulcie, I—"

The children, unable to contain their enthusiasm a moment longer, surged forward, pushing between Dulcie and Cal, eager to get to Fiona and Starlight. Even Robert seemed to have momentarily forgotten his chores as he deposited a tray on the table and moved to congratulate the happy couples. In the confusion, Dulcie slipped from the room.

Aunt Bessie, watching all the gaiety, turned just in time to see the hem of Dulcie's skirts as she disappeared up the stairs.

Dulcie stared around her big, comfortable room, then walked out to the veranda and leaned her arms on the railing. For as far as the eye could see were acres of green fields, divided by stately rows of palmettos. Along the shore, water lapped gently, shimmering in the morning light.

Had she only been here for a summer? How was it, then, that it felt so familiar, so comfortable, as though she'd been here all her life?

She would miss it. Tears stung her eyes and she blinked them back. She mustn't cry. Not here. Not now. Later, when she was back in Charleston, there would be time enough to give in to such weakness. For now, she must prepare to leave. And in order to do that, she must be strong.

There was nothing to pack. It should not be a shock to realize that she was penniless and homeless. Again. But she could find work. Perhaps she could work for a wealthy family. She had discovered that, despite her lack of experience, she was good with children.

Her eyes filled. The children. Her heart ached at the thought of not being with them to see them grow. But they would be safe here with Dar and Starlight. Safe and well fed and educated. And judging by the expression on Aunt Bessie's face whenever she looked at them, much loved. The children had become part of this family.

She saw Barc and Dar heading toward the shore to prepare the boat for the crossing to Charleston. She turned away, determined to say her farewells as quickly, as painlessly, as possible.

"Would you like to tell me what's wrong, child?"

Aunt Bessie was standing just inside the doorway to the balcony, watching her.

Dulcie's hand went to her throat. "I . . . was just preparing to say goodbye."

Though the older woman was shocked, she kept her tone easy as she stepped out onto the balcony and said, "Are you going somewhere?"

"It's time I returned to my home in Charleston."

"Nathaniel said your home was torched by the soldiers."

"It was. But the land remains."

"And you had, I suppose, a special fondness for your father's land."

Dulcie felt a sudden stinging at the back of her eyes and turned to stare out over the fields again. "I must go now."

"Just like that? What about you and Cal? It is plain that the two of you care very deeply about each other. I had thought . . . that is, I had hoped you two would marry."

Dulcie looked at her and swallowed. "You were wrong, Aunt Bessie."

The older woman's tone hardened. "Is it because of the loss of his hand?"

Dulcie bristled. "That's a terrible thing to ask. I've already told him that doesn't change who and what he is."

"Spoken like a woman in love."

Dulcie felt as though she'd been struck. She loved him so much her heart was breaking into millions of tiny pieces.

Aunt Bessie studied her, seeing the range of emotions in those expressive green eyes. "What is it then? If you love him, why would you not want to marry him?"

"Marry?" Dulcie tried to laugh, but it came out strangled. "Papa used to say..."

"What?" Aunt Bessie coaxed. "What did your father have to say about marriage?"

Dulcie tried to be light and flip, as Papa had always been. But the pain was such that the words sounded harsh and brittle. "Papa used to say that marriage was the goal of every woman and the ruination of every man. First he surrenders his heart, then his common sense, then his money and finally his freedom."

The older woman reacted with shock. "Did your father care so little about marriage, Dulcie?"

"It wasn't that he didn't care. But Papa... Papa had learned to close his heart."

"Why?"

Dulcie's gaze shifted away. She couldn't bear to see the mistrust that darkened Aunt Bessie's eyes. And soon, she knew, there would be more. There would be rejection. But what could it hurt now? After all, she was leaving.

"It's time you knew the truth, Aunt Bessie." She lifted her chin in that defiant way she had. "And when you do, you will agree that I must leave." She took a deep breath. "I lied about Papa. He wasn't a gentleman or a wealthy horse-breeder."

Aunt Bessie struggled to show no emotion. "What was he?"

"Papa chose to call himself a wanderer. I don't remember my mama. She died when I was just a baby. After that,

Papa just couldn't seem to settle down in one place. So he took me with him while he sold elixir.''

"Elixir?"

"Healing potions, love potions, even baby-making potions. Papa sold them all."

A traveling elixir salesman. Of course, Aunt Bessie realized, that would explain those oft-repeated quotations for every occasion. She should have suspected as much.

"Then, when I was thirteen, Papa decided I needed to learn how to be a lady. We were traveling through Charleston at the time, and he heard that a certain wealthy horse-breeder had a spinster daughter. So Papa became a horse-trader, and he acquired a filly that the breeder wanted, and in the process of selling the filly, Papa proceeded to sweep the spinster off her feet."

"You make it sound so cold and calculating," the older woman said.

"Oh, it was. Papa was a charmer. And when he wanted something, he found a way to have it. So when he wanted a mama for me, who would teach me the ways of a lady, he got one. But he didn't love her."

"And you found yourself with a new mama and a wealthy grandpa," Aunt Bessie said. "Were you happy with the arrangement?"

"For a short while. Belinda was good to me. And her papa doted on me. I had a home for the first time in my life. And I did become a lady of sorts. At least I learned how to dress like a lady, and walk and talk like a lady. But inside—" her voice lowered with self-contempt "—I was still just Dulcie Trenton, the elixir salesman's daughter."

"And your father?"

Dulcie looked away. "Papa squandered his new wealth. He enjoyed the life of a country gentleman—for a while. Grandpa built him a plantation on one hundred acres of prime land and set him up with some of the finest horse-flesh in all the South. But the truth was, Papa was still a wanderer. And when the war came, he was eager for a new adventure.'' Her eyes reflected the anguish she felt as she whispered, ''He looked splendid in his uniform. But when he rode away, Belinda fell into my arms, and suddenly I was the mama and she the helpless little girl.'' Her voice lowered. ''Papa broke that poor woman's heart.''

Dulcie fell silent for a moment, gathering her courage. ''When word came that Papa died at Bull Run, we weren't prepared. Papa had promised he would be back within a few months. I had thought—'' she took a deep breath ''—I had thought my papa would live forever.''

''How long was it before you found yourself alone again?''

Dulcie realized how astute the older woman was. ''Grandpa died that winter. With her fortune squandered and her husband dead, Belinda seemed to lose heart. She died the following spring.'' Dulcie forced herself to meet the older woman's eyes, knowing what she would see in them. ''I am my father's daughter. Not only am I a murderer and a liar, but a cheat as well. I did everything in my power to stay here, where we would be safe.''

''My dear, anyone else would have done the same,'' Aunt Bessie protested.

Dulcie refused to be persuaded. ''I am certainly not worthy of a man like Cal, nor a family as wonderful as yours. Cal is the finest man I've ever met. He deserves a woman who would be his equal in all things. As Papa always used to say, you can't make a silk purse out of a sow's ear.''

''Oh, my dear,'' Aunt Bessie cried. Tears filled her eyes and she made no move to hide them. ''Don't you understand that being a person of value, of worth, has nothing to do with wealth or breeding or family background? It has everything to do with goodness and strength of will and courage in the face of adversity. I see all those fine things in you, and more. Dulcie Trenton, I would be proud to have you as a member of my family."

Dulcie held herself stiffly, refusing to bend. If she gave in now to the feelings that threatened, all her resolve would be lost. "I've spent a lifetime cheating, lying, even stealing when necessary. It would be unfair to saddle Cal with someone like me. I must leave here, Aunt Bessie."

The older woman opened her arms and gathered Dulcie close for a quick kiss. "Your father's callous observance of marriage was wrong," she murmured. "Love between a man and a woman is a rare and wonderful thing. And it is not freedom that is surrendered, but loneliness and selfishness. Once, when I was young, I was fortunate enough to experience love before it was snatched from me. And I know that if there is a heaven, I will see my beloved's face smiling in greeting when I leave this world."

"Oh, Aunt Bessie." Dulcie could no longer stem the tears that clogged her throat and spilled from her eyes.

"A word of advice from one who knows. Do not squander your treasure, child." The older woman handed her a lace handkerchief before walking regally back through the balcony door and out of the room.

Dulcie wiped her tears and struggled to pull herself together. She must not let the others see her weeping when she said goodbye.

Hearing a footstep behind her, she whirled.

"Cal." She blanched. "How long..." There was no need to ask. She could tell by his mask of anger that he had heard everything.

"What do I have to do to make you trust me, Dulcie?" His tone was harsh.

When she said nothing in her own defense, he demanded roughly, "Do you love me?"

How could he ask such a thing after what they had shared? She would not dignify his question with a reply. She started to walk past him, but his hand shot out, holding her still.

"Tell me, Dulcie. Are there any other secrets you've forgotten to mention?"

"You mean killing, stealing and lying are not enough?"

"That's exactly what I mean. Will you promise me, just this once, that you will tell the truth? The simple truth?"

"I've held nothing back," she snapped. "If you heard what I told your aunt, you know everything."

He would not be appeased. "Your promise, Dulcie."

She was unable to meet his eyes. "I promise. It was the truth."

He heard the pain in her words and softened his tone. "I just want to be prepared. Now that I know you are your father's daughter—" the warmth of laughter crept into his voice, and he could no longer hold back his grin at the ridiculousness of the situation "—and that he was an elixir salesman and occasional horse-trader..."

She looked up and saw the way his eyes were dancing. "Are you mocking me, Cal Jermain? Are you laughing at me?"

"Now, Miss Trenton, what is there to laugh at? You invade my house—"

"Invade! How dare you."

He pulled her through the balcony door and into her room. Pulling her close, he finished, "—and bully me into dispensing medicine to all your strays—"

"They are not strays. Whether you like it or not, Mr. Jermain, they are your family now."

"—and you seduce me. For all I know, you might have used one of your papa's love potions."

"Oh! That is despicable!"

He pressed her hard against him and twined his fingers in her hair. "Are you going to stand here and deny that you seduced me?"

Though she tried to resist, her body strained toward his, and her breath backed up in her throat. She pushed against his chest. "I didn't exactly—"

"I'll remind you, Miss Trenton, that you promised to tell the truth."

She swallowed. "All right. I admit it. I did seduce you."

"That's better." He brushed his lips lightly over hers and felt her trembling response. "Now, about my earlier offer of marriage."

"You can't possibly want to marry me. Not after everything I've done, after knowing all about me."

"I'll be the judge of what I want, Miss Trenton. And at this moment, I want you more than anything in the world." He gazed with naked hunger at her lips, but resisted the urge to kiss her.

She couldn't believe what she'd heard. He wanted her. Even now, knowing everything. She brought her arms up to twine around his neck, but he put her a little away from him.

"Oh, no, Miss Trenton. I will not allow you to seduce me a second time. First I want your answer. Do you love me?"

"Yes," she whispered.

"That's better." His tone lowered. "Will you marry me?"

She pretended to consider his proposal very carefully. In truth, her heart was beating so wildly she wasn't certain she could speak. "I may. On one condition."

"And what is that?"

"I quite agree with what your aunt said at breakfast. You should not waste your talents. I don't think I want to be a farmer's wife. I would much prefer the life of a doctor's wife.''

"I've already told you, Dulcie. There is little use for a one-handed surgeon."

"But you still have your fine mind. Why couldn't you share your knowledge of medicine with others?"

"A teacher?"

She nodded. "If you'd like, you might even start a small school here on the island. Until, of course, your fame spreads, and you are called upon to travel all over the country sharing your knowledge. And then, I suppose, all over the world..."

His gaze narrowed. "Stop trying to sell me elixir, Dulcie."

She grinned. "I can't help doing what comes naturally."

He dragged her close again and pressed his hand to her cheek, knowing that if he didn't soon taste her lips, he would go mad. "All right. I'll consider teaching medicine." Two could play this game. "If you'll agree to marry me."

"Oh, Cal. You really don't mind about my past?"

"Dulcie. You are the most delightful woman I've ever met. Every time I thought about sending you away, I found another reason to keep you here. I couldn't bear the thought of losing you."

She stood on tiptoe and offered her lips. "Let's go downstairs and tell the others our news."

"Not just yet." With his lips mere inches from hers, he found the buttons of her gown.

"Cal, what are you doing? It's the middle of the morning."

"It's called seduction, Miss Trenton. And before Barc returns with the preacher, I intend to show you just how much I love you."

Love. Her protest died as his mouth crushed hers.

Oh, Papa, you were wrong, she thought. Marriage won't be the loss of everything. It will be the discovery of all of life's treasures.

"I might still have a couple of bottles of Papa's baby-making elixir," she murmured.

"I don't think we'll be needing them," Cal said against her throat. "I have some potions of my own, Miss Trent-on."

"Mmm," she said. "Indeed you do, Mr. Jermain."

As she gave herself up to Cal's love, she felt clean and fresh and whole. She had come here seeking only a place of refuge. But she had found so much more. Home. Family. Freedom. And the treasure of a lifetime.

As for Cal, he knew now that there truly were miracles. And he was holding one in his arms. And later, when his mind wasn't so clouded with desire, he would find all the clever words to tell her so. Or maybe he would simply show her. For the rest of his life.

* * * * *

Harlequin® Historical®

From the author of HEAVEN CAN WAIT
& LAND OF DREAMS comes another,
heartwarming Western love story

BADLANDS BRIDE

by CHERYL ST. JOHN

Keep an eye out for this delightful tale of an eastern
beauty who poses as a mail-order bride and winds up
stranded in the Dakota Badlands!

Coming this August
from Harlequin Historicals!

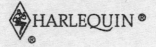

HARLEQUIN®

BIGB96-6

MILLION DOLLAR SWEEPSTAKES

SWP-M96

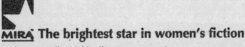

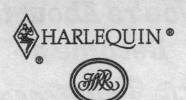

® HARLEQUIN ®

Get two times the pleasure in one convenient book.

A CONVENIENT MARRIAGE by STEPHANIE LAURENS

Delve into two captivating, full-length Regency romances and
discover the secrets of the Lester family.

THE REASONS FOR MARRIAGE,
and
A LADY OF EXPECTATIONS,

Two stories linked by family ties.

A CONVENIENT MARRIAGE—available this July
wherever Harlequin books are sold.

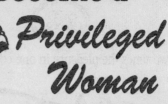

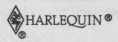